THE REVELATION CHRONICLES

THE REVELATION CHRONICLES

A novel by David Hume

Editing by Ligia Virginia Romero Soto
Cover illustration by Juan Jose Salinas Gallardo and Gabriel Ramirez Mendoza
Author photograph by Gabriel Ramirez Mendoza
Maps by Gabriel Ramirez Mendoza
Names, characters, businesses, places, events, and incidents are the products of the
author's imagination. Any resemblance to actual persons, living or dead, or actual
events is purely coincidental.

ISBN-13: 9780615937786 (David Hume)

ISBN-10: 0615937780

BISAC Codes
1. FIC032000 – FICTION - War & Military. 2. FIC002000 – FICTION - Action &
Adventure. 3. FIC020000 – FICTION - Men's Adventure

To my children:

Never stop seeking the truth.
Avoid those "sources of truth" that are based upon myth,
malice or ignorance.
Truth is the light that illuminates the darkness in this world.
(Summary of closing argument to the jury,
David E. Hume, Esq., 1962)

CONTENTS

PROLOGUE

The periscope broke through the water's surface, leaving a thin trail of bubbles in its wake. The seas were calm, and visibility, unlimited—perfect hunting weather. The USS *Jallao* was patrolling Colombia's northeast coast after being ordered to divert from their passage through the Panama Canal to the Pacific. The orders *Jallao* received were straightforward: intercept and sink a 485-foot German commerce raider, *Ingrid*, disguised as a Swedish merchant vessel. *Ingrid*'s radio transmissions were being monitored by the US Naval Intelligence Office in Key West. Her daily position reports to German Naval Headquarters in Berlin were decoded and then radioed to the submarine.

• • •

Two weeks earlier, *Ingrid* had departed Bremerhaven to resupply the five remaining U-boats operating in the southwestern Caribbean. Her cargo holds were loaded to the overheads with torpedoes, diesel fuel, and ammunition. The raider's 88 mm deck guns had been removed in order to make room for additional cargo.

After replenishing the U-boats off the Colombian coast, *Ingrid* was to proceed to the South Atlantic and enter the Brazilian port of Santos. There, SS security officers would supervise the removal of sixty wooden crates that had been covertly loaded in the ship's forward hold in Bremerhaven.

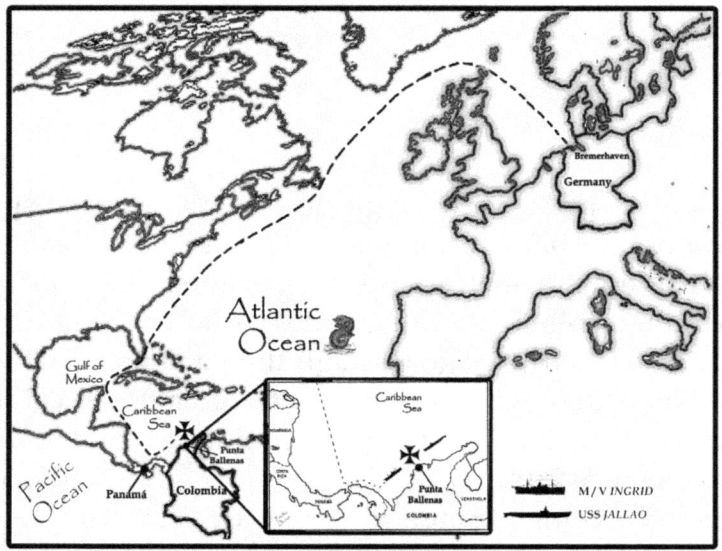

• • •

The *Jallao*'s captain looked through the search periscope, scanning slowly from east to west. The only surface activity he'd seen was caused by a V-shaped formation of pelicans diving into a school of sardines. He continued to scan the surface, moving the scope along the desolate coastline, when he felt a tug on his sleeve and drew back. His sonarman, a veteran of more than a dozen combat patrols, was smiling as he removed his padded earphones and glanced at the notepad he held in his hand.

"Skipper, I've got screws turning sixty-five revs, bearing zero-seven-zero degrees at a range of twelve thousand yards, eastbound. The contact's following the ten-fathom contour."

The CO gripped the periscope's handles and leaned into the eyepieces, moving the scope to the bearing the sonarman had given him. Silhouetted against the brown coastal dunes in the distance was a merchant vessel. The high, curling bow wave left no doubt that she was heading east at full speed. He switched to the attack periscope and adjusted the focusing knob. Within minutes, the light-blue hull of the German raider filled the scope's field of view. The vessel's name board, attached to the bridge railing, was clearly visible; it read *Ingrid*. Above the bridge, the Swedish flag flew from the steaming gaff. He walked the periscope around, making sure that *Ingrid* was alone, and she was.

"Man your battle stations!" the CO shouted out. "Make ready tubes one and two!"

He ordered two Mark-18 torpedoes set at a depth of six feet, not wanting to risk their running too deep in the shallow waters. The target's bearing; range, course, and speed were passed to the navigation officer and fed into the torpedo data computer. *Ingrid*'s course would take it to within 3,500 yards of the sub, close to the Mark-18's maximum range. The shallow depths prohibited *Jallao* from approaching any closer. The shot had to be perfect.

The CO brought the scope down and huddled with the XO and the navigation officer. After a second look, the torpedo data computer's settings were fine-tuned. The firing solutions remained constant, and the probability of a hit was optimal.

"Fire one; fire two!" the CO ordered.

He watched *Ingrid* through the attack scope, counting down the time to impact. With seconds left on the first torpedo's run, he saw a geyser of white water and heard a loud explosion.

"Dammit!" the CO yelled at his first shot, which had exploded prematurely, about 200 yards from the target.

Ingrid reacted immediately, beginning a turn to the right, toward the coastal shallows. But the second torpedo ran straight and true. Its 545-pound Torpex warhead struck the target amidships. Water shot skyward as the torpedo exploded just below her waterline.

A millisecond later, *Ingrid*'s cargo of torpedoes, fuel, and 88 mm high-explosive ammunition ignited. A flash of light was followed by a thunderclap as the raider blew apart. Even at a range of four thousand yards, the underwater pressure wave raked *Jallao*'s hull. The sky above the ship was filled with pieces of deck cargo and the arcing, smoky trails of burning phosphorous.

For a moment, the CO lost his target in the sea spray and smoke. He pressed his face harder against the periscope's eyepieces, looking for *Ingrid*. All he saw was a boiling, black mushroom cloud rising in the sky. Everything aft of the sinking bow section had simply vanished.

● ● ●

Ingrid's demise had an impact far beyond the Caribbean. Confirmation of her loss was received at the Kriegsmarine. Her radio operator had sent a desperate message reporting they were under attack off of Punta Ballenas; it was the last communication received from the vessel. The date and time, latitude, and longitude of her sinking and her crew and cargo lists were meticulously noted in the Kriegsmarine's records and filed away.

Days later, a copy of the Kriegsmarine's report was delivered to a twenty-six-year-old Swiss banker, Christian Rothmund, who was attending a black-tie party at the German consulate in Zurich.

Physically, Rothmund was the prototypical Aryan ideal: tall, athletic, blond, blue-eyed, with an air of superiority. Although he served as the personal secretary to the chairman of one of Switzerland's oldest banks, his allegiance lay elsewhere. Christian Rothmund was one of the Third Reich's most devoted agents.

He excused himself and walked to a nearby bathroom, locking the door behind him. After reading the typewritten sheets, he folded the documents, placing them inside his tuxedo jacket, and returned to the festivities. He was relieved that *Ingrid's* cargo manifest made no mention of the contents of the sixty wooden crates loaded in Bremerhaven. They were simply listed as "freight under consignment to the *Reichsführer* of the SS, Heinrich Himmler." Besides Rothmund, only three other Nazi officials had knowledge of the crates' contents, but he alone was responsible for their protection. Their salvage presented a logistical and security nightmare. Time was now his greatest challenge, and time was running out for the Third Reich.

FIVE BLIND MEN AND THE ELEPHANT

February 26, 1993
Lucerne, Switzerland
8:40 p.m.

Christian Rothmund eventually retired as the bank's senior vice president, in charge of investments for its wealthy South American clients. Although he continued to represent the bank in its philanthropic ventures in South America, he remained devoted to the cause of National Socialism.

He was watching the evening news when a special bulletin flashed across the screen. Unidentified terrorists had detonated a bomb in the bowels of New York's World Trade Center complex. Images of soot-covered survivors stumbling from the building mesmerized him. Even the mighty Third Reich had been unable to mount such an attack against the United States on its own soil. And although the death toll had been only six, he was certain that this group was worthy of the secret he'd protected; his *führer* would have been pleased.

But the challenge Rothmund faced was how to contact these people. News reports hinted at a murky Middle Eastern connection but gave no specifics. And certainly, they would have multiple filters set up for their own security.

Through a series of underworld connections he had nurtured in Argentina, he discovered that the group was known as al-Qaeda. They maintained an operating base of agents and training facilities in southern Brazil and in the remote eastern area of Colombia, near the Venezuelan border.

He called in old debts from some of his former clients. Within twenty-four hours, he was in direct contact with the group's leaders.

One day later
Austin, Texas
7:30 a.m.

Rothmund wasn't the only person interested in the identity of those who had detonated the World Trade Center bomb on February 26, so was Christopher Garcia.

Garcia had been the Eaton Group's director of intelligence for two years. Eaton had been looking for someone to fill the position when he happened to have dinner with the director of the DEA's El Paso Intelligence Center. The director, Eddie Vales, had worked closely with Garcia when he had been assigned as a DEA intelligence agent in Puerto Rico. Eaton was impressed by the recommendation Vales had given Garcia and hired him the following day.

The offices of the Eaton Group took up the top two floors of a handsome, glass-and-steel structure located near the main campus of the University of Texas.

Joe Eaton, a former assistant director of the FBI in charge of operations, managed the business in the same way he had when he was the special agent in charge of the FBI's New York office. He had zero tolerance for ineptitude, and anyone who did not meet his standards was soon looking for other employment. There were no slackers in Joe Eaton's shop.

• • •

Unofficially, the Eaton Group was referred to as "FBI West" because more than three-quarters of its staff were retired Bureau agents. Its CEO and founder, Joe Eaton, had retired from the FBI in 1995.

His father had worked as a geologist for Texaco, and he spent his early years in the Midland-Odessa area. He starred as a defensive end in high school and at Texas A&M University. But at five feet ten and 165 pounds, he realized he'd never get close to professional football. Instead, he entered the SMU Law School and, after graduation, opened a small practice in Dallas. However, civil litigation, contract disputes, and small claims court could not fill the void he felt. He longed for the same mental challenges he'd faced playing college football. In 1974, he joined the FBI.

• • •

Garcia's primary task upon arriving at the Eaton Group had been to improve the flow and reliability of information on international terrorism to the Eaton Group's multinational energy clients. During this early phase, he'd developed information linking three of the largest drug cartels in Mexico and South America with a group of Islamic jihadists based in Colombia and Brazil. Although initially involved only in money laundering, it soon became evident that this group was also involved in paramilitary operations and training. They called themselves "al-Qaeda."

His informant was none other than his old friend, Rafael Espinosa, now a major general and drug attaché in the Colombian embassy in Washington. Espinosa had tried to insert two undercover drug agents into the group. Their beheaded bodies were found a month later along a desolate road in the Guajira Peninsula.

Garcia's first report on al-Qaeda caught many of the federal intelligence agencies by surprise. But it was the FBI's reaction that puzzled Garcia. Instead of expressing interest, the FBI's response to Garcia's report was to attack each premise and discount the importance of the al-Qaeda group altogether. Eaton had called Garcia into his office.

"Chris, the Bureau's director of intelligence says that al-Qaeda is nothing more than money launderers for the cartels. And, according to him, no evidence exists to classify them as a threat to national security. They don't fit the mold."

"Joe, he's right about one thing; they don't fit the mold. These are not standing armies; they're terrorists. Al-Qaeda runs on a fuel that is abundant in the Middle East, hatred of the United States. There's no ideology involved. Their communiqués are increasingly violent, and they are scooping up volunteers by the hundreds from slums in Europe, the Middle East, and even in the United States of America."

Eaton winced and shot Garcia a look of disbelief. "I read your report. You laid out the background; you have names, places, dates, and actions identified. Why are government agencies ignoring it?"

"Because of the five blind men," Garcia answered.

"You need to stay off those hard drugs, Garcia," grumbled Eaton. "OK, I'll bite: what five blind men?"

"We'll call them FBI, INS, Customs, State Department, and CIA. Al-Qaeda is the two-thousand-pound elephant sitting in the living room with the five men. Each one reaches out and touches only one part of it. They don't share their information, so no one identifies it as an elephant. But it sits there right in front of them. Money laundering is only one part of al-Qaeda's structure. You've got a population of over five thousand unemployed radical Islamist soldiers who were trained by the United States for use in the Russo-Afghan war. They understand the importance of communications and logistics, and they operate in tight security."

"What about their leadership?"

"Their leader is a radical, religious-conservative Saudi who communicates directly with God. His name is Osama bin Laden. He's called for jihad against the Western countries who participated in Desert Storm, calling them 'infidels.'"

"Interesting," Eaton murmured, "but where's the threat? Bin Laden may talk shit from his soapbox, but where's the threat? Sounds like a wannabe army of terrorists to me."

"The Islamic world believes that the United States blindly supports Israel and ignores some pretty egregious human rights violations. We are the infidels, the new target for bin Laden's army of Islam. Jihad, as bin Laden and his followers define it, imposes a strict duty on each Muslim to join in an armed struggle against all nonbelievers and those who have committed crimes against Islam. These are religious zealots whose philosophy is no different from their ultraconservative Christian or Jewish counterparts. But they are telling us that our day will come soon. Why wait till that day comes? Let's hit them now!"

Eaton closed his eyes and rubbed his forehead, as was his habit when he was thinking.

"So you believe this is a religious war that's building up?"

"Not at all," Garcia shot back, "these are radicals who use Islam for their own purposes. Did Jim Jones represent the Christian faith when he slaughtered hundreds in Guyana? Do these Mormon splinter groups who abuse their children represent their faith?"

"But where are the holes in our security that you highlighted in your report?" asked Eaton. "This was a theme that really pissed off the assistant director."

"There are over one thousand people from Iraq, Pakistan, Syria, Kuwait, Jordan, and Saudi Arabia who entered this country on student visas, but no one knows where the hell they are. In most cases, these 'students' either never registered for classes or dropped out during their first semester."

"INS has that responsibility. What have they done?"

"Classified them as 'overstays' and left it at that. The addresses given by most are fictitious and INS wouldn't have the manpower to track them down in either case. Customs, State Department, and the FBI all maintain databases on suspected terrorists, but no one shares any information. Leads come in and are filed away. Interagency cooperation is nonexistent. The facts are in front of them. I know that the Colombian drug intelligence office has been sending out comprehensive reports to our embassy for the last two years regarding this al-Qaeda group, but the information just sits there. The FBI and the CIA have cut back on their intelligence budgets. The Bureau has two qualified Arab linguists; one is filling the slot of public information officer in San Francisco, and the other works as a liaison officer with the DEA. The al-Qaeda wire intercepts pile up, unread."

"And what do we know about al-Qaeda's funding?"

"They receive the bulk of their funding from money laundering commissions and drug sales, but that's our weak link right now. We know that funding is limiting their operations, but our sources have dried up."

"Christ," groaned Eaton. "So the elephant sits there growing bigger and more dangerous while we bicker among ourselves and piss away time. Now I can see it…Why can't the FBI?"

2

INGRID'S LEGACY

Two weeks later

Rothmund's chartered jet landed at a small airport in Foz de Iguaçu, Brazil, located on the Parana River near the Argentine and Paraguayan borders. He was picked up by his contact in an armored Toyota Land Cruiser and whisked away to a small pharmacy the man operated in one of Foz de Iguaçu's poorer barrios. It was noon, and the heat and humidity were at their apex.

Rothmund was escorted through the cluttered first floor to a room on the building's second floor. Air conditioners purred, and the walls were lined with racks of computer servers and monitors, a distinctly different environment from the street below. Pairs of unsmiling men dressed in desert camouflage and carrying flashy, chromed AK-47s walked about with a swagger. The majority were Somalis, with a few Yemenis thrown in for good measure.

After some pleasantries with the lower ranks, he was escorted into a room that served as a formal reception area, replete with overstuffed, red velvet chairs. He was served Arabic coffee and introduced to Mahmud Fayad.

From his demeanor and the deference shown to him by the others, there was no doubt in Rothmund's mind that Fayad was more than just another player. This man was a decision maker. Fayad was also physically different from those who gathered around him. His European features, fair skin, gray eyes, and ability to speak four languages allowed him access to the world—and made him dangerous.

Rothmund and Fayad met for two days at an isolated series of bungalows located on a ridge of land that looked down on the Iguazu Falls, some ten kilometers in the distance. They were accompanied by thirty uniformed men, who stood guard at various strategic points of the walled property. Rothmund was attracted to Fayad by his Aryan features and studied him as they walked along the tree-covered pathways perfumed by jasmine plants. He listened as Fayad described bin Laden's evolution from simple soldier to warrior, leader of fifteen thousand devoted disciples.

Sometime during the two short days, Rothmund realized that his führer and bin Laden were cut from the same bolt of charismatic cloth. But he was most impressed by the intensity of Fayad's hatred of the United States.

• • •

He returned to Switzerland, leaving Fayad in possession of a simple set of geographical coordinates—the latitude and longitude of a terrorist's dream. During the flight home, Rothmund thought about how perfectly timed these events had been. Two days before his Brazilian trip, he'd been diagnosed with advanced lymphatic cancer. It was terminal and inoperable. But that didn't matter now; he'd accomplished his mission.

He had sown the wind, and his newfound allies would reap the whirlwind. With his financial support and their neobarbarism, he could finally bring his hated enemy, the United States of America, to its knees. After all, the Americans and their Zionist-loving allies had destroyed his dream. He would pay them back with interest.

• • •

Christian Rothmund arose late the following day and threw on a long, beige silk robe. He stopped in front of the bedroom's full-length mirror, admiring the younger man he saw reflected in it, dressed in a formal white officer's tunic with the Knight's Cross hanging from his neck. He smiled and bowed respectfully.

After finishing his usual two cups of tea and scanning the morning paper, he walked to the den. This room had been built to his specifications and contained five hundred linear feet of walnut bookshelves. The numerous French doors allowed the entry of natural light. The oak-paneled floors were highly polished and added to the room's brightness.

The two-story, gray stone house overlooked the western limit of Lake Lucerne. The view from the den encompassed the entire length of the lake and the snowcapped mountains in the distance. The den was filled with the scent of daffodils and crocuses that had been placed in fluted crystal vases by his houseman.

He picked up a remote-control unit from the antique mahogany side table and pressed the play button. The stirring chorus of Wagner's, "Ride of the Valkyries," burst forth from the wall-mounted CD player. Rothmund stood still for a moment, visualizing the scene from Wagner's epic work: beautiful, nude maidens—daughters of the god Wotan—rode their steeds through a terrible storm, carrying the bodies of slain Aryan warriors to Valhalla.

Then he sat down in front of an oak writing desk and addressed an envelope to his attorney. He placed his original will along with a handwritten sheet of detailed instructions into the envelope and laid it carefully to the side.

He looked out at his property and Lake Lucerne in the distance, observing the rebirth of life in the bud-filled trees and shrubs that surrounded the house. It had been a mild winter, and spring had arrived ahead of schedule—another harbinger of future success, he thought.

Rothmund opened an old leather-bound book that contained handwritten, illuminated copies of classical literature. He turned the heavy parchment pages to a passage from the book of Revelation, chapter 6, verse 4, passing his fingertips over the words as he read.

"And there went out another horse that was red; and power was given to him that sat thereon to take peace from the earth, and that they should kill one another; and there was given unto him a great sword."

He reached into the desk's center drawer and retrieved the engraved 9 mm Luger that had been presented to him by the führer in 1940. As he gazed at the weapon, he remembered how intoxicating those days had been—the stirring martial music that was played during the victory parades celebrating the Third Reich's triumphs over Europe's best armies, intimate parties with the power elite, and the beautiful women who gave themselves freely to those in high positions.

Wagner's music approached its emotional crescendo as Rothmund inhaled deeply. He brought the Luger's muzzle to his head and pulled the trigger.

Austin, Texas
Eaton Group
9:15 p.m.

Garcia moved the cursor and clicked on the "Sum and Prioritize" command of the program he was working in. Key phrases began to fill in the columns in the tables displayed on the computer screen.

He had compiled twenty historical intelligence failures going back to Pearl Harbor and had asked the program to produce the three most common reasons for the failures. Within seconds, they appeared—language barriers, failure to distribute or analyze existing intelligence, and a misunderstanding of enemy strategy.

He thought about the recent bombings and shootings that had occurred in Holland, Argentina, Colombia, and Belgium.

Mysterious radical Islamic groups had taken responsibility for these acts. They had been referred to "practice sessions." Was this a bluff, or was it a trend?

Reports of these events were provided to the American embassy in each country. However, the reports were filed away without being read. Garcia felt a mounting frustration with those government officials who declared that the "terrorist problem" belonged to the Middle East and Africa. The United States, they explained, was too far removed from "these tribal conflicts" to be seriously targeted. One State Department official summed up the predominant philosophy in a single sentence: "Who would ever bite the hand that feeds you?"

Garcia's pleas to examine the evolving patterns of terrorism were not heard. The agency heads crowed a common theme—the Cold War had been won, the USSR was neutered and in shambles, and the dangerous days of the past when the super-powers were on the brink of a nuclear war were over. We'd survived the sixties, seventies, and eighties and were fast approaching the end of the nineties. The next millennium was in view. And the United States and its citizens were safe and secure.

This was the mantra that was repeated by the heads of the various federal agencies. And people in high places began to believe their own propaganda. Happy days were here again.

3

BARCELONA NIGHTS

Six months later
Friday
11:45 p.m.

The holiday crowds surged through the streets in Barcelona's bohemian Gothic Quarter. Spicy aromas of roasted onions and grilled seafood swirled around the sidewalk cafés, enticing the hungry pedestrians to stop and eat.

As midnight approached, strollers from Barcelona's broad avenues, Las Ramblas, mixed seamlessly with the partying masses in the Gothic Quarter. In this part of the world, midnight was the beginning, not the end, of weekend festivities.

A man carefully made his way through the crowds, walking northward. He'd just arrived on the ferry from Genoa, jammed with partying tourists and university students. But he wasn't looking for entertainment. He was al-Qaeda's chief of special operations, Mahmud Fayad.

Fayad was one of the modern Moorish invaders. Instead of a scimitar, he carried a black nylon laptop case. He was dressed in jeans, running shoes, and a dark-blue windbreaker—the ideal urban camouflage. Even his light-brown hair, pulled back in a short ponytail, fit in perfectly with Barcelona's bohemian surroundings.

His destination was a walk-up, sixth-floor apartment in a building whose cratered walls and pitted surface had earned it the unkind nickname of "La Luna." Even though the apartments were located within walking distance from the Gothic Quarter's pricy condos, no artists or poets lived in this building; it was home to those who required anonymity.

He slowed his pace and casually glanced up and down the streets. He observed the faces and body language of those he saw loitering near the dark alleyways, searching for the presence of the plainclothes agents of the Guardia Civil.

His journey had begun weeks earlier when he'd met with Christian Rothmund in Brazil. After the Swiss banker departed, he'd contacted al-Qaeda's leadership, describing Rothmund's offer. In the last month, Fayad had traveled more than ten thousand miles. He'd met with al-Qaeda operational cells in London and Somalia and with his superiors in an isolated camp near the Afghan-Pakistani border. He had arrived in Barcelona to initiate their request.

Fayad turned down a side street and stopped at a small sidewalk café and ordered tea. He sat with his back against the building's wall, observing any persons or vehicles that might have been following him. There were none. As he sipped the strong tea, his thoughts turned to Rothmund and his gift.

● ● ●

The sixty wooden crates that had been secretly loaded in *Ingrid*'s forward hold had contained more than seven hundred million dollars' worth of gold bullion, antiquities, and precious gems. This treasure had been looted from private homes, museums, and bank vaults throughout the Nazis' occupied territories. The plunder had been crated and loaded under the direct supervision of Heinrich Himmler, then Hitler's heir apparent. It was to have been used to fund the Third Reich in exile. The Nazi loyalists had selected a remote two-hundred-acre site in the Brazilian Highlands, where they would continue the fight. But a group of German industrialists and renegade army officers had argued for its use in Germany's postwar recovery. Himmler was the treasure's custodian. He would decide what was best for the future of National Socialism.

Shortly after receiving the news of *Ingrid*'s sinking, Rothmund had dispatched a team of agents to salvage the cargo. The bow section lay in only forty feet of water. They'd successfully recovered all of the crates from the vessel's forward holds, but their trucks had bogged down in the soft coastal dunes. Rather than risk discovery, they buried the crates less than a kilometer from the beach. The team of Nazi agents planned to travel to Panama and charter a transport aircraft capable of flying the cargo to Brazil.

But misfortune intervened again. The small plane that was to take them to Panama crashed shortly after take-off from Punta Ballenas, killing all onboard. Rumors began to spread among the Nazi hierarchy that the treasure was cursed—haunted by the souls of its true owners.

Rothmund was the sole surviving member of the original group tasked with the treasure's protection. He'd kept its existence a secret for almost fifty years. The meeting held in Foz de Iguaçu was the first time he'd revealed its location to anyone outside of the Nazi high command.

● ● ●

Osama bin Laden was incensed by his group's failure to bring down the Twin Towers. Their subsequent arrests had revealed an incompetent group of amateurs, not the sophisticated terrorist network he'd envisioned. He needed explosives, weapons, and better-trained cadres.

But terrorists' tools and training are expensive. Bin Laden realized he would have to reach outside of al-Qaeda for the experts he needed. Rothmund's bequest would more than satisfy these costs. The cash obtained from the sale of these items would fuel the international jihad bin Laden had promised his followers.

The gemstones—diamonds averaging three carets and emeralds the size of walnuts—were equal in value to the gold. But their sale through international criminal syndicates would take time, and time was a luxury that Osama bin Laden did not have.

The gold bullion, museum pieces, and coins were a different story. Collectors were ready to pay a price more than triple their fair market value. Bin Laden had given his operations chief two weeks to execute the plan's first phase: find and take possession of the treasure trove.

• • •

Fayad paid for his tea and made his way to La Luna's dark lobby, carefully stepping over the empty wine bottles, syringes, and used condoms scattered about the floor. After climbing the chipped marble steps to the sixth floor, he rested for a moment. Then he made his way down the dimly lit hallway, through the lingering odors of cheap disinfectant and fried fish, to his destination. He knocked lightly on the dented, black metal door. As it began to open, Fayad looked down the hallway once more to ensure that he hadn't been followed.

He stepped inside and was greeted by Ahmed Nazir, al-Qaeda's communications chief for the Mediterranean. "God is great, my brother," Nazir whispered and kissed Fayad reverently, twice on each cheek.

"I received your fax yesterday—wonderful news. We are blessed."

Nazir proudly pulled back a set of heavy, red wool curtains, revealing racks of computer servers connected to twenty-one-inch monitors. Two secure satellite phones took up the remaining space in what had been a bedroom. In the semidarkness, the twinkling blue, green, and yellow lights of the computer equipment created an almost surrealistic atmosphere, like the bridge of some alien, galactic cruiser.

Although Nazir held a degree in computer engineering, his specialties included more than website design. Next to Fayad, he had more foreign operational experience than any five people combined.

Fayad removed an envelope from a secret compartment sewn into his laptop case and sat cross-legged on the four layers of plush, multihued Persian rugs. He placed the envelope beside him, motioning for Nazir to also sit.

"We'll talk after we eat," Fayad said, as he reached toward the copper tray in front of him.

The mounds of hummus, lamb, plump figs, grapes, and honeyed dates were hard to come by in the mountain stretches along the Afghan-Pakistani border. Fayad ate voraciously.

After they'd consumed the platter's contents, Fayad lay back on the overstuffed, gold-embroidered pillows that surrounded him, sipping a glass of hot tea. Ever cautious of the presence of high-tech listening devices, he motioned for Nazir to come closer. Then he turned up the volume of a small TV set that was placed nearby; the sounds of a hotly contested Barcelona—Real Madrid soccer match filled the room.

"You have been selected to locate and recover our gift. Can it be done in two weeks?"

Nazir narrowed his eyes, looking directly at Fayad. "Of course it can be done."

"Open the envelope. You are now traveling on a Spanish passport; your new name is Alvaro Sanchez Mendez. Your Colombian work visa on the second page shows that you are a consultant, working for Harvard University on a project to catalogue historical sites along the Colombian coast. Obviously, one of those sites is the old stone church in Punta Ballenas. We were able to penetrate the weak computer system security at Harvard's research center and create a consulting history for Dr. Alvaro Sánchez Méndez; your cover story is airtight."

Nazir glanced quickly at each page of the passport, nodding his approval.

"And now for some homework…," Fayad said, pulling a sheet of notepaper from his laptop case. He wrote out a series of numbers. "These are the geographical coordinates of the buried crates—memorize them!"

After Nazir had repeated the numbers twenty times without error, Fayad withdrew a small plastic lighter from his pocket and lit the paper's edge, allowing the yellow-tipped flames to consume it as it lay in a glass ashtray. Afterward, he crushed the blackened remains into a fine powder with his index finger.

"Sheik Osama has agreed to support the Taliban in their jihad against the government in Afghanistan. In return, the Taliban will allow us to use their lands as training bases and will provide security. But the cost of their support is very high. The only way for us to succeed is for you to find and recover the treasure. Do you have any doubt that it can be done in the time allotted?"

Nazir looked unblinkingly at Fayad. "I will not fail!"

4

PIRATE'S GOLD

Four days later
Riohacha, Colombia
10:45 a.m.

The Trans-Colombia Airlines jet touched down hard on the tarmac, reversing its engines immediately on the short runway. It was midweek, and the flight crew outnumbered the passengers. Less than an hour before, the plane had departed Bogota in a hazy rain with temperatures hovering in the midforties. Now, the passengers deplaned under a cloudless sky and one-hundred-degree heat.

Nazir walked into the arrival area and saw the man wearing a white-and-blue soccer jersey, the prearranged signal for his contact. The young man acknowledged him by removing his ball cap and walked toward him.

"Good morning, Dr. Sánchez. Welcome to Riohacha," he said in Spanish. "My name is Ibrahim." The young man motioned toward the exit door and to a bright red, four-wheel-drive Nissan Frontier crew cab that was parked in one of the reserved spaces.

● ● ●

Within ten minutes, they'd navigated around the potholes that peppered Riohacha's main streets and were proceeding east on a broad coastal highway at high speed.

Ibrahim turned toward Nazir, offering him his hand.

"It is an honor to serve you," he said, now speaking in flawless Arabic. "All arrangements have been made."

"You have done well," replied Nazir. "And the items for logistics support?"

"I've leased two all-terrain trucks with five-ton cranes, as instructed. We also purchased the GPS receiver, lifting gear, and metal detector. The map of the coast is in your room."

"Excellent," said Nazir. "How soon before we reach your home?"

Ibrahim glanced at the face of his gold-and-platinum Rolex.

"Thirty minutes," he replied with a smile.

Exactly half an hour later, he slowed the vehicle and turned left, on what Nazir thought was a goat trail. Ibrahim gunned the Nissan, and the two were soon hurtling down the dirt road, leaving a rooster tail of light-brown dust behind them. As far as the eye could see, the land was covered by low, thorny shrubs, cactus, and sporadic clumps of stunted palm trees.

As they rounded a dune, an oasis of date palms and fruit trees appeared in front of them. A broad one-story, tan brick home, containing ten bedrooms, was located within the center of the thick stands of trees. Ibrahim slowed his speed and steered into the mansion's crescent-shaped driveway.

They stopped, and three men dressed in a desert-camouflage uniform appeared. Their faces were covered by red-and-white checkered *shemaughs*. Only their eyes could be seen. They carried AK-47s at the ready, with four sixty-round magazines snug in chest harnesses.

Ibrahim waved to them, and they melted back into the lush surroundings as quickly as they'd appeared.

Nazir nodded his approval, and Ibrahim noticed his look of satisfaction.

"You will be pleased with our security force. We passed more than ten on our way in here, invisible to the eye. They're stationed along the entry road twenty-four hours a day," he said, with just a touch of pride in his voice. "Ours is a united force made up of volunteers from Yemen, Pakistan, and Somalia. Even the Colombian guerillas, the FARC and ELN, fear them. They know these are not ignorant peasants dressed like soldiers; they are the real thing. My men are fearless and devoted to God, not money."

Nazir exited the truck and gazed at the tall Moorish fountain, the fruit trees, and the manicured flower beds. "This is what Paradise must look like, my brother," Nazir said, taking in the coolness and the sweet lemon scent of jasmine.

Towering bougainvillea plants climbed the rear walls of the property and provided a palate of color: purple, yellow, orange, and white mixed with the various shades of pink and scarlet.

"My father, who died when I was young, named this place 'Wadi Aman' because it provided safety and security in the middle of a hostile land."

"It is the perfect name," said Nazir, glancing at the arid landscape that surrounded the house. "Ibrahim, I'd like to meet this afternoon to review all our procedures. I want nothing left to chance."

"We look forward to it," Ibrahim replied.

"We?" asked Nazir.

"God is with us!" replied Ibrahim.

The following day
Wadi Aman
4:30 a.m.

Nazir had risen early and studied the coastal map, plotting the coordinates he'd memorized. It appeared that the crates' burial site was within a half mile of the beach. The two landmarks described by Rothmund—the low wall of an ancient stone church and the beached wreckage of an old wooden schooner—would narrow the search area even more. All was in order except the weather.

After driving for forty-five minutes, they turned onto the coastal highway that led to Punta Ballenas. The scudding, dark clouds obscured the rising sun. A low-pressure system was passing over the north Colombian coast.

Nazir focused on the four-inch LCD display window of the GPS receiver as Ibrahim drove on.

"We're getting closer to the area. We should be able to see our target by now."

The red dot on the LCD display moved steadily toward a circle that marked the location Nazir had preloaded. It was about to intersect the circle's boundary when he felt the truck brake hard.

In the distance, he could see rows of industrial lights, groups of metal buildings, and a serpentine network of white thirty-inch pipelines. A large sign on the side of the road provided an explanation.

ECOPETROL COLOMBIA

PUNTA BALLENAS GAS PROCESSING PLANT

Nazir continued to stare ahead, as if he were looking at some terrible apparition.

"According to the GPS, we're within a kilometer of the site," he muttered. "This can't be. A gas plant built over the site?"

The two got out of the truck and stood on the side of the deserted coastal road, studying the topography. Nazir raised the GPS unit and double-checked the data he had entered.

"Human error," he growled. "I'd loaded degrees, minutes, and seconds, but I forgot to confirm the 'seconds' box. It was working with degrees and minutes only."

Nazir reentered the data and let out a loud sigh of relief.

"Thank God!" he yelled out. "Our target's to the west of this plant. Let's go find that stone church."

• • •

For the next hour, they drove down sandy lanes and trails on the western side of the plant, searching for anything made of stone. Occasionally, they would pass a solitary Wayuu, one of the local indigenous inhabitants, walking with their goats. Nazir felt a building desperation until he saw a broad trail leading into some foliage. There, covered by a few vines, were the remnants of an old stone wall.

They parked the truck and ran to the site. Except for a few isolated Wayuu settlements, there was no other human habitation for twenty miles—only stunted trees, cactus, sand, and a few goats.

Nazir looked toward the beach, searching for the second landmark, the ribs of the old wooden schooner. But after he saw the force of the heavy surf, he realized that this landmark had long since disintegrated.

Nazir retrieved the metal detector from the truck and began to sweep the area of the wall's west side. The metal detector's head was so sensitive that it could penetrate three meters of soil and locate a soup can. The wooden crates had been buried at a depth of one meter, and each was banded with five heavy chromium-nickel stainless-steel straps.

In another thirty minutes, the audible alarm began to squeal loudly. Nazir placed the metal detector on the ground and picked up three large conch shells, marking the spot.

"Let's get back to the house and wait for darkness. We're only half a kilometer from that plant. We've got to be careful."

• • •

The console operator in the gas plant's security office had noticed the red Nissan Frontier driving around the plant's perimeters. He reached out for the camera control joystick and brought one of the large cameras around to where the truck had stopped. There was nothing overtly suspicious about it, but at least it was more interesting than watching the Wayuu and their goats.

He panned the camera's 300 mm lens toward the two men who were standing in a clearing and depressed the zoom button to its maximum setting. He could see that they were engaged in an animated conversation. One of them placed seashells he'd been cradling in his arms on the ground in front of him. Then he moved the camera toward the truck's rear, recording its license plate. The next thing he did was to call the security supervisor.

"Good morning, sir. A red Nissan truck has been driving around the perimeter. The two men appear to be tourists or shell collectors. I just thought you'd want to know. They are in camera four's sector."

The security supervisor punched in the sector's code on the CCTV system's control panel and glanced at the monitor on his desk. Nothing appeared to be abnormal in the men's actions, but he wanted to keep his staff alert.

"OK. Call the National Police in Riohacha and ask them to send a patrol through here. Also, mark the time, so we can retrieve the scene if they need it. This is not a tourist resort, it's an industrial site!"

The console operator was thrilled; anything to break the boredom of observing seagulls, sand, and goats was a welcome gift.

• • •

Heavy rains continued to pound the coast well into the night. Nazir decided they would begin again at daylight. Although he was close, Nazir realized that the clock was ticking. He had only eight days left to perform a miracle.

The following morning dawned cloudless and cooler. Nazir and Ibrahim sped to the site in agonizing silence. After digging below the surface where he'd placed the seashells, Nazir made his initial find: a heavily rusted, metal gas-line valve, nothing more.

They continued sweeping areas just to the south of the old stone wall when the audible alarm started its high-pitched wail. The area that set off the alarm measured ten square meters.

Nazir drove a hollow steel probe into the ground and struck an object a meter below the surface. When he pulled the probe up, the unmistakable sight of creosote-treated wood stuck out of the probe's tip. It was just as Rothmund had described the crates, heavily creosoted to protect their contents from the elements. Nazir tearfully hugged Ibrahim.

"My brother, God is great."

He decided to retrieve the shovels from the truck's bed, but before he'd taken three steps, a battered, olive-drab Toyota Land Cruiser appeared at the end of the stone wall. The white-and-green *PN* logo of the Colombian Policía Nacional was visible on the driver's side door. The vehicle pulled up slowly to where Nazir was standing and stopped.

"Good morning," the man in the passenger's seat said with a smile, "are you having vehicle problems?"

Nazir smiled back, noticing the rank on the man's forest-green epaulets.

"No, Captain, we're conducting research on historical sites. I'm Dr. Alvaro Sánchez Méndez, a consultant with the archaeology department at Harvard University. The project is tedious; we're trying to locate the original foundation of the Capilla de Punta Ballenas. This church is over five hundred years old and doesn't want to share its secrets."

The captain shook his head sympathetically. He understood the frustration of detective work.

"But," Nazir continued, pointing toward the old stone wall, "it looks as if we have finally found its remains. We should be finished in another day, and then we will conclude our scientific research in one of the bars in Riohacha. Even archaeologists need a little diversion!"

The National Police captain laughed and extended his hand.

"OK, Doctor. Perhaps we'll meet you this weekend in Riohacha…for some scientific research."

Nazir pulled the forged Spanish passport out of his shirt pocket and handed it to the officer.

"Captain, here is my passport with the work permit attached. You are welcome to verify our project."

The man took the passport and opened it to the photo page, glancing quickly at Nazir. Then he turned to the work visa. He smiled and handed it back to Nazir.

"That won't be necessary, Doctor. We must continue our patrol. We were concerned that you may have broken down."

Nazir and Ibrahim waved politely as the battered Toyota slowly drove off, disappearing in the heavy brush.

Nazir exhaled and turned toward Ibrahim.

"Let's pack up and return tonight. High winds and the possibility of rain are forecasted. Those lazy pieces of shit would never venture out in bad weather. This has to be done quickly before anyone else gets curious. But if they return, we'll have to kill them!"

● ● ●

The two National Police officers drove westward, back to their headquarters in Riohacha.

"You've been uncharacteristically silent since we stopped back there, Sergeant. What's on your mind?"

"The archaeologist did say Capilla de Punta Ballenas and that it was over five hundred years old?"

"That's correct."

The sergeant shook his head.

"That site is the Capilla de San Rafael, and it's less than three hundred years old. We studied the site's history when I was in high school. Our teacher was a Jesuit brother, from the same order that founded the church. It seems odd that an archaeologist from Harvard University would make such a mistake."

"I see. Shall we return and inform Dr. Sanchez that he flunked Colombian history?"

"No, Captain, but—"

"So which are they, Sergeant, drug traffickers or contraband smugglers?"

The sergeant didn't reply and looked straight ahead, ignoring the question.

"OK, Sergeant, when we get back to the office, you may call Bogotá and confirm that a valid work visa was issued to Dr. Sanchez Mendez. Then, I will authorize a call to Harvard, where you can confirm whether he is conducting historical research for them."

"Thank you, Captain," the sergeant replied, savoring his small victory.

"However, in the future, I suggest you read fewer mystery novels and more of our intelligence directives."

"Actually, Captain, I asked the plant's security officers to save the digital images of those two people. I'll send them to headquarters in Bogota when I receive them. And that's in accordance with Intelligence Directive 27."

"OK, Sergeant. You win. Keep me informed."

Later that night
11:25 p.m.

Nazir's luck held. The weather had deteriorated during the late afternoon, and now the area surrounding the gas plant was being lashed by strong winds and blowing sand; but the rain hadn't materialized. He used a night scope to scan the area from the top of a tall dune.

The plant had lost its commercial power and was operating on emergency generators; the outer perimeters were dark, and the surveillance camera system had no backup power source until commercial power returned. They were downwind from the plant; any noise they made would not be heard.

In addition to their red Nissan, two heavy-duty, six-by-six Tatra transport trucks equipped with five-ton cranes had accompanied them. The crew consisted of ten trusted members of Ibrahim's security force—now manning shovels, not weapons.

The crane's boom would be extended and swung over the crate's location. After digging around the box and sliding the lifting straps under it, the crate would be lifted from its sandy grave and swung into the open truck bed and covered by a heavy canvass tarp.

The group huddled together in the darkness at the edge of the road, reviewing and coordinating their plan. When Nazir was satisfied, he motioned for four of the men to put on the night-vision goggles Ibrahim had purchased earlier. They were dispatched to act as perimeter lookouts, equipped with secure voice radios. The remaining six would be involved in the digging and loading operation. He glanced at the phosphorescent numbers on his watch.

"Let's get this done!" he shouted. "We have only four hours before daylight."

At two thirty, hours ahead of schedule, the last crate was lifted into the trucks. Nazir marveled at the pristine condition of most of the crates. They'd been impregnated with creosote, and he could still make out the Nazi eagle stamped into the surface on many of them.

Only one of the crates had collapsed while hoisting it from the sandy pit. The canvas bags of gold coins it contained were quickly transferred to the Nissan, and the pieces of shattered wood were tossed into the brush.

Nazir had just secured the Nissan's tailgate when he heard one of the perimeter lookouts calling him on the radio. Commercial power had returned; the entire plant perimeter was lighting up, sector by sector. Soon the cameras would be operational. He yelled for the trucks to leave immediately.

In a little more than an hour, the entire convoy entered Ibrahim's driveway and parked next to the house. Nazir exited the red Nissan with clipboard in hand. The men stood silently by their vehicles. Ibrahim had doubled the security detail. From now until departure, the contents of the crates would be under twenty-four-hour guard.

Nazir walked into the house and picked up the secure satellite phone, punching in the numbers from memory. The call was answered in a sixth-floor walk-up apartment in Barcelona. Nazir didn't waste time with the usual flowery greetings.

"We have all sixty crates. The inventory has started, but it may be larger than we thought."

After finishing the description of the major items of the find, Nazir gave Fayad the GPS coordinates for the runway that was being constructed by Ibrahim's group and the time for rendezvous.

"You have given us the sword, Nazir," Fayad said. "My lord Osama will be told of this immediately. God is great. I will see you soon."

After ending the call, Nazir stood still for a moment, trying to slow down the evening's events. The enormity of his accomplishment was just beginning to sink in.

After a quick breakfast, they began the task of inventorying every item and repacking the contents into the reinforced aluminum-alloy shipping cases that Ibrahim's contact had fabricated. The inventory and repacking took place in a large tent, performed by eight handpicked security men. Every one of them had sworn a blood oath of allegiance to Ibrahim and his family.

The next day
Maicao, Colombia
10:35 p.m.

The two men sat across from each other at a small table outside the thatch-roofed bar. Multicolored Japanese lanterns of Chinese manufacture were strung between the Acacia trees that surrounded the small structure, giving the place a party atmosphere. But it was a weeknight, and the men had the place to themselves.

One was a native of Maicao. He had arrived from Palestine some thirty years before to escape the endless poverty and strife that was tearing his homeland apart. He was a devout Muslim who had established a thriving construction business in the Guajira Peninsula.

The other man was a member of the Colombian National Police's Anti-Narcotics Group. He was the chief of intelligence for the Guajira sector of Colombia.

"About a week ago, a young radical, Ibrahim Said, leased two of my six-by-six Tatra trucks," the old man said, reaching out for the arm of the intelligence agent.

"At first I thought nothing of the transaction until my nephew described his conversation with Ibrahim. He told my nephew that he needed the five-ton cranes to lift buried valve assemblies for an Ecopetrol construction job."

"So you are upset that this young man beat you out of a contract and—"

"I know all the construction jobs that Ecopetrol has in this area," the man said. "None of them have anything to do with valves—buried or otherwise. Ibrahim has never worked. His father left him a lot of money. He employs a number of Arab mercenaries who are in this country illegally."

"That's a problem for Immigration isn't it?"

"Not when their purpose is to advance bin Laden's revolution," the man replied, "Ibrahim has known my nephew all his life; they grew up together. He confides in my nephew. Ibrahim tried to recruit him for jihad. He told him that one of al-Qaeda's top commanders is in Colombia for that purpose. However, when my nephew didn't react, Ibrahim told him the man's name to impress him, Ahmed Nazir, al-Qaeda's chief of communications."

"Ahmed Nazir," the intelligence officer growled, "He's on Interpol's wanted list for assisting ETA with terrorist activities in Madrid. He's much more than a communications chief. Are you absolutely sure of this?"

"One hundred percent," the man replied certainly.

The intelligence officer shook his head.

"So now, in addition to the cartels, we have to worry about al-Qaeda in Colombia?"

"I don't know what to make of it," the man replied, "but to have a high-ranking al-Qaeda operative here makes me nervous."

The intelligence officer glanced out into the distance, watching the squadrons of flying insects spiraling around the hanging lanterns.

"Can you contact Ibrahim?"

"He will be returning the trucks to my warehouse in Maicao in two days' time."

"Let's meet at your warehouse in two days, but I want to be sure that Ibrahim will be there. Keep in close contact with me. I'll have an interrogation team with me."

"It shall be done," the man responded as both rose from their chairs, "As-salaam."

"As-salaam alaykum," the intelligence officer replied.

• • •

One day later at precisely 10:00 p.m., the chartered C-130 touched down on the sandy runway that had been prepared. The aircraft reversed the thrust on all four engines, sending clouds of fine dust forward.

The C-130 had been chartered by one of bin Laden's front companies in Venezuela and was crewed by al-Qaeda mercenaries. Even before stopping at the end of the crude runway, the aircraft's rear cargo door had begun to open; time was of the essence. The aircraft turned around quickly and stopped. Its engines were cut back to their minimum throttle setting.

The rear cargo door finally came to rest on the ground, and four crewmen ran out and assembled a series of loading ramps. Twelve heavily armed members of al-Qaeda's special operations unit deplaned and fanned out to preassigned positions. Their orders were simple: protect the aircraft and its cargo.

They were followed by Mahmud Fayad, wearing a heavy flak jacket over his khaki overalls. He walked to where Nazir was standing and embraced him heartily, kissing him on each cheek.

"Well, my brother," Fayad shouted over the noise of the aircraft's engines, "it's time to load our prize!"

The men watched as the contents of both all-terrain trucks flowed up a series of roller ramps placed between the trucks and the aircraft.

Nazir stood stoically, clipboard in hand, while each of the one hundred fifty reinforced aluminum cases was loaded into the aircraft. Then they were placed in cargo containers, and these were lashed securely to the aircraft's deck fittings.

As the last case was loaded, Fayad guided Nazir by the arm, up the aircraft's loading ramp.

"I must speak with Ibrahim. Wait for me here; I'll be right back."

Nazir couldn't contain his curiosity and peered around the aircraft loading door. Fayad and four of the security guards walked toward the red Nissan Frontier and the two all-terrain trucks where Ibrahim and his security entourage waited.

As Fayad approached the red pickup, Ibrahim and his men bowed reverently. The four security guards who had deplaned with Fayad raised the short barreled H&K machine guns and opened fire on the group. In a matter of seconds, it was over.

Thirteen bodies slumped on the ground surrounding the red Nissan. Then one of the guards walked forward and tossed a phosphorous grenade into the Nissan's cab. The pickup began to burn rapidly. Then the bodies of the thirteen men were tossed into the flames.

There was a sudden pop as one of the two large all-terrain Tatra vehicles parked behind the Nissan began to burn.

Fayad trotted back to the rear door, followed by his security detail. As the last man entered, Fayad gave a thumbs-up sign to the loadmaster. The engines revved up, and the rear door closed.

Nazir followed Fayad to a row of plush leather seats that had been installed just aft of the cockpit. As they made themselves comfortable, Fayad turned toward him. "Ibrahim truly disappointed me. Two of his men had spoken about the operation in a bar in Maicao; they were drinking alcohol. We couldn't trust them after that. We had to mitigate our risks quickly."

Nazir nodded his concurrence without speaking.

The C-130's prop wash bathed the area in blinding dust as it began its take-off roll down the crude air strip. In less than twenty seconds, it had lifted off and disappeared quickly into the darkness.

After an awkward period of silence, Nazir finally spoke.

"I am glad that I didn't disappoint you."

Fayad grinned.

"On the contrary, my brother, your work was spectacular. You would have been invited to join Ibrahim and the others for the meeting by his truck if that had been the case."

Then Fayad gently placed his hand on Nazir's shoulder.

"Remember, my brother, we are the guardians of true Islam. We must protect it from these Sunni mongrels."

"God is great," replied Nazir as he clasped both of Fayad's hands and bent forward, touching them with his forehead.

As he rose, Nazir felt himself being violently pulled away from Fayad. He was gagged and bound. Fayad leaned close to him and held his head in both hands.

"Someone identified you. We couldn't take the risk of your being captured and interrogated. This would have put the operation in jeopardy. God will reward you in paradise for your deeds. Your sacrifice for our cause will become a legend."

Nazir tried to struggle free, but the ropes bound him tightly. Two men placed him upright and dragged him to the rear of the aircraft, where he saw the cargo door opening.

As Nazir's body tumbled through the cold air toward the jungle below, the C-130 reached its cruising altitude of twenty-five thousand feet and continued flying south toward its destination, a small airport near Foz de Iguaçu, Brazil.

5

PICKING UP THE PIECES

One day later
Punta Ballenas, Colombia
10:40 a.m.

The set of digital photographs transmitted to his headquarters in Bogotá by the National Police sergeant had set off more than alarm bells. The National Police Intelligence Unit was in full panic. Interpol's Bogotá office and Spain's intelligence directorate had identified Ahmed Nazir, a member of a terrorist group calling themselves "al-Qaeda." The security guard's close-up of Ibrahim's pickup truck's license plate allowed the National Police to trace its ownership to a jihadist mosque in Maicao.

Now, the director of Colombia's National Police unleashed every resource available to him. His most pressing concern was to secure Ecopetrol's gas-processing plant. He was sure that given Nazir's presence in Colombia, their target was the destruction of the plant, which would deny Colombia 80 percent of its natural gas.

The flight of three Blackhawk helicopters landed at the western side of the plant, emptying the combat-equipped squads of soldiers and explosive experts onto the sandy ground. Two of the EOD specialists ran toward the site identified by the National Police captain who'd first seen Nazir.

As they approached the old stone wall, they found a swath of shallow holes but nothing more. The only things that Nazir had left behind were tire tracks and questions.

But a short distance from the site in some thick brush, the National Police Intelligence Unit made an odd discovery. One of the team members noticed pieces of dark stained wood on the ground. When these were picked up and examined, the outline of a bold Nazi eagle stared back at them.

The burned-out hulks of the red Nissan Frontier and two Tatra trucks had been found by some local goatherds next to an improvised airstrip. The presence of a clandestine runway was nothing new for this part of Colombia. However the presence of thirteen charred, unrecognizable bodies inside the Nissan's wreckage was unique and created a field day for the national and international press. The media was told that the carnage was a result of drug cartel squabbles, and they took the bait and ran with it.

Four days later
Washington, DC
Colombian Embassy
9:30 a.m.

Garcia sat in General Rafael Espinosa's high-security briefing room, reviewing the photos taken at the Ecopetrol gas plant and the airstrip.

"The National Police feel that Nazir was there to sabotage the plant. But I don't see the connection," Espinosa said.

"And the holes dug in the sand," Garcia said, "what were they for? They are too far away from the plant or its pipelines for the placement of explosives. The first situation report described the scene as looking like a prepared graveyard; all that was missing were the coffins. But there were forty or fifty excavations. That's a hell of a mass burial."

Espinosa pondered the question.

"Buried treasure," Espinosa laughed. "Nazir said he was an archaeologist. This must be a sequel to *Indiana Jones and the Lost Ark*! We even have a piece of wood with a Nazi eagle on it."

But Garcia wasn't laughing. He was thinking about the piece of wood.

"Rafa, go back to the video you showed me with the red pickup truck in it."

They watched the camera panning to the license plates and then moving toward Nazir and Ibrahim.

"Stop it there!" Garcia shouted.

It seemed like a blur before, but when Espinosa stopped the footage, the freeze-frame image showed the flat, circular head of a metal detector jutting over the truck's tailgate.

"Have the National Police intelligence team return to that site and sweep the entire area. You may have been joking about buried treasure, but they were after something *in* the ground; why else would you use a metal detector? The sabotage theory is way over the top!"

Espinosa reached toward a file folder on his credenza and handed it to Garcia.

"Chris, this is a summary of an interview conducted by one of our intelligence officers over a week ago. The person he was interviewing was the owner of the two heavy-duty trucks that were burned near the airstrip."

Garcia opened the file and began reading the interview that had been conducted at a bar on the outskirts of Maicao.

"Al-Qaeda, Nazir, and the requirement for a five-ton crane...," Garcia repeated. "Has he done a follow-up interview?"

Espinosa shook his head.

"Our informant and his son were gunned down in broad daylight the day after the first interview. But the person of interest, Ibrahim Said, is probably one of the thirteen badly burned bodies that were found in the Nissan pickup truck. We're waiting for the forensic tests to come back. That leaves us with no witnesses."

Garcia handed the file back to Espinosa.

"So where do we go from here?"

"We still have that piece of wood—the oil-stained plank with the Nazi eagle on it. Do you have any suggestions on finding out its origin?"

"The Smithsonian Institute, right here in Washington, would be the place I'd start with, Rafa. Their historical forensic section has the best experience tracing items from World War II, if it's really that old. But how the hell did it get there, and what was it used for? Those are the questions for us now."

Espinosa stared at the photo of the wood plank laid out on his desk.

"You know, Colombia was very anti-Nazi as war broke out in Europe. The German nationals who had built up the predecessor to Avianca, SCADTA, were forced to sell their shares and leave the country. We researched all incidents involving German espionage activity and found nothing. But I will have the plank sent to the Smithsonian."

• • •

Three months later, the Smithsonian solved part of the mystery. The wood was a species of durable white pine that was treasured for its straight growth pattern and grew only in the Black Forest region of Germany. The creosote impregnated in the wood was traced, using a new technology, to its origin. A sample was subjected to analysis using a gas chromatograph. Then the sample's "fingerprint" was compared to a worldwide set of petroleum "fingerprints". This particular sample contained synthetic hydrocarbons that matched a sample from the Ploiesti, Romania, oil fields and laboratories—a German possession in 1944.

The broad-winged Nazi eagle that had been pressed into the wood wasn't just the National Socialist emblem. It carried a small, almost unseen coat of arms in its claws that identified the contents of the wooden crate to be the personal property of the infamous Reichsführer of the SS, Heinrich Himmler.

• • •

Although Ibrahim and his shadow army had been linked to Nazir and a radical mosque in Maicao, Colombia, their supporters appeared to have disappeared without a trace. The Colombian National Police intelligence teams had torn Ibrahim's Wadi Aman apart without finding anything of substance. The case file was marked as an "attempted sabotage of a petroleum facility" by the CIA and remained open.

Garcia had come closest to providing an answer. In his final report to Eaton, he had stated, "From the evidence provided by the Colombian police attaché and his intelligence units, it appears that all persons of interest, numbering about forty, have abandoned Colombia; homes, vehicles, and high-value items have been left behind. The existing Colombian Immigration and Customs records have revealed that approximately three-quarters of the group departed on Air France flights from Bogotá to European and Middle Eastern destinations. Ten persons departed Colombia on a Brazilian-based chartered aircraft. All members of this group share one common characteristic—radical jihadist beliefs. These radicals, in the opinion of this writer, represent the gathering storm that will exhibit itself within the next few years. Their stated intention is to harm the United States and its citizens. This threat should be taken seriously."

6

THE GATHERING STORM

One year later

It was just after five in the afternoon when a line of violent thunderstorms rolled across the forests of northwestern Pennsylvania. Lightning forked through the dark olive skies as two isolated storm cells came together, forming one wall of raw energy.

Throughout the upper Allegheny valley, ancient stands of hardwood trees groaned and popped as they were assaulted by the storm's violence. An old stone hunting lodge sat just below a mountain ridge on the leeward side of the storm. It was completely surrounded by towering evergreens that bent obediently as sheets of rain, hail, and wind pummeled the earth around it.

However, the five men who were meeting inside paid no attention to nature's blitzkrieg. They'd been seated for hours in the lodge's living room around a circular wooden table. The table-top and nearby hunt board were littered with plates of partially consumed sandwiches and empty foam cups, mute evidence of their intense ten-hour meeting. From their casual style of dress, they could have passed for participants in a corporate retreat. Monogrammed golf shirts, Nikes, and khaki Dockers were the uniform of the day. But this was a multinational corporation of a different sort.

Some were hardline jihadists, dedicated to the spread of their ideology and fired by religious fervor. Others professed no religious motivation at all. They were mercenaries who unemotionally traded their technical expertise for money.

● ● ●

The final stages of the plan had been hammered out during the morning and early afternoon. But there was one last thorny problem to solve.

"That's not what we agreed to, Rashid. I asked specifically for the Czech long-period delay detonators. We're a week away from executing the plan, and you want to make substitutions. What gives you the right to change what I ordered?"

A heavy set man with closely cropped white hair leaned forward on the table, glaring at the speaker.

"Jack, shut up! We'll use what we have. I don't see a problem!"

"You never see a problem because you buy cheap crap and sell it at a premium—just like you did in Nicaragua. You're nothing but a bloody thief, Rashid!" Jack Riley screamed back.

Tension caused by hours of complex planning began to threaten the group's unity. Their leader, Abdul Hamsa, stood up.

"It's been a long day, my brothers, and we are tired. Jack, you will have what is necessary to accomplish our mission. You and Rashid have been invaluable to our effort; we must stay united."

Both men involved in the dispute were old enemies who'd been brought together for this one operation. Clearly, their wounds had reopened. Hamsa had defused a situation that could have destroyed the mission.

● ● ●

Jackson Xavier Riley was a short and wiry extrovert with a shock of red hair and a ton of attitude. He was an innovative explosives expert who had plied his trade for a time in the Provisional IRA.

But the Provo leadership had struggled to rein him in; his taste for violence surpassed even their limits.

He fared no better with the CIA. Once after being criticized for "overkill" in Nicaragua, he'd promptly detonated four pounds of plastic explosive under his supervisor's Jeep Cherokee, lifting it fifty feet into the air and spraying the surrounding campsite with shrapnel and car parts. Even in the liberal atmosphere of covert operations in the 1980s, Riley became an instant liability. Among criminal psychopaths, he had no equal. Riley maintained a "body count" list that he'd started years before. After every operation, he scanned the newspapers to cut out articles for his scrapbook, making certain that the number of additional dead was accurate. The updated list numbered 7,984…and counting.

The heavyset man that Riley had argued with, Rashid al-Bakar, was one of Miami's most infamous personalities—an amoral arms dealer with the reputation of selling to the highest bidder, no questions asked. His arms transactions were conducted in total secrecy. To the public, he was known simply as an "entrepreneur," and that kept everybody happy. He socialized openly with personalities from Miami's sports and music worlds, attaining A-list status in a town that prided itself for its diversity.

Al-Bakar had emigrated from Pakistan in the midseventies and had set up an import-export business in a tiny industrial park near the Miami International Airport. But he knew how the game was played. The favors he had done for the president's men during the Iran-Contra days guaranteed him freedom from prosecution. And more importantly for al-Bakar, these favors had made him very rich.

• • •

The meeting had finally ended, and the plan was complete. The five men walked outside, where al-Bakar and two others embraced Hamsa before entering their vehicles. Riley had purposefully distanced himself from the group. He stood with his back turned, wanting to show his contempt for al-Bakar.

The storm had passed, and faint rays of the setting sun reflected off the mountain's ridgeline. The scent of rain-soaked moss and honeysuckle perfumed the cool evening air.

After watching the taillights of the cars disappear down the gravel lane, Hamsa and Riley returned to the living room. Immediately, a servant, wearing the traditional white *thawb* and sandals, appeared with a glass of hot tea and two shot glasses filled to the brim with bonded Irish whiskey, the latter for Riley.

• • •

Abdul Hamsa had been a "true believer" for only eight years. He was a convert. And like most converts, his religious fervor was more intense, more demanding, and less forgiving than others'. Although he was well-known among his terrorist peers as "Abdul Hamsa," he maintained a secret that very few knew about. His birth name was John Thomas Cronin.

He'd been raised in the heart of upscale San Diego County, just north of La Jolla. His was an environment that was high on privilege and low on moral values. He'd never held a job and was repulsed by physical labor. His father was a mediocre lawyer who struggled to maintain the family's lavish lifestyle. The majority of his father's income came from distributing pirated Anthony Robbins business coaching videos. His mother, a burned-out flowerchild, subsisted on a little homegrown weed and a hefty country-club schedule.

Hamsa had a superior IQ and had moved effortlessly up the California private-school ladder. Physically, he was unexceptional: average height and weight, black hair and brown eyes, with a permanent pout. During his senior year, he affected dark lacquered nails and numerous body piercings. He wallpapered his room with posters of Marilyn Manson and Michael Jackson.

His ever-tolerant parents clung blindly to the hope that their son was merely passing through some tough times. His increasingly bizarre behavior was off-limits in their conversations. Then came the drug arrests for possession with the intent to distribute seven pounds of methamphetamines.

Hamsa returned from his six-month jail sabbatical with a new purpose; he'd found God. His parents were thrilled, until he informed them that the cost of finding God was a twenty-five-thousand-dollar donation to an unpronounceable Middle Eastern charity and an airline ticket to a place called "Islamabad."

He'd spent the next three years in religious studies that included demolitions training and ambush techniques. He'd become part of the violent jihadist cadres created through the kindness of the Swiss banker, Rothmund. Only 2 percent of the original group survived their final phases of training. Other candidates who were unable to hide their obvious Middle Eastern features or who were constrained by an average intelligence waited impatiently in various European ghettos to be called for the jihad.

The honor graduates were inserted into western communities, where they led unassuming lifestyles, awaiting orders. But the candidates would not be alone. A network of jihadist supervisory agents, whose job it was to maintain contact with the newer recruits, had been in place for years in these communities. Some had Caribbean roots that allowed them to enter under the government's radar. Others hid behind academic credentials. But they hid in plain sight. Their occupations ranged from postal workers to electrical engineers, and they were never far away.

The first thing that Hamsa did upon returning to the United States was to have his name changed legally from John Thomas Cronin to Abdul Hamsa. His intensity and self-discipline impressed even the most ardent radicals. He was totally fluent in Arabic and had been bathed and purified by the teachings of jihadist clerics.

The one-time lost soul was on the verge of fulfilling his newly discovered ambition. He would enlighten the world as Abdul Hamsa, a modern prophet. He would destroy the decadent, godless country that had nurtured him and replace its corrupt democracy with the one true religion—the amalgamation of jihadist ravings according to the gospel of Osama bin Laden.

• • •

"Jack, what was the real reason for your battle with Rashid: detonators or who selected them?" Hamsa asked. "He's very valuable to this operation. And just so you know: it was Rashid's connection who confirmed our target's schedule."

Riley gulped down the two shot glasses of whiskey before answering.

"Rashid," he rasped as the liquid burned its way to his stomach, "may have all the connections in the world, but he's greedy. He's charging us triple over the market price. He shouldn't be allowed to select a damn thing; he's nothing more than a buyer. How about listening to your experts, Abdul! That's what you're paying us for!"

Hamsa thought for a long moment before responding. "Aside from the detonators, are you satisfied with everything else that Rashid provided?"

Riley looked down at his hands and then raised his head. "I suppose so, Abdul, but that fat bastard talks too much. I've heard that from a number of people in the arms business. Mark my words: he'll get us into trouble one day."

Hamsa was relieved. He could handle al-Bakar in the future. His only concern now was the success of his plan.

• • •

The old hunting lodge where the men had gathered had been this group's safe house for over ten years. Its isolated location and the Constitution of the United States guaranteed their privacy. The lodge's entry foyer led down a dark paneled hallway that was decorated with framed oil paintings. But one painting, measuring five feet by three feet, attracted more attention than all the others. It depicted a grotesque, web-winged angel flying high above the fiery pit of hell. In one hand, the angel held an upraised sword; in the other, a severed head. A brass plate affixed to the base of the painting's frame identified the subject: ABADDON—REV 9:11.

The painting's presence was not accidental. It had been one of Christian Rothmund's favorites. It was rumored that Hitler himself had painted it during his early twenties. Hamsa had been instantly drawn to it, gazing into the eyes of the creature and tenderly stroking its face. He knew the passage from the Book of Revelation, chapter 9, verse 11, by heart: "And they had a king over them, the angel of the bottomless pit, whose name is Abaddon."

A ten-foot-wide stone fireplace was the living room's focal point. Groupings of priceless antique flintlocks and medieval armor were mounted on each side of the stone chimney as it progressed twenty feet up the wall. Two steel breastplates at the collection's apex dated back to 1191 and were of particular value to this group. They'd been removed from the bodies of slain Templar Knights during the Third Crusade by the Islamic vanguard.

Below the ascending display of armor and centered just above the roughly hewn oak mantel was a gold-plated, engraved 9 mm Luger mounted in a shadow box. Its German inscription read, "Presented to Major Hans Rothmund, the Third Reich's finest—Adolf Hitler."

Finders Keepers

One week later
Austin, Texas

Garcia strolled through the Longhorn Mall after work, look-ing for a pair of running shoes. But as he passed by one of the bookstores, a thick volume placed in the new-releases section caught his eye. It was entitled *History of the German Commerce Raiders, 1938–1944*. Maritime history would be a welcome alternative to the daily demands of intelligence reporting, he thought, and he bought it.

That night after dinner, he began reading the table of contents. It listed the vessel's name, history of operations extracted from the Kriegsmarine's records, and descriptions of their voyages taken from the ship's logs. The names of the vessels were legendary: *Atlantis, Kormoran, Möwe, Wolf II*, and *Ingrid*. Each chapter was heavily illustrated.

Garcia thumbed through the black-and-white photographs until he stopped at one that was a periscope camera shot of the *Ingrid* sinking. The image showed a black mushroom cloud boiling skyward and the barely visible bow section of *Ingrid* submerging. But it was the photograph's caption that caused him to stand up and reread it:

USS *Jallao* sinks the *Hilfskreuzer Ingrid* on
August 14, 1944, off Punta Ballenas, Colombia

He turned to the chapter on *Ingrid* and read down the page that listed her missions until he reached the page describing her last voyage.

• • •

For this mission, the *Ingrid*'s captain had chosen a longer, but less traveled, route. The direct passage from Bremerhaven would have forced him to transit the busy Atlantic shipping lanes. A chance encounter with a curious allied warship could prove fatal. The raider's complement of six 88 mm deck guns had been removed in order to make room for the additional cargo of critical provisions and canned goods.

To avoid any confrontation, *Ingrid* crossed to the north of the shipping lanes and navigated through the treacherous "Iceberg Alley," two hundred fifty miles east of Newfoundland. After clearing the ice fields, *Ingrid*'s captain turned southward, skirting the North American coast, and made his way toward the Gulf of Mexico. He transited the Yucatan Pass between Mexico and Cuba and entered the Caribbean Sea.

Flying her false Swedish colors, she appeared to be just another freighter making its way to the Panama Canal. But fifty miles from the canal's entrance, she changed course to the east and began a sprint along the Colombian coast toward her rendezvous with the U-boats near Cabo de la Vela. The raider's steam turbines drove her ahead at a speed of eighteen knots. But it was a footnote at the end of *Ingrid*'s log entry that turned out to be the jackpot for Garcia.

The Department of Justice had been investigating Swiss involvement in the hiding of Nazi funds during World War II. One of the targets of the investigation had been Christian Rothmund, a high-ranking Swiss banker. But just before the investigators could close in on him, Rothmund committed suicide.

Because he had been listed as a subject of the investigation, members of the Lucerne Canton Intelligence Unit had descended on Rothman's home. They were looking for a suicide note but found nothing. Rothmund's attorney had retrieved the letter his client had written just before he'd decorated his den with pieces of skull and brain.

However, in going through his closet, one of the forensic agents had found a Kriegsmarine report on the sinking of a German naval vessel, *Ingrid*, in the inside pocket of a tuxedo jacket. It was dated August 14, 1944, and contained blood-red "Top Secret" stamps in each page's header and footer. This dated document might not have gained the attention of a standard police group, but these were specialists looking for connections between Swiss banks and the Third Reich. The last line of the vessel's cargo manifest jumped out at the technician—sixty wooden crates loaded in Bremerhaven, listed as, "freight under consignment to the *Reichsführer* of the SS, Heinrich Himmler." The crates' construction was described in detail: matching the exact details Garcia and Espinosa had seen in the photographs that Espinosa had in his office in the embassy.

It had been common knowledge that Himmler had been sneaking funds and valuables looted from the occupied countries out of Germany. And the sixty crates were rumored to contain gold ingots, coins, jewels, and antiquities to be used to support the Fourth Reich that was to be established in the barren stretches of the Amazonian basin. Its value had been estimated to be close to nine hundred million US dollars.

But this information went nowhere. It was recorded and filed away in 1993 by the Swiss Lucerne Canton prosecutor's office until it was discovered by the author of the book. The young PhD had tied together the *Ingrid*, her last voyage, and the sixty wooden crates.

And now Garcia connected the dots between the mounds of sand in Punta Ballenas and Ahmed Nazir's mission to Colombia. The mystery surrounding the origins of the oil-stained plank was finally solved. And a major funding source for al-Qaeda had been identified.

The next morning, Garcia called Espinosa to break the news to him. That call was followed by a personal visit to Joe Eaton's office.

8

The Infidel's House

Two weeks later
Washington, DC
2:15 a.m.

Two weeks later
Washington, DC
2:15 a.m.

Aside from a few crack dealers trying to hustle some business along the shadowy stretches of New Hampshire Avenue, the city had finally settled in for the night. It was the time of the August doldrums, when the sidewalks and pavement radiated the solar energy they'd absorbed during the day. The putrid scent of methane, not magnolias, perfumed the air.

A light-gray Ford F-350 pickup drove down Sixteenth Street NW and turned into a side street as it neared the Rittenhouse Hotel. The pickup's driver maneuvered through the narrow alleyway and stopped in front of a black metal entry gate. He reached out and pushed the call-box button.

Inside the Rittenhouse's security office, the night duty officer pressed the speaker button as he observed the driver and passenger on his video console.

"Can I help you?"

"We have the backup compressor for your number one A/C unit. We're here to change it out."

The security officer moved the joystick to the right, panning the camera toward the pickup's bed. A large wooden box took up every square inch of the bed's available space. He saw the words "COMPRESSOR-URGENT DELIVERY-RITTENHOUSE" stenciled in bold black letters on the box's side.

"Just a minute," the security officer said as he turned toward the night supervisor.

"Were we expecting a compressor for the A/C unit?"

The supervisor opened the security department's logbook and leafed through some pages, stopping when he came to today's date.

"Yep, here's the entry in the night orders. Management wants the new compressor installed tonight. Let him in. I'll meet them at the freight elevator."

The security officer pressed a button on his console, and the gate began to slide open.

"Sorry for the delay," he said. "The security supervisor will meet you at the freight elevator."

"No problem. We'll have you hooked up in no time," the driver answered pleasantly.

The pickup entered the service area, turned, and stopped. Then the vehicle backed into the loading platform.

The security supervisor walked toward the two men, pointing to a piece of equipment. "The pallet truck is over there. I'll go up in the elevator with you to unlock the roof entry doors."

"Thanks," replied one of the technicians as he and his companion slipped on leather gloves.

As the freight elevator reached the roof level, the security supervisor locked the door open with the cylindrical firefighter's key, revealing a view that few people in Washington had. Lafayette Park lay directly below them. And to the south, just across Pennsylvania Avenue, was the White House—bathed in the light of fifty metal halide flood lamps. A large American flag hung limply in the still air, above the portico.

They pushed the pallet truck containing the heavy wooden box to an open area next to the air-conditioning units and removed the crate's top.

The security supervisor, who had worked under the name of Kenneth Allen for the past eight months, looked into the box, examining its contents. Abdul Hamsa was pleased with what he saw.

"Our years of waiting are almost over," Hamsa said. "The infidel's time has come. Jihad is here."

"God is great!" the men replied.

Hamsa smiled and walked toward the roof's corner.

"You've got to lift off at one hundred fifty feet. I've marked that point with white tape. But it's exactly one hundred seventy feet from here to that four-foot lip on the west side," he said, pointing to the low concrete wall that surrounded the roof. "That's the same distance we've used in practice. It'll be tight, but you can do it."

The man who had trained to fly the craft for this mission began walking a diagonal line toward the roof's southwestern corner. Hamsa walked beside him, reviewing each step of the takeoff run.

"Any questions?" he asked as they arrived at the wall.

"None," the man replied bluntly. The pilot stood silent for a moment, mentally measuring and remeasuring the distances, heights, and angles. Then he turned toward Hamsa. "I am ready."

The three walked to the wooden box, and the pilot handed Hamsa a pair of blue latex gloves, which he pulled on. The box's hinged side was released, and they rolled out what appeared to be an oversized tricycle with a sturdy, high-backed seat in its center. Bolted behind the seat was a water-cooled, 65-HP Rotax engine equipped with a four-bladed propeller.

Hamsa called the ground-floor security center on his radio, informing them that he would stay with the technicians until repairs were accomplished. Then they pushed the machine to the northeast corner of the roof, where the pilot laid out the parasail canopy behind it, lining up the risers. After some quick preflight checks, the pilot gave them a thumbs-up.

Hamsa reached inside the box and retrieved the last item—a black nylon tactical vest that Jack Riley had designed. It contained twenty pounds of C-4 military-grade plastic explosive separated into four five-pound bricks sewn into each of its four vertical pockets. The detonators, which resembled metal pencils, were wired into each pocket and connected to a switch connected to the vest's front.

Hamsa looked up from the equipment and out toward the White House. "Your reference point is the flagpole. As soon as you clear the perimeter fence, veer right and point your nose at the double windows between the flagpole and the end of the West Wing. Your optimum point is ten feet from those windows. The blast wave will penetrate eighty feet, far enough to kill the infidel dogs sleeping inside."

The pilot smiled as he put the vest on and tightened the straps securely. He glanced at his watch and looked out over the roof's end, concentrating on his takeoff path.

"At four twenty-five, I will take off, and at four twenty-six, I shall destroy the head of the crusader's government and his family. God is great!"

"We will see you in paradise," Hamsa said as he kissed him on both cheeks.

Hamsa and the other man then turned and walked toward the freight elevator. As they exited on the ground floor near the loading dock, Hamsa leaned toward him. "Start the truck. I'll clear you to exit. Park it in the long term lot on Sixteenth Street. Then meet me in front of the coffee shop. The van is waiting for us there."

Hamsa began walking briskly. But just a few feet from the hotel's rear-access door, he stopped and looked at his hands in disgust. He tore off the blue latex gloves and tossed them into a nearby Dumpster. He'd almost walked into the hotel's security office wearing them.

Hamsa entered the security office and saw his two security officers monitoring the banks of video monitors.

"Clear that A/C truck, please. They need to pick up another part," he said and then added, "and speaking of need, could you guys use some donuts and fresh coffee?"

The two young men were delighted.

"I'll be back in fifteen minutes," he said, glancing at his watch. "They should be turning out a fresh batch of their famous glazed donuts right about now."

• • •

At 4:23 a.m., the pilot strapped himself into the seat and turned the ignition key to the right. The Rotax engine fired up immediately. Even with his earplugs in, he could still hear the reverberations as sound waves bounced off the taller buildings in the area.

He pushed the throttle forward from its idle position and felt the craft begin to roll. The ram-air canopy lifted off the ground and inflated as more air was forced into the parachute's cells.

He pushed the throttle completely forward, concentrating on the building's southwest corner. He could see the four-foot-high wall rushing at him. With twenty feet to spare, he saw the white tape pass under him; he was airborne. He felt a rush of emotion as the machine began to lift higher. But his joy was tempered by the thud he felt as the rear wheels bounced off the wall's lip, barely clearing it.

The pilot pushed the rudder tube to the left, correcting his course to aim directly at the flagpole over the White House. Within seconds, he was nearing the center of Lafayette Park. He glanced at the illuminated altimeter that read fifty-five feet. He pulled back on the control stick to gain more altitude.

A police officer patrolling Lafayette Park looked up in disbelief. He heard the engine's high-pitched sound echoing off the nearby buildings as the manned parasail passed directly over him. The officer switched his handheld radio to channel 3, the Secret Service's tactical channel.

"Breach! Breach!" he shouted into the radio. "There's a powered parachute crossing Lafayette Park, southbound, bronze canopy, coming at your twelve."

The Secret Service sniper, seated under a covered observation post just to the left of the portico's peak, heard the report in his headset. He brought the microphone close to his mouth and leaned forward, glancing through the 50 mm tactical scope mounted on the Remington M700. He saw the target immediately.

"I have him," he said calmly.

"You are free to fire, Post One. Post Two, back him up," said the senior Secret Service agent from inside the White House's control room.

The sniper moved forward, checking his weight against the rifle's bipod. The pilot's torso filled the scope as he placed the reticle's crosshairs on the pilot's center of mass. The sniper exhaled, watching through the scope as the pilot reached for something connected to the front of his vest.

The semijacketed .308 Remington Ultra Mag bullet left the barrel at 3,000 feet per second. It struck the pilot just below his sternum, passing through his heart, and exploded in the cylinder heads of the Rotax engine. The man involuntarily jerked backward, trying to rise in the seat, but was restrained by the safety harness. An instant later, the second shot entered the pilot's upper right chest and exploded, severing his arm from his body.

The craft appeared to stop in midair and then fell, slowly picking up speed as the forces of gravity pulled it back to earth. It landed about thirty yards inside the White House's high wrought-iron gate, in the middle of a manicured rose bed. The canopy fell over the dead man like a shroud.

The sniper had performed flawlessly, as he should have. As a young marine corporal, he'd learned his trade from Master Sergeant Carlos Hathcock, the legendary marine sniper against whom all snipers are measured.

South of Alexandria, Virginia
4:45 a.m.

The dark-blue Chevrolet conversion van navigated its way through the early-morning traffic in the southbound lanes of Interstate 95. The van's occupants chatted nervously and had their eyes fixed on the fourteen-inch monitor that was tuned to a local Washington, DC, station. Suddenly, there was absolute silence. A "Breaking News" banner flashed across the screen. One of the men reached forward, punching up the TV's volume.

The face of a female reporter appeared as she adjusted her earpiece. Behind her, the screen was filled with the flashing blue, red, and white strobe lights of police cars and fire department vehicles. The group inside the van began to cheer and shout.

"Silence!" shouted Hamsa, trying to hear the reporter.

"A Secret Service spokesman has reported that a man attempted to fly a small ultralight craft onto White House grounds. But we may never know the reasons behind his actions," she said as the camera zoomed in for a tight shot of a group of White House Police Force and Secret Service agents looking under the folds of a bronze-colored parasail.

"There is a no-fly zone for the radius of a mile around the White House, and according to the Secret Service, they were forced to shoot as he approached. The dead man is described as a white male, approximately twenty to twenty-five years old. The Secret Service also reported that the president and his family were unaware of the event until awakened by agents after the incident. This is Carla Garces, reporting live from the White House."

The camera pulled back from the reporter, focusing on the well-lit American flag that now waved slowly above the portico in the early-morning breeze.

"Turn it off," snapped Hamsa.

"We planned this to the last detail. How could this have happened!" one of the men shouted.

"Everybody take a deep breath," Hamsa growled. "He was killed before he had a chance to set the charge. You heard what the reporter said; he was killed as he approached."

The others looked at him and nodded their heads respectfully.

"But I promise you that we will avenge our brother's murder," Hamsa said as he looked out at the early-morning traffic on I-95. "We must concentrate on our trip. It's still a long way to Atlanta. Watch your speed! Getting stopped by the police is not something we need now."

WINDS OF CHANGE

Two days later
Washington, DC
FBI Headquarters
8:15 a.m.

Assistant Director Colby Sabinson, in charge of the FBI's Terrorism Task Force, sat alone at the end of the long wooden conference table. He was one of the most respected agents within the FBI, known for his intelligence and tenacity. Sabinson had grown up in the farming areas of southern New Jersey. He joined the Marine Corps on his seventeenth birthday and, within three months, found himself in Vietnam, refueling the A-6 Intruders of Marine Corps All-Weather Attack Squadron VMA-224.

One night after a heavy mortar attack killed thirteen of his fellow marines, he promised himself that if he survived, he would return to school and do something with his life. Eight years later, he'd received a master's degree in forensic science from Rutgers University. Three months after graduating, he was hired by the FBI.

Sabinson refused to be pigeonholed in a technical specialty and opted for assignments in the FBI's busiest field offices. His greatest success had been the capture and prosecution of seven IRA terrorists who had been funneling money into and weapons out of the United States.

Now, he sat alone, staring at a photograph of a bloodstained tactical vest that lay in a bed of bright yellow roses in front of the White House. In forty-five minutes, he would present the Bureau's report of initial findings to the Terrorism Task Force. And for the first time since his days in Vietnam, he felt an uncomfortable sense of foreboding. He'd reviewed the information gathered by the Secret Service and knew just how close the pilot had come to accomplishing his mission.

• • •

Sabinson's agents had swept into the Rittenhouse Hotel within ten minutes of the incident and had found the wooden box that had been used to bring the aircraft to the roof. They'd interviewed the two night security officers and obtained the videotape of the air-conditioning truck entering and departing the hotel service area. But the quality was so bad that it was considered useless.

The hotel's security officers on duty had mentioned that their supervisor had accompanied the two men to the roof. They identified him as Ken Allen, stating that he'd worked at the Rittenhouse for almost a year. Shortly after the air-conditioning truck departed, Allen had left to get donuts for them but hadn't returned.

At first, the agents feared Allen might have been taken hostage, until they asked to see his personnel file. It was missing, and his desk had been cleaned out and wiped down. However, one of the security officers located a payroll list in the accounting office. It contained a roster of all employees by name, social security number, and date of birth.

One of the agents called the Bureau's tactical intelligence section and requested background information on the thirty-eight-year-old Allen. Within ten short minutes, the mainframe computers on the third floor of the FBI's headquarters had produced the first inkling of a larger problem.

Kenneth J. Allen had served in the US Air Force as a missile technician and had been honorably discharged in 1991. Since then, he'd worked for a small security company in Dalton, Georgia. He was found murdered in Atlanta the day before he supposedly began working at the Rittenhouse. Kenneth Allen would not be returning with the donuts he'd promised his security officers.

This may have been the end of the evidence trail had it not been for the persistence of one FBI forensics' supervisor. Just after daybreak, while his team combed the roof and elevator for prints and other evidence, he and two assistants drew out a grid of the service area. He volunteered to explore a nearby Dumpster that contained the daily kitchen discards.

On top of the fish parts, carrot peelings, and other discards, he saw two light-blue latex gloves. What he did next was based on weak logic and a nonscientific procedure called "a hunch."

He had his team contact both the kitchen and housekeeping supervisors. They returned quickly with the answer. The hotel used only standard, opaque white gloves. He carefully placed the gloves in an evidence bag and sealed it with a bright orange "URGENT" label. The FBI's Forensic Lab technicians had been able to raise two latent prints of a thumb and index finger on the outer portion of the left-hand glove. After comparing the prints against the Bureau's database, an exact match was found.

At 2:05 a.m. the next morning, three FBI agents walked into the Rittenhouse's security office. They showed the two security officers some photographs: both selected the same man, responding with a shout. "That's him!"

The captions on the back of the photo read, "John Thomas Cronin: alias Abdul Hamsa, Byron Werner, and Abdullah Hamsa." He'd been arrested in San Francisco twice for possession of cannabis and possession with intent to distribute methamphetamines. He'd served six months in the Marin County Detention Center. The last entry showed that his mother had filed a missing-persons report on him in 1995, but nothing else.

The aircraft was traced to its original owner in Ocala, Florida. It had been purchased by a white male driving an older model dark-green Chevrolet Suburban. The man had paid cash for the ultralight, but that's as far as the evidence trail went.

A fingerprint check of the dead pilot was negative in the national and international databases. He carried no identification and had no tattoos or scars. His clothing and watch were off-the-rack K-Mart. His origin continued to mystify the FBI's top forensic experts, although the majority of the team concluded that he was of Middle Eastern descent. His cadaver photo had been enhanced and sent to Interpol.

The ATF had confirmed that the twenty pounds of military-grade C-4 found in the vest didn't explode because the detonator's fuse had burned for less than a second and failed. The vest had been manufactured in Ireland; the detonators, in China. A faulty six-dollar detonator had saved the president's life.

The C-4 contained microscopic batch-identification tags. The tag codes matched those from a shipment that had been stolen from an army supply depot in Homestead, Florida, two years before.

Sabinson was particularly worried about what he hadn't seen in his review of the information. No motive had surfaced, and no calls had come in taking responsibility for the act.

• • •

Sabinson jumped slightly as he realized that the conference room was filling with people. In addition to his Bureau agents, senior intelligence agents from the Secret Service, NSA, INS, and ATF were also present. A black three-ring binder had been placed in front of each person's seat. The binders contained the initial report of findings. Sabinson had good news and bad news. He decided to start with the good news.

"The director is briefing the president at this time. The basic findings we have will be released publicly this afternoon. Your notebooks contain only the initial intelligence, so please feel free to take notes. There were at least three men involved. Only one has been identified."

After finishing the briefing and returning to his office, Sabinson made a call to someone he was sure could help him. He'd been Sabinson's mentor when he'd first entered the FBI and was someone he could trust. His name was Joe Eaton.

Austin, Texas
Eaton Group
11:45 a.m.

The intercom buzzed in the office of its intelligence director.

"Mr. Garcia," the woman's voice said, "Mr. Eaton would like to see you in his office for a short meeting."

Garcia walked through the foyer entrance to the CEO's office, trying to mentally assemble a status report he was sure Eaton was eager to hear. He looked at the CEO's secretary as he approached the closed entry door, trying to elicit a hint about what might be awaiting him. But she merely smiled and said, "Go right in, Chris; he's expecting you."

Eaton was seated at a round conference table near the floor-to-ceiling windows. He waved Garcia toward one of the chairs while he finished reading some notes he'd made. Eaton removed his half glasses and gave Garcia a nod.

"I just reread your 1993 report on Middle Eastern terror cells in Colombia and Venezuela. You predicted that they would fund other cells in Europe and the United States—that the funding was the forerunner of a new wave of world terrorism. You also predicted that al-Qaeda would hit soft targets in Africa. Obviously the 1998 embassy bombings support your trend statement. Do you believe there is more to come?"

"More than ever," responded Garcia. "What we saw in Washington is connected to these groups."

"Even though no one has been identified or taken responsibility for the act?"

"Correct!" responded Garcia.

Eaton paused for a long moment, glancing again at the notes he'd made of Garcia's report.

"Chris, I got a call today from an old Bureau friend of mine. He asked me for some help, and that's why you're here."

Eaton described Colby Sabinson's plea for assistance; the information pouring into the FBI's intelligence group was overwhelming their personnel. In order to control the mountains of data, the FBI was forming an international team of analysts under contract to complement their existing Terrorism Task Force. Sabinson had requested Eaton Group's top candidate, and Eaton was making it very clear who his choice was for the job.

"You'll be living on base at Quantico, where they've set up an isolated site. You'll be in charge of the lead intelligence team."

"What about my responsibilities here?" Garcia asked.

Eaton smiled pleasantly. "I think one of your senior analysts is more than capable of moving up temporarily, if you know what I mean, Chris."

Garcia sat still for a moment, not saying anything. He could only think of a term used in the ancient game of chess—*checkmate.*

"When do I leave?"

"In a week," Eaton answered. "Sabinson will meet you when you arrive. Now get your shop in order. If Sabinson's right, what we saw in Washington is a preview of coming attractions."

10

Behold...the Red Horse!

Five days later
Boston, Massachusetts
1:30 p.m.

Gulls squawked and dove near the crowded public pier in Boston's historic harbor area. Although there was a stiff breeze out of the east, the sun beat down unmercifully on the crowds of people. The USS *Constitution* stood tall at her berth, decked out in brightly colored signal flags.

A couple wearing matching "I Love Boston" T-shirts had been standing at the end of the serpentine queue for almost an hour, waiting to tour the vessel. So far, they'd moved a total of forty feet. The man glanced at his watch and then leaned close to his companion.

"Let's find another location. We have to be on the road by two thirty."

The woman looked around, examining the buildings and parking area that surrounded the pier.

"Over there, near the ship's gangway ramp: we'll get something to eat and sit on the curb."

"Perfect," he said as they both left the line and walked toward the food stands.

As they sat down on the nearby curb, the pair took off their backpacks and casually placed them behind a group of wire recycling bins that were filled with discarded foam food contain-ers and soda cans.

• • •

Within a few minutes, they'd reached Interstate 95 and were headed south toward Atlanta. At exactly 2:32 p.m., the woman made a call on her cell phone. The call closed the detonator circuits, and the six Claymore mines that had been fitted into the backpacks exploded with a hellish roar. Hundreds of hardened steel balls cut a swath in the crowd.

Seventeen people who had been standing in line to visit the USS *Constitution* were killed instantly, and sixty-five were badly wounded. Among the most seriously maimed were young children who had been standing in line to have their faces painted. A stroller holding two twin girls had been cut in half; the tiny girl sitting in front had lost both her legs.

Sabinson would soon have a partial answer to his motive question. It was found in raised letters on the rubberized face of each Claymore: "THIS SIDE TOWARD ENEMY."

The same day
South of Houston, Texas
Southland Refinery Complex
2:30 p.m.

The truckers lining up to enter the Southland Refinery were furious. Someone had telephoned a bomb threat to the refinery's human resources office, and the security guards were stopping and inspecting each tanker as it entered.

This had caused the usually free-flowing highways to take on the appearance of rush-hour traffic in Manhattan. Massive tandem tankers sat in a stalled line while others had pulled off on the highway's shoulder.

One of the older single-tank rigs parked next to the cyclone fence near a group of fuel storage tanks. Thick, black smoke began belching from the tractor's dual exhaust stacks.

The driver jumped from the cab and raised the truck's heavy hood. He climbed the built-in engine-inspection stairs and, after a short examination, climbed down. He shut the engine down and began trudging his way on the dusty shoulder toward a truck service center located a half mile away.

About a hundred yards down the road, the driver of a black Dodge Ram pickup traveling away from the refinery swerved to the shoulder and rolled down the passenger's side window.

"Need a lift?" he shouted.

"You're right on time," the tanker's driver replied as he leaped into the big Dodge.

As they reached the outskirts of Houston, the driver reached into his shirt pocket.

"I figured you could use this," he said, handing the cellular phone to his passenger. "Our Boston team had great success."

The man smiled as he flipped open the cell phone's lid and pressed the "speed dial 1" button. Then he turned in his seat, looking out the truck's rear window.

A massive mushroom cloud of orange flame billowed upward in the southern sky. He turned quickly to face the driver.

"God is great! We will have a lot to celebrate when we get to Atlanta. So tell me about the Boston team."

The call had triggered a detonator placed in the center of more than ten tons of compressed ANFO, a lethal mix of ammonium nitrate fertilizer and fuel oil. The supersonic blast wave flattened people, vehicles, buildings, and storage tanks within a radius of three hundred yards. Fires were fed by the fuel and volatile chemicals. It looked like an ancient apocalyptic painting; the ground spewed sulfurous flame and smoke. Forty-five people were killed, and hundreds were injured by the blast and resulting fires.

• • •

After an initial stumble, Hamsa had two successes on the same day. The al-Qaeda leadership was thrilled as they watched the live feeds on CNN. Their followers celebrated by firing their weapons into the air. Shouts of "Death to the crusaders!" and "Destroy the infidels!" echoed throughout their Swat Valley encampments.

Bin Laden and his inner circle finished discussing their new strategy. The time was right to come out of the shadows and to take responsibility for what had happened.

Al-Qaeda's new communications chief was ordered to send e-mails, drafted by the leadership, to all the international media. But their pièce de résistance was the video recording that was made by bin Laden and sent via anonymous e-mails to the major worldwide electronic media sources. The text was something most residents of the Western world had not heard before. But the words would have been familiar to those who had fought near Jerusalem almost eight hundred years before. The English version was read by a turbaned, chubby young man sporting a disheveled, patchy black beard. His accent left no doubt that he had been raised in the United States. He sneered and glared at the camera as he read the script.

"Praise God, lord of the worlds. Paradise is for the believers, and the unjust shall burn forever in the pit of hell. You have felt the first attack by al-Qaeda on your soil; many more shall follow."

• • •

A group of men sitting in a bar in Huntington Beach, California, watched the TV as they ate their burgers. One of them stopped and elbowed the person to his right.

"Dude!" he yelled out. "That's Adam! Remember the guy with the longboard who told us he was going to Hawaii. That's him!"

The other man looked up at the TV and nodded affirmatively as his friend continued.

"He's freakin' me out; listen to what he's saying."

"Yeah," said the third man, "he's pissed about something. Pass the ketchup please."

• • •

"You and your children are easy targets. The attacks will not end until the nonbelievers and their spawn are wiped from the earth. Our brothers will go forward in the road of jihad, fighting to defend our religious nation. Prepare your caskets and coffins. The decadent reign of the Christian nation called the United States is over. We shall provoke war and reap the conquests. You shall taste the bitterness of famine and death. The streets of America shall run red with blood. The sword shall bring everlasting peace to the new world that we create. Victory is for God, his messenger, and the mujahedeen."

11

AFTERSHOCKS

The next day
Washington, DC
FBI Headquarters
6:45 a.m.

Sabinson sat at his desk, reading the reports that had arrived from the Boston and Houston offices. In fifteen minutes, he would meet with the task force. The incoming intelligence and field reports had already overwhelmed his staff. He had to gain control of the information, or he would drown in it. He reached for his coffee and glanced at the *Washington Post* that had been delivered earlier. The ominous headline read, "TER-RORIST GROUP CLAIMS RESPONSIBILITY FOR 62 DEAD IN BOSTON-HOUSTON BOMBINGS—FBI SILENT."

The article quoted the communiqué they'd received from al-Qaeda verbatim. It mocked the deaths of the children killed in Boston, saying that they were the "perverse offspring of infidels" and their killing was justified by jihad. It also threatened to target children in the future. Then it rambled on for five more paragraphs, belittling the ability of the US security forces to defend their own citizens. Ominously, it warned, "The best is yet to come!"

Houston
8:10 p.m.

The al-Qaeda communiqué published in the newspapers and the video sent to TV stations were the ideal tinder needed to inflame an already nervous population. The media frenzy merely fanned the flames. Many youth sports events had been cancelled, and some people were afraid to go to work. The more vicious points in al-Qaeda's propaganda were hotly debated.

A regularly scheduled show on a local Houston TV channel, *Religious Round Table*, featured a nervous Muslim cleric who did his best to defend Islam as a "religion of love, compassion, and toleration." He pleaded for patience, citing the fact that the religious justifications for the bombing deaths didn't really exist; they were fabrications. He also accused al-Qaeda of "hijacking Islam."

But the words in al-Qaeda's terror transcript held greater weight with the public. The panel of local clergy who accompanied the man listened to the caller response in amazement. A young Episcopal priest decided to try to blunt the hatred that was spewing forth from the incoming call speaker.

"Wait a second," he said. "Don't you see what's happening? Someone wants us to start killing each other. That's what their objective is! It's not Islam. It's al-Qaeda, and al-Qaeda is a criminal group. They're nothing more than our own neo-Nazis in different clothes."

The priest's attempt at peacemaking was overwhelmed by the continuing flood of calls. Within minutes, the terrified Muslim cleric was hustled out the station's backdoor by three heavily armed members of the Houston PD.

Just south of Houston, a group of refinery workers packed a local bar and watched the play-by-play of the explosions on the bar's widescreen TV, seething with frustration and anger. Others stood in groups in the bar's parking lot, discussing how they could identify terrorists and the best manner to dispatch them to the next life.

Hans Rothmund would have been proud. Violence and misery had merged with hatred and mistrust.

12

SEMPER FI—THE BRASS BALLS BRIGADE FORMS UP

The next day
Quantico, Virginia
10:45 a.m.

The unassuming two-story, brick colonial building sat at the end of a paved lane, surrounded by a grove of oak, beech, and poplar trees. The hardwoods had started to change into their autumn colors, creating a scene that resembled a college campus more than a government installation.

The FBI's newly formed Anti-Terrorism Intelligence Group was billeted in the comfortable efficiency apartments on the building's second floor. It was international in its makeup, consisting of Interpol intelligence analysts who would be working side by side with their US counterparts and a small group of Arabic linguists.

The first floor resembled something out of *Star Wars*. Small working cubicles containing secure phones and data lines were encircled by rows of servers and other electronic gear. The windows were covered with dark shades, and white-noise generators were affixed above each window frame. The lights were constantly on—this was a true 24-7 operation.

Garcia had been issued his ID card and keys when he'd checked in with the Administration Office on the first floor.

77

He'd finally finished unpacking the clothes he had brought with him and was looking forward to relaxing before the hectic time ahead.

Just as he was making his way toward the television set, he heard a light tapping on the door. As he opened it, a stocky man in his midfifties stared back at him. He was dressed in a plaid flannel shirt, faded jeans, and hiking boots.

"Christopher Garcia? I'm Colby Sabinson. Welcome to Quantico." Sabinson shook Garcia's hand warmly.

"Joe Eaton sends his regards, Colby," Garcia said as he offered Sabinson one of the two chairs near the breakfast table.

"His recommendation of you says a lot, Chris. Joe's not known for gratuitous praise, and he went on about your abilities for almost fifteen minutes," said Sabinson, who now seemed to be staring at Garcia, as if he were sizing him up.

"You don't look anything like your baby picture," Sabinson said. "Your dad, Christopher Garcia Sr. was an A-6 Intruder pilot with the 224th Marine Attack Squadron in Vietnam, wasn't he?"

Garcia's puzzled expression turned to a smile.

"Yes," he replied, "it was the 224th."

Sabinson leaned back in his chair and smiled broadly.

"I was a PFC in the corps then. I refueled your dad's aircraft—sometimes twice a day! It's a small world, Chris. I reviewed your background application, and when I saw your name and home address, I almost fell out of my chair. He taped your baby picture to the instrument panel, right next to his weapons switches—used to brag that you flew with him on every mission! I'm sorry to hear he passed away, Chris. He was a great man and a fine pilot."

Garcia remembered the late-night phone call he'd received from his mother less than a year ago. His father had complained of feeling nauseated. Within a few hours, he suffered a massive heart attack and died in her arms at their ranch in Eagle Pass, Texas. He still felt the pain of loss, but Sabinson had brought the happy memories back to life.

"You may not know it, but your dad went through officer's basic training just down the road," Sabinson said. "It was called the PLC-A: Platoon Leader's Course, Aviation. So now you've come full circle!"

"I'd forgotten about Quantico," Garcia laughed. "All Dad ever talked about was Pensacola!"

"Let me tell you something about your dad," Sabinson said, leaning toward Garcia. "He had his weapons officer, a real artist, paint a figure near the nose of his Intruder. It was a Longhorn bull mounting a smiling Ho Chi Minh, giving it to him up the ass." Sabinson was attempting to talk through fits of laughter. "One day, the commanding general for Marine Air in Vietnam showed up with a group of touring congressmen. When they got to your dad's Intruder, one of the pansy politicians began to complain to the general that the nose art was 'offensive.' The general didn't even break stride. He looked for the pilot's name that was stenciled just under the canopy and turned to his aide. 'Make a note for Captain Garcia!' he shouted, looking directly at the congressman. 'Tell him to change Ho's smile to a grimace! The congressman's right. It's offensive to see that son of a bitch enjoying himself so much!'"

They both rocked with laughter. Garcia was seeing a side of his father he'd never known. But Sabinson wasn't done yet.

"He returned from a mission up north knocking out SAM sites, and we found a total of fifteen holes in his A-6. You could've put a basketball through some of the holes in his starboard wing. Most pilots would be weak in the knees after going through something like that. But I'll never forget it," Sabinson said with a look of amazement. "As we walked around the aircraft, your dad said, 'Colby, we're going to beat these bastards. If they can't shoot any better than that, they don't deserve to win.'"

Both Sabinson and Garcia laughed until tears came to their eyes. Without a doubt, there was a lot of his father in Garcia.

Sabinson ordered sandwiches to be delivered, and the two sat at the kitchen table while he finished the last of his Vietnam war stories. During their long lunch, Sabinson laid out the task force's findings and leads for Garcia. Later that afternoon, Sabinson returned to Washington, after giving Garcia his home phone number and a dinner invitation.

Garcia already sensed the urgency in Sabinson's voice. He wanted to put the pursuit of Hamsa on the front burner.

• • •

The next morning, Garcia met with the day-shift supervisor and support personnel he would be working with. Most of the people in his section were Interpol analysts from Spain and the United Kingdom. Garcia was paired with Leonardo "Leo" Montiel, who had been Interpol's Spanish liaison officer at FBI headquarters in Washington before being selected for the Terrorism Task Force's analysis team.

Tall and athletic, Montiel didn't look like the stereotypical intelligence analyst. Born in Toledo, Spain, he'd graduated from the Catholic University of Madrid with a degree in criminology and served five years in the Special Operations section of Spain's Guardia Civil. He'd also spent three years working as a senior analyst for the CNI, Spain's National Intelligence Center, before his Interpol assignment.

Their soundproofed, modular cubicle contained a STU-IV secure telephone, twenty-one-inch flat-panel monitors linked to the FBI network and the National Security Agency through secure servers, printers, and the ever-present crosscut shredders.

It took them the better part of three days to work their way through the background files and reports, but now they had a clearer picture of why the FBI had asked for assistance. Somewhere within the geographical boundaries of the United States, a group of people had begun a terror campaign. There were no established patterns and not much physical evidence.

Their first assignment was to review the initial ATF field reports from the Boston and Houston bombings, to determine if any new investigative leads existed. Garcia had chosen the Boston files, and Montiel, Houston's.

Garcia scrolled down through the first report and stopped at the fourth paragraph, reading and rereading the same line. A small, deformed metal tag, less than a centimeter in length, had been recovered near one of the bodies. It contained a serial number that had been traced to a Motorola cellular phone. Garcia thought for a minute, remembering the conversation he had had with Montiel during the welcoming reception a few days before.

"Leo, didn't you work on a kidnapping case in Madrid where you located the kidnappers by tracking their cell phone use?"

Montiel looked up from his monitor and turned his chair toward Garcia.

"Exactly four years ago, Chris. We had their cell phone numbers and used data received from the microwave relay towers."

"How did you track the group?"

Montiel smiled broadly, remembering one of the toughest cases he'd ever worked. "Cell phones constantly search for the strongest signal. It's done automatically—no need for the phone to be turned on. Cell phone towers are usually set up at fixed distances: let's say, about five to ten miles apart. Assuming the cell phone is moving, the signal is switched to a tower that gives it the strongest signal. All you need is the cell phone's number and the provider database. In our case, we sat in the provider's switching room and had the locations real-time."

Garcia leaned back in his chair and stared at the monitor.

"So the database could also identify calling numbers as well as numbers called."

"Exactly, NSA has the database you would need."

"Then take a look at this," said Garcia as he slid his chair to the side.

Montiel read the ATF report, noting the possible lead.

"Chris, that's the serial number for the phone itself. Motorola should be able to track this to the dealer that sold the unit and give you the actual phone number. Once you have that, we'll contact NSA and ask them for the Boston and Houston data."

Three hours later, Garcia and Montiel were in possession of the number for a prepaid cellular phone with a 412 western Pennsylvania area code. The NSA Boston database search had revealed a mysterious five-second call made by another prepaid cellular phone with the same area code. The call had been made within three miles of the USS *Constitution*'s pier at the exact time of the blast. The same western Pennsylvania area code showed up on the Houston list; a call had been made seven miles from the bombsite at the same time the device exploded.

The NSA's mainframe computers had also produced another find. The Houston cell phone had called the Boston cell phone at 10:23 p.m. that same day. The call had been made somewhere in eastern Louisiana on I-10, the major east-west interstate. The call was received by the Boston cell phone just south of Baltimore on I-95. The call lasted for fifty-seven seconds. No calls were made by either phone after that. Their batteries had either been pulled out, or the phones destroyed.

The prepaid phones had been sold by a company in Pittsburgh, Pennsylvania. A priority message was sent to the FBI's field office in Pittsburgh.

The following day
11:00 a.m.

The Pittsburgh senior agent in charge called Sabinson as soon as his two agents had returned to the office. The cell phones had been purchased six months before by a corporation—Liberty Enterprises. Both the address and business history of Liberty Enterprises proved to be fictitious. The cellular bills were paid on time, every month, by money orders sent from all over the United States.

Although it may not have been a total success, they'd finally begun to peel back some of the mystery. It was a beginning that Sabinson had prayed for.

13

Escape from the Tangled Web

Two days later
Miami
Biscayne Causeway
Tequesta Yacht Club
7:05 p.m.

Abdul Hamsa sat stiffly in the passenger's seat of the armored Mercedes G55 AMG that was parked near the yacht piers. The majority of the yachts moored there were over two hundred fifty feet in length. Some carried helicopters on their upper decks, while one had a pair of his-and-her minisubs snug in a custom-built cradle on the stern.

The Mercedes's usual luxury status was diminished by the assortment of Rolls Royces, Bentleys, Ferraris, and Aston Martins parked nearby. Dark window tints and six-figure price tags hardly raised an eyebrow in this part of Miami.

The setting sun painted the tops of the towering thunderheads a dark pink as gusts of cool wind stirred up the choppy waters of Biscayne Bay. A storm was building to the east.

"Abdul, your face is all over the Internet! Last night, *America's Most Wanted* featured you in their lead story, and they used your real name. You've put me in a very difficult position by requesting this meeting."

"Rashid, please stop being so melodramatic. Those idiots used a mug shot from the nineties, from the Marin County Jail. They're looking for a man with black hair, brown eyes, and a mustache."

Hamsa grabbed the rearview mirror and turned it toward himself. He glanced at his closely cropped blond hair and the blue eyes, thanks to a new pair of contact lenses. He was satisfied with his handiwork and released the mirror.

"It was the detonator, Rashid! Jack was right!" he screamed.

Al-Bakar jumped at the sudden outburst and looked away, refusing to acknowledge Hamsa's accusation.

"But no one, outside of you and me, will know about this," Hamsa continued, "because I need something special. Let's call it a tradeoff—your assistance for my silence."

Hamsa handed him a sheet of paper containing a series of schematics and a list of materials. Al-Bakar read the document and then glanced at Hamsa.

"Abdul, you are insane! No one will touch this. Nothing here is off-the-shelf. It's all controlled. This is absolute madness!"

"Rashid, this is not a request!" muttered Hamsa.

Al-Bakar gripped the steering wheel hard and stared out over the hood. "No! Absolutely not! It's too risky."

"That's unfortunate, Rashid," Hamsa said, his voice now radiating all the warmth of a Siberian winter. "I was hoping that you were a true believer. Some might take your refusal as treasonous—or worse, blasphemous."

Al-Bakar whipped his head toward Hamsa; his face was ashen. "I know of only one person who could provide you with what you want, but contact with him will be very difficult."

"Why is that, Rashid? Have you lied to him too, just as you lied to us at the meeting in Pennsylvania?"

"Abdul, I...I...," al-Bakar stuttered.

Hamsa smiled, showing his teeth.

"Rashid, I need the information in one week."

Al-Bakar sat motionless in his seat, seething.

"Abdul, I swear that it cannot be done in a week! You must give me more time."

"I have protected you up to this point, Rashid. If you won't help us now, I can't guarantee your safety any longer, or the safety of your family."

Al-Bakar surrendered.

"Call me on my cell. I'll be in Bar Harbor, at my summer place. I will have what you need. That's a promise."

Hamsa got out of the car without saying another word and slammed the door hard. Then he walked slowly toward his rental car as torrents of rain began to drench the parking area. He sped out of the parking area, destined for West Palm Beach and the condo of one of his supporters. He would rest for the night. Tomorrow would be hectic.

The following day
Coral Gables, Florida
Ritz-Plaza Hotel
2:20 p.m.

Hamsa took the elevator to the fifteenth floor and tapped lightly on the door as he'd been instructed to do. It opened, and he was greeted by a man who had a sumptuous late lunch waiting for him. Mahmud Fayad hugged him tightly, kissing him on both cheeks. But this was not a social call. Fayad had been ordered by the Supreme Council to meet with Hamsa. Rumors concerning the detonator's failure had reached bin Laden. His orders were direct: investigate, determine the truth, and mitigate all vulnerabilities.

They relaxed and chatted about the past while consuming plates of fruit and lamb that had been ordered from room service. Hot jasmine tea was served after the lunch, and the formal meeting began.

"Abdul, the sheiks are very impressed with your plan and believe that it can be accomplished. They have made the deposits you requested to your account. And most importantly, my lord Osama sends his personal greetings, may God be praised."

Hamsa smiled and bowed his head reverently.

"It was you who taught me these skills, Mahmud. I praise the day we met."

Fayad looked pleased and lit one of his favorite Djarum clove cigarettes before continuing.

"We have only one concern, and that is for your safety."

"I appreciate the council's concern."

Fayad smiled and took another puff from the dark-brown cigarette. "How well do you know Rashid al-Bakar?"

"Is there a problem?" Hamsa asked, trying to maintain his composure.

"I am not sure," said Fayad, gazing at his cigarette. "I know he has been a critical part of our operations, but we've heard some disturbing rumors. I am also concerned about his present motives."

"May I ask what rumors you have heard?"

"They relate to his fidelity, Abdul. It appears that he's become westernized far beyond his clothing. Jihad is becoming less important than nightclub appearances with his entertainment friends. He consumes alcohol in public, wears diamonds on his fingers like a woman, and seems to be sliding into an abyss of broken promises. He has lost sight of God."

Fayad shot Hamsa a look that reinforced his concern.

"And then there are the questions about the detonators," he said without breaking his gaze.

Hamsa now understood the reason for his visit.

"Abdul, did you know about the detonator problem before the operation?" Fayad's eyes narrowed as he inhaled the cigarette's smoke.

Hamsa was walking on a slippery slope. He had to lie and it had to be believable.

"Rashid promised me that he had replaced the detonators with those that Riley had asked for. The pilot confirmed that they were the correct ones. Only after the failed attempt did we find out the truth. This I swear by God."

Fayad continued his stare for a long five seconds; he then turned away and stood.

"Al-Bakar is dead!" Fayad hissed. "I will have this pig taken care of."

"No, Mahmud," replied Hamsa, "I brought him into the operation. He is my responsibility. I will personally exact justice."

Fayad nodded, and a smile replaced the fury Hamsa had seen on his face. He stubbed out his cigarette on his plate.

"Abdul, I will leave the matter in your hands. Now that you know what he has done, show him no mercy. God is great."

14

Treason and Treachery— Guilty as Charged

Two days later
Washington, DC
FBI Headquarters
9:15 a.m.

Sabinson was putting the larger pieces of the terrorists' puzzle together, but the failure to catch Hamsa was weighing heavily on him. NSA had reported a sudden increase in coded Internet and cellular traffic between Florida, Pakistan, and Afghanistan—something was brewing.

West Palm Beach, Florida
10:00 a.m.

Hamsa closed the condo's door and took a cab to the airport, leaving the car he'd been driving in the visitors' parking space. He took a taxi to the Palm Beach airport, where he rented a nondescript blue Ford Taurus, using a false driver's license he carried. The five-thousand-dollar cash deposit he laid on the counter took care of the bothersome credit card. After all, he'd signed for a "local rental only," promising not to take the car out of the state.

As he approached the I-95 entrance ramp, he swerved into the parking area of a 7-11. He bought a large coffee and two sixty-minute telephone cards and proceeded on his way north.

Hamsa made good time in the light traffic, and by noon, he was entering the outskirts of Fort Pierce. He exited I-95 and found a service station, where he filled up the car's tank and made a phone call to al-Bakar, using one of the cards he'd purchased earlier.

There was no answer to his first two calls; the phone continued to ring without the voicemail kicking in. However, his third attempt yielded results.

"Hello."

"Good morning, my brother," replied Hamsa. "I love Bar Harbor this time of year."

"I didn't recognize the area code on the caller ID," al-Bakar said. "Where are you?"

"I'm traveling."

"I won't have the information until tomorrow," al-Bakar responded coldly.

Hamsa had been prepared for his response.

"When you have it, I want you to meet me in Portland. I'll call you in the afternoon to let you know where I am."

"No, I can't do that. It's too dangerous; the—"

Hamsa cut him off in midsentence.

"That information is worth fifty thousand dollars. I have it in cash."

Hamsa had learned which buttons to push.

"See you tomorrow, my brother."

One day later
Portland, Maine
Municipal Park
10:20 p.m.

Hamsa watched al-Bakar's Mercedes enter the parking space near his own car and come to a stop. He opened his door and stretched.

Al-Bakar was nervous and edgy as Hamsa entered the passenger's side door. He placed the gearshift in the park position with the engine running and the lights on. Then he reached into his jacket pocket and handed Hamsa a folded sheet of paper.

"Here's the information you asked for: name, cell phone, house phone, e-mail, and fax. Abdul, this is it. I really have to distance myself from you now. You are drawing a lot of unnecessary heat."

Hamsa glanced at the name and numbers that al-Bakar had written on the note paper.

"Thank you, my brother," he said as he folded it and placed it in his windbreaker pocket.

"And the fifty thousand?" al-Bakar asked.

"Fayad was right...," Hamsa murmured.

"What did you say?" said an agitated al-Bakar.

He got a quick glimpse of the 9 mm semiautomatic that came out of Hamsa's jacket, but it was too late. He covered his face as Hamsa fired four quick shots into his chest.

"What else have you done for money?" Hamsa asked, looking at al-Bakar's motionless body leaning limp against the driver's side door. He reached over and felt for a pulse. The hollow point rounds had done their job. He'd already stopped breathing.

Hamsa picked up the empty shell casings and exited the Mercedes, walking briskly to his rental car. He got in and looked around, making sure that he hadn't been seen. Then he drove away.

• • •

At about 11:30 p.m., a police cruiser pulled up next to al-Bakar's silver Mercedes G55 AMG. The vehicle's lights were on, and the engine was running. As the two officers illuminated the vehicle's interior with their flashlights, they realized that this was not some lover's tryst. The man's body could be seen through the blood spattered windows.

• • •

Hamsa had checked into a small boutique hotel along Portland's harbor. The TV show he was watching was interrupted by news coverage of al-Bakar's death. But most importantly, the reporter explained that the Maine State Police had set up roadblocks and were swarming the area. He was going to have to change his plans. Instead of the leisurely trip to Utah he'd envisioned, he would have to walk out of the trap that had been set for him.

The next morning, Hamsa checked out, leaving his rental car in the hotel's parking lot after wiping down its interior. He walked to the ferry terminal, where he purchased a round-trip ticket on the large car ferry, the *Scotia Prince*.

That afternoon, the ship departed its pier-side berth, and he was on his way to Yarmouth, Nova Scotia, along with hundreds of other late-autumn tourists.

15

OUT OF THE MOUTHS
OF BABES

The next day
Washington, DC
FBI Headquarters
7:05 a.m.

Sabinson watched the CNN broadcast of the events that had occurred in Portland.

"Police theorize that international arms dealer Rashid al-Bakar became lost when he took the wrong exit from Interstate 95. It appears that he may have stopped to ask directions and unwittingly became the victim of an attempted carjacking. Police report that al-Bakar's silver Mercedes G55 is valued at more than one hundred fifty thousand dollars. The arms dealer had a vacation home in Bar Harbor. He leaves a wife and two children. And now, on to other news…"

Sabinson picked up the TV's remote and pressed the power-off button. The murder of a notorious international arms dealer with shady connections to a former president's security advisors was intriguing enough. But unknown to the general public and to the press, Rashid al-Bakar was to have testified secretly before a federal grand jury in less than two weeks. The carjacking motive seemed too convenient.

Al-Bakar and his attorney had begun negotiations with the Justice Department. There had been strong suspicions among the Terrorism Task Force agents that al-Bakar had been involved with supporting terrorist groups, along with his other clients, drug dealers.

Sabinson decided to expedite the process. He reached for the intercom's handset and punched in the numbers for his liaison officer with the attorney general's office.

"Bart, it's Colby; let's go ahead and contact al-Bakar's attorney. See if he will voluntarily produce the files. There's no more attorney-client privilege; his client's dead. I'll give our Quantico analysts a heads-up. If these files contain half of what I think they might, our guys will be putting in double shifts for the next month."

Portland, Maine
FBI Field Office
8:15 a.m.

Special Agents Jim Schneider and Alan Bernstein had been assigned to the Portland office for ten years. They had enjoyed their time in the backwaters of crime: fishing, hunting, and taking care of monthly reports to headquarters. The occasional bank robbery and interstate car theft kept them on their toes, but the last twelve hours had turned their world upside down.

Nancy Blakely al-Bakar sat in front of them, finishing her third Diet Coke. She was an attractive blue-eyed brunette from Miami, who had been married to the arms dealer for the last twenty years. They had met when al-Bakar was in his late forties and she had just turned eighteen. She was a dancer in a gentleman's club named Red Velvet, and al-Bakar married her a week after first meeting her. But she had adapted well to the millionaire's lifestyle. She was dressed in a Dolce & Gabbana sundress and sweater and Manolo Blahnik sandals.

"Tell us more about the call you said your husband received before he was killed," said Schneider.

"The call came in on his cell, the day before yesterday. I could hear the caller's voice because Rashid always held the phone away from his ear and had the volume maxed out. He had some phobia about cancer caused by microwaves."

"Did he say who it was?"

"No, but I recognized the voice. He had called before. They always spoke in Arabic."

"Do you speak Arabic?" asked Bernstein.

"Only *thank you* and *good-bye*!" she laughed. "Rashid never took the time to teach me. But I know Arabic when I hear it."

"Do you remember how long ago this person called your husband?"

She hesitated, turning the four-carat diamond ring she wore on her index finger nervously with her thumb.

"It was sometime last summer, maybe July…yes, July because my oldest son left for Europe in August. He had to look something up for Rashid, some information the man asked for."

"OK," said Schneider, "we'll get back to that in a minute. You said the call your husband received two days ago upset him. What was the problem? Why did it upset him?"

"Rashid told me the man wanted him to drive to Portland; he didn't want to. But something the man said convinced him it was OK."

"Do you know where the man was calling from?"

"No," she answered.

"Rashid took the calls on the same cellular phone that you gave us?"

She nodded affirmatively.

Special Agent Schneider flipped through a yellow legal pad that contained his case notes.

"What information did this man ask for when he called last summer?"

She scrunched her face and looked away for a moment. Then her eyes lit up as if the answer had just arrived in her cerebral inbox.

"This is going to sound weird," she mumbled.

"Try me," said Schneider with an edge of frustration in his voice.

"My son was working as a summer intern in Congressman Miranda's office. Rashid asked my son to confirm that the president would be in Washington in August. He said one of his clients was interested in arranging a meeting with him. It was really anal. The man kept calling Rashid, asking him to confirm the dates that the president would be in the White House."

The room fell silent. Neither Schneider nor Bernstein showed any reaction.

A moment later, Bernstein asked, "Is this the same Congressman Miranda who was arrested for money laundering?"

She smiled and shook her head. "I don't pay attention to politics," she answered. "Now, if it's a sale at Julian Chang or Fendi Casa, I'm on it!"

Bernstein merely nodded.

"Did Congressman Miranda pass on the information regarding the president's schedule to Rashid?" continued Schneider.

"Yes," she replied, "Congressman Miranda was only too happy to get it for him. Miranda was always trying to line Rashid up for business. But he didn't do this out of love for his country. Miranda got some of the pie too," she said and smiled.

"Some of the pie?" asked Schneider, unable to hide his frustration anymore.

"A commission…a percentage of the contract," she replied dryly.

"You're sure about the month. You are sure it was August?" Bernstein asked.

"Yeah," she answered, "because about two weeks after that, some wacko tried to fly into the White House. My son was in Europe when that happened."

"Was Rashid in Florida when the man tried to fly into the White House?"

She didn't answer but appeared to be thinking about the event. Eventually, she turned toward Schneider.

"He was in Florida, and he wasn't," she murmured. "He began drinking...hard. I'd find him on the patio in his underwear, really out of it. He kept on saying, 'I'm fucked...I'm fucked.' And he must have been hallucinating because he was worried about a leprechaun. He usually drank heavily when a business deal fell through, but this was different."

The two agents merely stared at her without saying a word.

"You don't think he had anything to do with that White House thing?" she asked, looking thoroughly confused.

"Nancy," said Bernstein, copying her bewildered look, "I think you know the answer to that question...and more. But this interview is over for now. We'll be in touch."

Schneider excused himself and walked to the receptionist's desk.

"Get Assistant Director Sabinson on the phone now. I'll be in my office—it's urgent."

16

VANISHING ACT

Two days later
Chester, Nova Scotia
9:45 a.m.

The realtor was pleased that she'd been able to rent the small, sparsely furnished cottage. It sat back in a thick stand of pines, hidden from the road, and had been vacant all summer. The tourist industry in the Maritimes was in a slump. The economy was stagnant, and the high gas prices had cut the normal flow of tourists from the States by more than half. It was late October and the rental had been a godsend for her family. Her husband, a cod fisherman, had been out of work for nearly a year.

She'd been impressed with the renter. He'd driven to her office in a plain, gray compact. He was pleasant and well-mannered, and he had paid six months' rent in advance with US dollars, without questioning the rental price. The man told her he was a writer, trying to finish his first manuscript. With an artsy name like Winslow Braswell, she was sure he'd be successful.

He'd been concerned about privacy, stating that he wanted a location that would allow him to concentrate without being interrupted. She laughed and assured him that the only visitors he might have would be a stray fox or porcupine.

Before leaving the office, he'd also given her a five-thousand-dollar cash deposit, asking that she obtain phone and Internet service for the cottage in her name. His reason was absolutely plausible; he had no credit history in Canada. And he emphasized that he could give her more cash when she needed it. She happily agreed to start his phone and Internet service.

• • •

Abdul Hamsa sat back in an overstuffed chair in the cabin's living room and yawned. He was beginning to relax after his long journey from Portland. He would begin contacting his network in the morning.

Portland, Maine
FBI Field Office
10:15 a.m.

Special Agents Schneider and Bernstein sat in front of the computer's twenty-one-inch flat-panel screen alongside Portland's chief of police and their chief of criminal forensics. Earlier in the morning, they had submitted four digitally enhanced fingerprints that Portland's forensics team had lifted from the back of al-Bakar's Mercedes rearview mirror. The prints didn't match al-Bakar or his wife's. It was a long shot, but it was all they had. The group sat, waiting for match results from the Bureau's digital index in Washington.

The phone rang, and Schneider picked up the handset. He listened for a moment and then pointed toward the computer's monitor. The musical chime of an incoming e-mail resonated in the hushed room. Bernstein typed in his access code, and the screen filled with three mug-shot photos and side-by-side comparisons of the digital prints that had been sent.

The document's header contained the subject's identification in bold print: "John Thomas Cronin; aliases on record: Abdul Hamsa, Byron Werner, John Thomas, and Kenneth Allen."

The agent thanked the caller and hung up. His next call was to Colby Sabinson.

One week later
Quantico, Virginia
8:30 a.m.

Sabinson had not exaggerated the number of al-Bakar's files or the time it would take Garcia and Montiel to review them. His attorney had turned over the seventeen cardboard file boxes of paper documents without a fight. He didn't want anything pertaining to al-Bakar to be within five hundred miles of his law office.

The bulk of the six thousand documents related to contacts and sales made during the Iran-Contra days. Those were shipped to the Department of Justice for their ongoing investigations.

It wasn't until Garcia and Montiel reached box number fifteen that their interest was piqued. This box contained hundreds of multipaged phone bills. Garcia pulled out the first of the batch: a nine-page cell phone bill for one month.

As he reached the third page, a number stared back at him—one he'd seen before. It had a 412 western Pennsylvania area code. Using his database, Garcia began to search for the number. It came up with a match in two seconds.

Al-Bakar had called the same number that showed up as an outgoing call on the day of the Boston bombing. Although his grand jury date had been cancelled, al-Bakar was testifying from the grave.

"Leo, I've got something for the NSA cell tower database. How long will it take them to run this?"

Montiel picked up the handset of the STU-4 secure phone and punched the second speed-dial button, the FBI's liaison officer with the NSA. After a short conversation, he turned toward Garcia. "Ten minutes!"

● ● ●

The mainframe computers on the National Security Agency's fourth floor searched through the databases they had tapped into from all the cellular phone providers in the United States. The computers had identified and followed one of the microwave relays as far west as Logan, Utah, where the electronic trail went cold.

"I'll write up the report for the task force right away," Garcia said as he assembled the notes from the NSA's analyst.

But box fifteen, the one they referred to as "Pandora's Box," yielded one more clue. This time it was Montiel's turn to score.

He pulled a plain, letter-sized manila envelope from the first file folder. It contained a single photograph of al-Bakar. There were snowcapped mountain ranges in the distance, but the immediate surroundings looked like a typical desert—cactus, brush, and sand.

Its subject was a smiling al-Bakar, wearing desert camouflage fatigues and holding an M-16 equipped with a 40 mm grenade launcher. He leaned casually against a signpost that read, "DENT DE SCIE GUN CLUB—NO TRESPASSING." There was an indiscernible Arabic script on the back of the photo.

Garcia and Montiel shouted out at the same time, "Alex!"

• • •

Alexander Masood Khamis was the section's Arabic linguist and probably the most sought-after person in Quantico. He was fluent in Arabic, Spanish, Portuguese, French, and German. His parents, both physicians, had grown up in Abu Dhabi, in the United Arab Emirates. They'd met while attending medical school in London and had immigrated to the United States in order for his father to pursue his specialty, tropical medicine.

Khamis had been born in Baltimore, where his father was completing his advanced studies at the University of Maryland's School of Medicine. He'd been named after his father's best friend in medical school. His nickname, "Alexander the Great," was earned after he'd broken a code used by Brazilian drug dealers that had been written in a little-known Portuguese dialect.

At five feet five, he was muscular and compact. He'd been a consensus all-American lacrosse player for three years in a row at Johns Hopkins University. However, two years after graduating and joining the FBI as a field agent, he'd suffered severe spinal cord injuries while skiing in Canada, rendering him a paraplegic. But he had never slowed down. And more importantly, the FBI had never given up on him. Instead of a medical retirement, Alex Khamis was granted a transfer to the intelligence section.

Khamis read and reread the writing on the back of the photo. Then he turned the picture over, gazing at the scene. He grasped the small joystick in his right hand and pulled back hard. His electric wheelchair shot back, and then he spun the chair ninety degrees, facing one of his bookcases.

He reached out and grasped a road atlas and returned to his desk, thumbing through the pages until he reached the section he'd been looking for.

"Does the Arabic writing say where he is?" asked Garcia.

Khamis looked at Garcia and nodded slowly.

"He's in northern Utah, close to the Idaho border, west of the Sawtooth National Forest."

Their mouths dropped in amazement.

"It says all that in Arabic?" exclaimed Montiel.

"Not exactly," Khamis laughed. "I recognized the mountain range behind them, the Raft River Mountains. I used to cross-country ski in that area. The clincher was the gun-club sign. It says, 'Sawtooth,' in French. The Sawtooth National Forest is probably east of where he is. The Arabic says, 'Training Camp,' and lists the date, March of 1998."

Garcia and Montiel left Khamis's office feeling slightly less intelligent than they had when they'd entered. They spent the next hour and a half assembling the information they'd gathered and scanned the photo in as the last exhibit. Garcia decided to call Sabinson directly.

"We've tracked down eight phone calls to the same isolated area—about thirty-five miles from Logan, Utah. It sure fits the ideal site for a training base. I think it's worth the time to have some agents take a look."

Sabinson didn't need any further convincing; the photo had taken care of any doubts he may have had. He would begin immediately with ground surveillance.

17

ALEXANDER CUTS THE
GORDIAN KNOT

At about three thirty in the morning, an FBI surveillance team found the sign in the photo. The entrance to the site was located just off State Route 30. The gate was pad-locked, and an older-model Jeep patrolled the inner perimeter, sweeping the area with a spotlight. Two heavily armed figures dressed in desert camouflage had exited the Jeep to check on the series of chains and locks that secured the entry gate. They missed the FBI vehicle parked thirty yards away behind some brush.

Agents had conducted an online search of the land records for the site and found a deed for the two-hundred-acre tract in the name of the Sawtooth Gun Club, Incorporated, Yost, Utah. Sabinson had authorized an aggressive surveillance.

Northwest Utah
8:30 p.m.

The unmarked C-130D maintained its altitude of twenty thousand feet as it orbited slowly over the barren stretches of desert just west of the Sawtooth National Forest. Its complement of sophisticated visual surveillance gear and electronic sensors swept the desert floor.

The forms of two large Quonset huts glowed brightly in the FLIR operator's screen. He could even make out a group of people about half a mile away, conducting target practice in a narrow gully. The muzzle blasts of their weapons twinkled on his screen like fireflies. The sensor operator glanced at the panel in front of him. A small amber light began blinking, telling him that the cellular intercept equipment was picking up a call. The Arabic linguist adjusted his earphones and pushed the toggle switch on the panel in front of him to record. The receiving cellular's ID popped up on a small screen above the linguist's writing table.

"The call's coming in from Madrid, but it's a patch from some other location," the sensor operator explained. "The point of origin is blocked. The receiving cellular is a prepaid disposable, area code 412."

The linguist concentrated on the first words of the conversation.

"Are you on schedule with Cascade?" asked the caller.

"We're ahead of schedule. We will depart in two days."

"Excellent," said the caller. "Your visit shall leave them deaf and blind."

"We have watched them carefully. They are more interested in drinking coffee and filling their bellies than security. Karim and his group will disable the alarm systems. Then it's just a matter of placing the soup on the legs. We'll use the caps recommended by your friend. They are one hundred percent reliable."

"There will be no more problems with caps. I took care of that problem," the caller growled. "God is great!"

"And the triad is doomed," the man replied, and the call ended.

The linguist passed a typewritten copy of the conversation to an FBI agent seated beside her. After reviewing the notes, the agent reached for the secure phone and called Sabinson in Washington.

Quantico
Terrorism Task Force Intelligence Center
11:30 p.m.

Garcia, Montiel, and Khamis had been placed on stand-by earlier in the day. They had been assigned one task: review and analyze any intercept information from the C-130 flight, and have their analysis ready for Sabinson as soon as possible.

Sabinson had wanted to wait and continue covert surveillance of the Utah group in hopes that Hamsa would show up. He pressed Garcia for a definite plan—a go or no-go on taking the group down.

• • •

By quarter to six the next morning, Garcia, Montiel, and Khamis had hammered out a rough analysis of the voice intercept. Their review of the recording had identified two immediate problems: the use of a slang that was particular to the Arabic language used in south Yemen and the misinterpretation of key phrases by the linguist. Khamis had solved these riddles after consulting a sixty-year-old reference book that he kept in his library. Garcia and Montiel then put together the rest of the puzzle by identifying the group's objective and worked backward from there. Even though it may have been early in the morning, Sabinson was wide awake and attentive.

The word *soup*, mentioned in the sentence "Then it's just a matter of placing the soup on the legs"—Khamis had found it in the sixty-year-old text, whose uniquely bizarre title read *Guide to Ordnance Terminology for British Army Operations in the Middle Eastern and North African Theatres of War*. *Soup* was the slang term for "a mixture of TNT-based explosives or charges." *Cap* was another slang term, used for "fuse" or "detonator." These words had been adopted by the native Arabic speakers and had been passed down to the present generation. However, the term *legs*, used in the phrase "placing the soup on the legs," had to wait for the solution to the term *triad*, from "And the triad is doomed."

Khamis replayed the last phrase twenty times. He struggled with two or three alternatives, and then he had it.

The word in Arabic that had been used was not a literal translation of *triad*, but the cardinal number three, *thalaathatun*. The linguist translated what she heard to mean *triad*, or "three closely related things."

Khamis had written out variables for the Arabic word *thalaathatun*: "tri," "triumvirate," "triple," and he threw in "trinity" for good measure. When the team began discussing the possibilities, Garcia launched himself from his chair toward a map of strategic Department of Defense sites in the United States.

Trinity referred to a major telecommunications site located outside of Golden, Colorado. It was so named because of the three towers installed at one of the highest areas in the southern Rockies. This site relayed all military telecommunications and satellite-image transmissions worldwide. The towers were set above a series of reinforced "legs" that anchored the structures in place.

The team's final challenge was to add flesh to the word *cascade*. Once the towers were taken down by explosives, their failure would begin a chain of events where the back-up systems would overload at an increasing rate. One after the other would fail as the momentum cascaded down the series of systems. The initial failure would become a torrent, leaving the DOD "deaf and blind."

● ● ●

"So, putting the facts together," Garcia said, "This is a terrorist group ready to depart on a mission that could destroy or disable the military and intelligence capabilities of the United States for a period of weeks, if not months. You wanted our advice, so here it is. Go after these people now—today—and stop them.

Hit them hard because whoever was talking will never speak in the clear again."

Sabinson thanked Garcia and his team. His next call was to the FBI's director.

The next day
Northwestern Utah
3:15 a.m.

The decision to take immediate action had been made, based on Garcia's urging. The conversation that had been intercepted left the Terrorism Task Force with few options. Although Garcia listed the probability of Hamsa being there as low, Sabinson could only hope that Garcia was wrong this time.

The three MH-60 Pave Hawk helicopters flew through the darkness at an altitude of one hundred feet, full bore at 185 mph. Each helicopter carried twenty members of a combined FBI-ATF SWAT unit and all their gear. They'd assembled and coordinated the operation in less than twelve hours.

Behind them, a fleet of ten armored Humvees had just veered off State Road 30. They were jammed with additional FBI agents and Utah State Police officers. Their task was to back up the units landing in front of them. The armored Humvees, equipped with heavy-duty, dragon-tooth front bumpers, accelerated as they plowed through the locked gate and dashed toward the Quonset huts located a mile inside the fence line.

The Pave Hawks flared and landed three hundred yards from the two Quonset huts. The SWAT teams disembarked, and the helicopters lifted off immediately. The group ran forward, as fast as their ammo bags and other gear allowed.

One of the sentries posted near the command hut ran around the side of the building when he first saw the dust being kicked up by the flaring Pave Hawks. He hadn't heard the helicopters coming in because he'd been listening to a Bollywood soundtrack on his headphones. He brought his weapon up to his shoulder and began firing wildly into the darkness. At that instant, he was cut down by an ATF sharpshooter. Two other armed sentries appeared at the corner of the building and were taken out in the same fashion.

Panic and disorientation ruled inside the Quonset huts. Men tried to find their weapons and ammunition in the dark but only succeeded in stumbling into each other.

Then the Humvees arrived, forming a crescent shape fifty meters to the east of the buildings. They lit up the huts with their fifty-million-candlepower searchlights. A two-thousand-watt loudspeaker was directed toward the larger hut.

"This is the FBI! You are completely surrounded! Come out with your hands up, and no harm will come to you!"

No response was heard. After waiting for sixty seconds, a CS gas canister was shot into each hut. Gas vapor wafted out from the broken windows, but no one came out. Finally, a voice inside one of the huts shouted, "God is great!"

An explosion ripped through both huts, nearly blinding the converging government forces. Fires burned for about thirty minutes and finally died down. The smell of explosives and burning flesh lingered in the frigid air.

• • •

Sabinson ordered two teams of forensic specialists to be flown in immediately. He wanted to determine whether Hamsa was among the dead. The answer would disappoint him even further.

Although the absence of Hamsa was a blow to Sabinson's efforts to cut the head off the monster, his forensics team did find one item that would give them an insight into Hamsa's ultimate objective. It was contained in a single, scorched two-gigabyte thumb drive that survived the explosions and fires that had consumed both Quonset huts.

The innocuous, red, plastic flash drive contained thousands of e-mails. Some were personal communications between Hamsa;

Mahmud Fayad, al-Qaeda's chief of operations; Ayman al-Zawahiri, bin Laden's deputy; and bin Laden himself. Although the flash drive had been placed in an evidence bag with other bits and pieces of documents salvaged from the inferno, its electronic analysis would open the eyes of many Western intelligence experts to the counterintelligence adage "Simple may be slow but it's safer."

The process that al-Qaeda had used was built on strict discipline; no exceptions to the communications rules were tolerated. Messages were typed on computers without an Internet connection. After completion, they were saved using a flash drive. Then a courier would travel to a distant Internet café, never using the same location twice in a row. At the selected Internet café, the courier would plug the memory drive into a computer, copy the message into an e-mail, and send it. The process was merely reversed for any incoming e-mail, where the message would be copied into the flash drive. Messages were never read online, and e-mail addresses were changed weekly. It was a labor-intensive process, but it worked.

18

FRIENDS AND FAMILY

Four days later
Quantico, Virginia
9:30 a.m.

Garcia and Montiel strolled back to their cubicle from the morning briefing. One of the FBI's behavioral-science profilers had presented a summary of Hamsa's survivalist skills, noting that he enjoyed the role of the "faceless assassin," similar to the Bruce Willis character in *The Day of the Jackal.* But she had opened and closed her presentation with the same questions: How did Abdul Hamsa get out of Portland? Did he get out of Portland? And where was he now?

As they sat down, Garcia turned to Montiel and snapped his fingers.

"How did Hamsa get out of Portland? The answer's in the investigation report we've been reviewing!"

Garcia picked up the thick document and flipped forward until he came to the page he had marked with a purple Mylar tab. He glanced at it for a moment and then turned toward Montiel.

"This is the summary of actions taken by FBI agents and Portland police when they canvassed the public transportation sites after al-Bakar's murder. They passed out flyers at every location with Hamsa's photos, a day after al-Bakar's murder. They interviewed sales personnel in every transportation site in

Portland: rail, air, car rental, and the ferry terminal. But no one could identify Hamsa. What photos did they use?"

"They used the booking photos from his drug arrest—the 1993 booking photos," Montiel responded.

"Right," said Garcia. "He's changed his appearance. His face wasn't on those flyers, but his name was. We missed it. He was trained in escape and evasion. The lecturer said it herself."

Garcia snatched Hamsa's mug shots they had taped to one of their bookcases and began drawing in different features.

Montiel watched Garcia's doodling for a minute and then nodded his head in approval.

"I struck up a friendship with the forensic-science supervisor. She just finished updating a program that can give us aging and facial changes within a few seconds. How about if we ask her to do a little collage for us—some hair color options and different facial hair styles for our friend, Sheik Hamsa?"

"That's a great idea, Leo, but every time you 'strike up a friendship' with one of the ladies in the forensics department, you end up disappearing with her for the weekend. Have they figured out the pattern yet?"

"I think that they consider it sharing a 'foreign asset,' Christopher. No property rights are involved."

"You are a shameless man!" growled Garcia.

• • •

It was mid-December, and the vacation schedule had begun. But the three stalwart bachelors in the analysts' section—Garcia, Montiel, and Khamis—had decided to work through the holiday period. On Christmas Eve night, the Officer's Club was running its half-price special from three in the afternoon until midnight. A massive snowstorm had swept down from the north, leaving them in sole possession of the bar. The three lived only about a hundred yards from the club.

Montiel had retrieved his guitar and he, Khamis, and Garcia had entertained the skeleton staff in the bar, who found themselves stranded by the storm. Montiel's renditions of classical flamenco music became as intense as some of the new lyrics that were added by Garcia and Khamis.

With a few hours to go before closing time, the bartender placed the chafing dishes filled with lobster, shrimp, and sirloin tips on the table beside them.

"Gentlemen," he said, "Merry Christmas. We were expecting a crowd, but the weather changed that. You three have been our best—and only—customers. Please don't let this go to waste."

He didn't need to repeat himself. The three dug into the fare immediately. He returned with two pitchers of cold Michelob Dark, making it a very Merry Christmas.

They watched the end of the news report on the wall-mounted fifty-inch flat-screen that featured a segment on the blizzard-like road conditions. At this point, Khamis put his fork down and lifted a handsome color print of a sailing ship from his lap, placing it in front of Garcia. It was a print of one of the first revenue cutters commissioned by Alexander Hamilton, secretary of the Treasury in 1790—the US Revenue Cutter *Massachusetts*.

"Merry Christmas, Chris, this is from Leo and me for being our team leader and making us look good."

Garcia held the print in his hands and, after a long moment, glanced at Montiel and Khamis. Although Garcia tried to hide it, he was impressed.

"I have nothing for either of you that would ever equal this," he said, recovering from the initial wave of emotion.

At that instant, two more pitchers of cold Michelob Dark arrived, and they did something they had promised not to do. They talked about Hamsa.

"Sometimes I think we'd have more luck finding Hamsa by throwing darts at a map of the world," Montiel said. "It would be a lot easier if he were on some 'family and friends' cellular plan, so we could tap in and listen."

"The Bureau interviewed Hamsa's family," Khamis said. "They weren't much help. The father kept insisting that we had fabricated his son's crimes and that he was really being held captive by a cult religious group in Texas."

"Leo," Garcia said grinning, "say that again…the 'family and friends' thing."

Montiel looked over his glasses at Garcia. "Why do I have a feeling that something bad is about to happen?"

"Not 'friends' in that sense, but associates: do we have a list of Hamsa's past associates?" Garcia asked.

"The only information we have is from ATF and the FBI's criminal files. But you're right: no associates list."

"I think we need to see *all* the interagency files on Hamsa, not just what the Bureau has!"

Montiel rocked back in his chair, looking at Garcia.

"I know, Chris. You don't have to say it. 'Leo, can you call your friend in the liaison office and have her send us any collateral intelligence reports for that *son of a bitch* Hamsa,'" Montiel said, mimicking Garcia.

Their laughter echoed throughout the empty bar, but it was cut short by the entry of three snow-covered women from the base Administration Office who had attempted, but failed, to drive to their apartments located off base.

Montiel was the first to recover and uttered, "There is a God," followed by Khamis, who said, "And he is a wise God," followed by Garcia, who completed the praise, by saying, "And he is a most generous God, with excellent taste!"

Garcia stood immediately and waived them over to the table. They were thrilled by the invitation—all second lieutenants, long legged and looking for adventure. Hot spiced rum was ordered, and the real party got underway.

After closing time, Khamis led the way through the increasing blizzard conditions in his powered chair. One of the women sat in his lap, holding four bottles of Bailey's Irish Cream. Garcia and Montiel and the accompanying admin staff were towed behind Khamis's chair on large aluminum trays, borrowed from the club and tied in line by some tablecloths that had been provided by the barman.

The party continued until early the next morning. Loud snoring replaced the music as the sun rose.

19

Abaddon Rises

Two days later
Near Chester, Nova Scotia
9:00 p.m.

Abdul Hamsa was furious. He'd been watching the evening news when a follow-up report on the FBI's Utah raid was aired. His plans were now in shambles. He'd planned to attack a number of power transmission centers in the Rocky Mountains after the Trinity attack, but the entire cadre of trained terrorists had been wiped out.

The news report contained no specifics about how the FBI had discovered the site and the Bureau remained strangely tight-lipped about their sources. And this began to bother him. He considered all the possibilities, thinking them through. He reached the same conclusion after analyzing each of the scenarios. Someone inside his group was cooperating with the government.

Three days later
Quantico, Virginia
1:15 p.m.

Garcia and Montiel finished preparing the collage of computer-generated photos for Hamsa's updated features. The new images would be distributed worldwide in early January. They'd convinced Sabinson to begin arresting some of Hamsa's lower-level sympathizers in order to diminish his comfort level and disrupt his network. They were also promised a list of Hamsa's prior associates in two weeks.

New Year's Eve
Chester, Nova Scotia
11:15 p.m.

Abdul Hamsa was in a foul mood. He'd made several calls to a pay phone in Atlanta at the prearranged time, but no one answered. After trying for two more hours, he finally made contact, but he wasn't pleased with the conversation.

FBI agents had descended on al-Qaeda cells in Los Angeles; Newark, New Jersey, and Dearborn, Michigan, arresting thirteen of Hamsa's supporters. The once-faceless group was beginning to feel the pressure. Their protection was being peeled away, one layer at a time. Hamsa's frustration was intensified by the fact that it was hazardous for him to travel and his communications were limited to a few prearranged phone calls and an occasional e-mail. The only good news Hamsa received was that Jack Riley had been contacted and would be arriving in one week.

Now, as the crowds of East Coast revelers celebrated the New Year's arrival, Hamsa stood alone outside of his cottage, swilling down the remainder of a bottle of Screech Rum his landlady had dropped off as a Christmas gift. He wore a light flannel shirt and felt the wind cutting through the fabric in the ten-degree weather. It had been snowing for days, and the weather only added to his misery. As he drank, he thought about the two great tragedies in his life: the family of infidels that had raised him and his association with al-Bakar. He cursed them all to hell as he stumbled through the snow.

One week later
Halifax, Nova Scotia
5:10 p.m.

Hamsa drove away from the airport, heading west toward Route 103 and Chester. With him was Jack Riley.

"The trip's shattered the nerves, Abdul, my boy. I'll need just a taste to settle me down a bit," Riley said, pulling the fifth of bonded Irish whiskey from his suitcase. He broke the seal and downed about four ounces in one swallow.

Hamsa remembered a few years back when "just a taste" for Riley meant two bottles. The Irishman had been one of the most sought-after explosives experts in the world. He'd trained five cadres of young terrorists in the isolated desert stretches of Yemen. One of his teams had initiated the attack on the USS *Cole*.

Most recently, he had distinguished himself again. He'd received a five-hundred-thousand-dollar bonus after instructing the Colombian FARC guerillas in the fine art of turning propane gas cylinders into guided missiles.

Hamsa glanced at him as Riley consumed the bottle's contents.

"I'm glad you haven't changed, Jack."

"No need to, Abdul," Riley said bitterly, "I'm rich and retired…And I've run out of challenges."

Riley was becoming more morose by the minute until they passed by Halifax's busy seaport. He glanced out the window toward the large merchant ships and suddenly perked up.

"Abdul, we're passing a place that used to be called Old Halifax. During World War I, an ammunition ship waiting to transit the Atlantic exploded in this harbor. It wiped out almost two square miles of city in a few seconds and killed over two thousand people. It was the biggest manmade explosion until Hiroshima. The blast wave created a tsunami that took out people on the shoreline for miles. Compared to what we use today, those explosives are considered primitive, but look what they did! Explosives—aren't they grand?"

Hamsa smiled, not saying a word as Riley opened another bottle and downed four ounces in one gulp. He turned toward Hamsa, putting his hand on his shoulder.

"That lying bastard al-Bakar—he got what he deserved. Bugger 'em all!"

"I should have listened to you, Jack," said Hamsa. "I don't know how much damage he did. But I need a solution to another problem now—my communications. Were you able to contact that friend of yours, the IT security consultant?"

Riley took another swig from the bottle and nodded.

"You mean the IRA hacker who found religion," Riley laughed. "Abdul, the solution is foolproof. It'll take those knobbers ten years to figure it out. Most e-mail is encrypted and routed through IP servers to a destination. My guy wrote an encryption program to allow e-mails from your group to be diverted to a remote server, just like your own private post-office box. Then, you make a visit to the post office and pick up your mail. And no one else can read it. Not even those bloody FBI twits."

Hamsa shot a glance at Riley.

"And what if someone tries to track the e-mail, trace it to its point of origin?"

"His program contains a new type of firewall. It interrogates all incoming e-mail. If your security credentials aren't registered, you get sent to a dummy server that's buried under a trillion layers of electronic bullshit. Basically, the tracking attempt ends up in outer space, going round and round." Riley laughed heartily. "The software's in my bag. We can install it when we get to your place."

Hamsa, for the first time in weeks, was genuinely pleased. After a number of failures, something was finally going right.

For the remainder of the trip, Riley occupied himself with the destruction of the bottle's contents. Hamsa was deep in thought and hardly paid attention to his companion, other than an occasional grunt when Riley tugged on his sleeve during one of his tirades.

They finally pulled into the driveway, and Hamsa helped a heavily listing Riley into his cabin. Because of Riley's "exhaustion," Hamsa decided to present his plan to him in the morning. Riley curled up on a large sofa and, in minutes, was snoring loudly.

Hamsa made sure that Riley's encryption software was loaded and working before retiring. For the first time in weeks, he slept a full eight hours.

The next day
10:15 a.m.

Riley had fully recovered his senses, but only after consuming a pound of fried Canadian bacon, washed down by five cups of strong black coffee and two bottles of Molson Ale as a chaser. Hamsa had gotten up at six and remained entrenched behind the computer, sending a flurry of e-mails. He walked to the sofa where Riley had collapsed after breakfast.

"Do you still have your contacts with the FARC in Colombia?"

Riley looked at him for a moment and then sat up, offering Hamsa the other half of the sofa.

"Abdul, I never lost touch with those boys. They're my retirement fund. What do you need?"

"Jack, I can't trust anyone else with this. It'll be one of the biggest challenges you'll ever face in your life. I need you to close a deal for me. Can you do it?"

Hamsa handed Riley two documents he'd prepared in the early morning. Riley reviewed each document, and his eyes began to dart back and forth across the page.

"This is a dream come true. Hell yes, I can do it!"

Hamsa couldn't help but laugh. The old Jack Riley was still somewhere in that body.

"And I'll need one more thing before you go."

"Name it!" hollered Riley, now fully energized.

"I'll need a sketch of the device you wanted to use in London."

"I'll have it for you in an hour."

Riley was in heaven. He was needed, and there was more killing to be done.

20

A Mother's Love

Two days later
Guatemala City, Guatemala
US Embassy
8:15 a.m.

A slightly built middle-aged woman with strong Mayan features shuffled her way forward in the serpentine queue near the main gate of the American embassy. She wore her best skirt and blouse for the occasion and had even purchased a new pair of shoes. She held a tattered manila envelope close to her. Although she had been in line for three hours, it didn't matter. She was ready to stand in line all day, all week if necessary.

The woman finally reached the security checkpoint and tendered her identification card. When asked to state the reason for her visit, she replied that her son's photograph had appeared on an American television show, *America's Most Wanted*. She'd been told that the embassy could help her get her son's body returned to Guatemala for burial.

Within minutes, the embassy's regional security officer appeared at the security checkpoint. He escorted the woman to his office and began to interview her.

He'd been skeptical about her story until she reached into the manila envelope and produced three photographs of her son that matched the postmortem pictures of the ultralight's pilot shown on AMW. He called the ambassador immediately.

Quantico, Virginia
10:45 a.m.

Sabinson finally had a solid lead in the failed August attack on the White House. After finishing his conversation with the US ambassador to Guatemala, he'd contacted Garcia. One of the FBI's Cessna Citations had been fueled and was ready to proceed to Guatemala City. But there were more questions than answers. It was up to Garcia, Montiel, and Khamis to fill in the blanks.

They dashed to Dulles in one of the specially equipped vans that lifted Khamis and his chair aboard. They would structure the interview during the flight to Guatemala. It would start at eight sharp the following morning.

The next day
Guatemala City
US Embassy—Visitor's Conference Room
9:10 a.m.

The forty-nine-year-old woman, Gloria Beltran, sat stoically at the end of a long wooden table, with the well-traveled manila envelope in front of her. She rested her hands on top of the envelope, touching it gently as she spoke.

The RSO had made copies of the original photos for the Quantico analysts. Garcia sat to her side, and she faced Montiel and Khamis.

She had seen the television program while visiting her brother, just before Christmas. She had never learned to read, and he translated the Spanish subtitles for her. She saved her money and finally was able to afford the bus fare to the capital.

She had first met the pilot's father when he and a group of Middle Eastern immigrants had arrived in Guatemala in the midseventies. They had three sons—one of whom was the ultralight's pilot. Her husband had joined a radical mosque in Guatemala City, but she did not like the subservient lifestyle she was subjected to. She had grown up in a male-dominated society but had never been treated like a slave. The last straw came when the husband demanded that she wear a burka that covered her entire body. He destroyed her perfume and refused to let her listen to the radio or leave the house without his permission. He whipped her with a cane pole so badly that she'd been hospitalized. While she was in the hospital, her husband had taken the three boys and moved from their village, refusing to let her see them.

Her eldest son, Enrique, had maintained weekly contact with her. But she worried because he'd become very religious, expressing his hatred for all nonbelievers. Then in the early 1990s, the father had taken all three boys to Pakistan and then on to Afghanistan.

During July of the past year, Enrique had reappeared. He told her that he'd been chosen for a great honor but was very secretive about what it was. He'd left some photos with her.

"The night before he left, Enrique sat on the edge of my bed. He cried, telling me that he would not see me again, but he loved me. I begged him to tell me why I would never see him again. He said he was part of a great jihad; he called it the 'first strike.' He said the second strike would take place this year…at a place and on a date of great significance to the United States."

"Did he say any more about the second strike?" asked Garcia.

"No," she said, "after that, he would only talk about Islam—the type of Islam that he was being taught. I begged him not to leave, but he told me that he was happy. And he gave me these," she said as she opened the manila envelope and withdrew three photos, placing them in front of her.

Garcia stood and walked around the end of the table where he, Khamis, and Montiel could see them. Staring out at them was her son, the pilot. He stood proudly beside an ultralight aircraft, with desert and mountains in background. Barely visible was an old, weather-beaten sign that read, "DENT DE SCIE GUN CLUB—NO TRESPASSING."

"Remind you of another one we've seen before?" asked Khamis.

Neither Garcia nor Montiel responded. Their gaze was fixed on the photos as more of the puzzle pieces came together.

The second photo showed her son and three others standing at attention and smiling broadly. They wore desert fatigues, and everyone except Enrique wore full beards. In front of the four men were items usually not found in any gun club—an RPG-29 and a stack of Claymore mines.

The third photo showed her son posed beside the ultralight, giving the thumbs-up gesture.

The room was still as Garcia walked back to his chair.

"Has anyone contacted you since your son's death?" asked Garcia.

"Yes," she said, pursing her lips, "a young man from the mosque came to my village after I had seen the television show. He offered me twenty-five thousand US dollars as payment for my son's sacrifice. I told him to go to hell—that it was blood money. I told him that no amount of money could bring my son back. He slapped me in the face and left."

Garcia leaned closer to the woman and looked directly into her eyes.

"You came here to ask for help. Do you want to bury your son here?" asked Garcia.

She nodded slowly, showing no emotion.

"We will have your son's body returned, and we thank you for the help you have given us."

Although tears began to run down her face, she maintained the same stoic expression she had during the interview.

"He was never raised to do what he did," she said. "I don't know where I lost him."

As the woman rose from the chair, she reached into the manila envelope and withdrew a small, laminated card containing Arabic writing.

"He left this in his old room. I found it one day when I was cleaning. I have no use for it."

Garcia handed the card to Khamis, and the woman was escorted out of the room.

"It's a prayer for the dead," said Khamis, "but the last paragraph is meant for those who have died in this jihad: 'And you shall rise again after the second strike and come back into this life. God will reward you for your bravery, and you will have peace for the rest of your days."

Dulles International Airport
12:35 a.m.

The Cessna Citation touched down and taxied to the restricted government hanger. Garcia had sent copies of the three photographs to the task force and Sabinson before leaving the embassy. The flight back had been quiet; each man was involved in his own thought processes. But some of the secrecy had been stripped away. Hamsa's advantage had been reduced, but by how much?

21

MERCHANT OF VENICE—
MERCHANT OF DEATH

Four days later
Willemstad, Curacao
Hato International Airport
2:10 p.m.

Riley exited the Air Canada flight from Halifax, bounding down the shaky, aluminum passenger stairs two at a time. He was a man on a mission, and after years of boredom, he was finally back in the game he loved.

During the five-hour flight, he'd read and reread the detailed instructions that Hamsa had printed out. He remembered the phrase that Hamsa had used—"One of the biggest challenges you'll ever face"—and realized that his friend had not understated the task.

After passing through the customs checkpoint, he maneuvered his roll-on suitcase through a maze of tourists to the white microbus with a tropical Marriott logo.

• • •

After checking in at the high-end resort, he quickly unpacked and waited for his contacts to arrive. Within minutes, he heard a faint knock on the door. Riley glanced through the fisheye door viewer and slowly pulled the door open. Standing just outside of the threshold were two men, clean-shaven and dressed in white cotton guayaberas, linen slacks, and Reef sandals. Riley gave each man a hearty abrazo and directed them into his suite. He glanced down the hallway and then closed and locked the door.

Riley's visitors had traveled for a week to meet with him. They had started their journey in the jungles of Ecuador, flying in a chartered helicopter to Venezuela and then a commercial jet to Curacao. They were members of the ruling junta of the Revolutionary Armed Forces of Colombia, the FARC—Colombia's most violent terrorist group. To ensure their anonymity, they'd shaved their revolutionary beards before leaving their camp. The taller of the two was Enrique "Quique" Cano, chief of operations for the FARC, and the other was Jairo Jimenez, known as "JJ," the organization's banker and chief financial advisor. The three sat in cushioned wicker chairs set up around a minibar, attempting to catch up on past events.

"Christ almighty, Quique, how long has it been…five years?" Riley asked.

"Five long years, Jack. We thought you were dead."

Riley smiled broadly as he filled the highball glasses with four-ounce shots of Old Parr whiskey.

"It would take more than a few government troops to kill old Jackie," Riley scoffed.

Riley had been the IRA's "Caribbean liaison officer," representing the Sinn Fein in Cuba. Eventually, he moved on to Colombia, where he initiated explosives training for the FARC terrorists. He'd barely escaped a government ambush that captured three IRA members and placed him on the IRA's blacklist. The reason for his unpardonable sin was classic Riley. He'd gotten very drunk and overslept, missing the patrol.

"I've been reading the newspapers," Riley said. "That Leticia attack was excellent; it was a textbook encirclement—ambush and kill." He passed the glasses to his visitors. "And you put my training to good use. The mortars did their job."

"We killed almost three hundred after we trapped them in a church. And then, poof!" Cano said, motioning with his hands as if creating a billowing smoke cloud.

"The place burned so fast that we heard only a few screams before everyone was turned into charcoal."

"Was there any fallout from the bleeding-heart press about the children?" chuckled Riley.

"We explained to the few who criticized us that the children were being used as shields, so we had no choice. They would have grown up to be government soldiers anyway." blurted out Cano, "Better to take them out now!"

The incident that was being discussed involved the massacre of two hundred ninety-eight civilians, including over one hundred children, just outside the Amazonian town of Leticia on Colombia's Pacific coast. The children had been especially targeted because most were dependents of local police and Colombian army soldiers assigned to duty there. The gas-cylinder incendiary mortar had been invented by Riley in 1995. The weapon, consisting of a 55-gallon drum with a large propane gas cylinder inserted in it, was first used by the IRA in Ulster.

In Leticia, Riley's invention had been used to incinerate the people after they had taken refuge in an old church during a FARC assault. There had been other massacres, but this one in particular was Riley's favorite. In truth, he'd taken credit for the death toll and added the clippings and grisly photos to his scrap book.

But there were more important matters at hand, and Riley chose to press forward with the business that had brought him to Curacao.

"Quique, JJ, thank you for coordinating today's meeting. I know you had to pull some strings, and I appreciate that. I don't know Pollard, but you do. Can he deliver my order?"

"He has the merchandise you need," Cano responded coolly.

"Would the FARC be interested in purchasing a few pieces of our order? I mean, once the Colombian government realizes what you possess, they would have no other option but to agree to your demands."

"That would not be possible," JJ answered. "First of all, the cost would consume our entire operational budget and second..."

He hesitated, giving Riley a hard look.

"We must be realistic, Jack. Aside from a few ideological differences, the FARC is still a business. We can't afford to alienate our international funding sources."

Riley smiled sarcastically and sighed. "What a bunch of knobbers you people have become. I saw the FARC website on the Internet. You're selling T-shirts and ball caps! Has it gotten that bad? I mean really...T-shirts for God's sake! You should tell your marketing manager to switch to the Che T-shirt. It's a big seller in Europe and the United States!"

"It's worse than that," JJ replied, ignoring Riley's barbs. "The government has gained momentum with its security program, and kidnappings have been cut by almost two-thirds. Carjackings have fallen more than ninety percent. Revenue's a problem, Jack."

"Well that's a bloody shame because I was hoping to get some help with costs. Let's hope that Pollard's open to negotiations."

"Not Pollard," Cano shot back, "he holds all the cards and knows it—there are no other sources, Jack. We tried to get the cartels involved, but they wouldn't touch it. They have their own problems."

Riley thought about Hamsa's words again and tried to think of other ways around the monopoly issue.

"Do you have any other information that may help me? I need a bargaining chip that can turn this guy around."

Cano nodded his head slowly, showing no emotion.

"I'll tell you up front that this is only a rumor, but it makes sense. One of our European weapons contacts passed it on to us."

"I'll be the judge of its quality!" snapped Riley. "So what is it?"

"When Peru and Ecuador were involved in the Alto Cenepa War in early 1995, Pollard made a deal with the Ecuadorian government to sell them ammunition, about five million dollars' worth. He used his contacts in the Israeli mafia to dupe some of the senior

Ecuadorian military officers into releasing a letter of credit based on a sample of a box of one hundred rounds these officers looked at outside of Tel Aviv in the desert. The money went into his account in Miami, and then the shipment mysteriously disappeared. The war ended a month later, and the Ecuadorian military couldn't complain because their attempt to get the ammo had been against international sanctions. He has no respect for anyone because he's being protected by the Israeli mafia. Be warned that he will do everything he can to take advantage of you. It's the money that he worships, not the cause. So be prepared for some difficult bargaining," Cano said bluntly. "He's an obnoxious asshole."

"Well," Riley said, raising himself from his chair, "no use to keep the obnoxious asshole waiting. Let's go."

Riley picked up his laptop and secure cell phone, placing both in a dark-blue attaché case. The three then proceeded to the hotel entrance, where a chauffeured black Lincoln Town Car picked them up. They drove through the city and then followed a newly paved road along the sea. Within ten minutes, they pulled up in front of an ornate steel entry gate that opened swiftly.

In front of him stood a two-story manse that sat high on a bluff, surrounded by the turquoise Caribbean Sea. Riley could make out the high-powered halogen spotlights and large PTZ surveillance cameras encased in weatherproof cases, spaced at fifty-foot intervals along the wall's crown.

As the Lincoln entered the circular driveway, he saw two groups of armed men standing near the domed portico.

"Quique, are these local boys?"

"No, Jack, they've been recruited from every slum in Central America. They're supposed to be his security force, but they're no more than ghetto gangbangers. Also, rumor has it that he's a little too devoted to a few of them."

"Ah, devotion…," said Riley. "It's been the downfall of many a man. But who knows: if this guy is as tough as you say he is, I may have to drop my knickers for him to pull this deal off. Let's hope it doesn't come to that!"

Their laughter took the edge off the tension that had been building since they left the hotel.

Riley and his two FARC contacts exited the vehicle and were immediately ushered into the mansion's foyer. The floors were a highly polished light-green marble that reflected the brown-and-gold batik wallpaper.

One of the security guards, a thin, heavily tattooed teenager, approached Riley and his two companions and motioned with his AK-47 for them to raise their hands. After all three had been searched, another young man instructed Riley's group to walk down the long corridor that led toward the dining room by pointing his AK-47 in that direction and grunting.

"Sweet mother of Jesus, what have I gotten myself into?" Riley muttered as he walked away from the group of young thugs.

At the passageway's end, Riley saw a lone individual seated at the head of a polished-ebony dinner table. The man stood and motioned for them to come forward. As Riley approached him, the man walked away from the table and introduced himself as Larry Pollard, shaking Riley's hand warmly.

"Welcome to my home, Mr. Riley. Please, gentlemen, sit down. I know it's been a long trip, but we have some business to transact. And I understand that your time here is limited."

He was deeply tanned and about the same height as Riley; he had his thick, black hair heavily moussed and combed straight back. He wore a black silk guayabera over a pair of brightly colored hibiscus-print surfers' pants and was barefooted. He'd lived in Venice, California, and continued to maintain its free-flowing lifestyle.

To Riley, Pollard looked and acted more like the stereotypical sports agent than an international arms dealer. And he was immediately struck by two things: Pollard's torturous New York City accent and his vast collection of Japanese *hentai* jade sculptures placed in groups on an intricately carved ebony hunt board.

Riley placed his attaché on the table and pulled out the laptop and cell phone. Pollard sat and opened a small leather-bound notebook, turning toward Riley.

"Your group gave us quite a challenge with this order. But in my business, solutions, not apologies, win customers."

Riley looked at Pollard intently, deciding to do some quick ego stroking.

"Without getting into trade secrets...Just how did you manage to pull this off? I've been on the operational end of your business for thirty years and was told that no one had the capability to fill our order."

Pollard's smile lit up the entire room. Now Riley knew what fueled him.

"I went right to the source—the Moscow boys. Between them and facility guards who were making a top salary of fifty dollars a month, we found a way."

But before Riley could interject a few more compliments, Pollard's face became sullen, and he regained the stiff, formal façade he'd projected earlier.

"But you didn't come here to discuss history; you came here to do business," he said, glancing at the leather-bound diary in front of him. "The terms are FOB Elizabeth, New Jersey, with delivery in two weeks. Payment will be made within thirty minutes of our agreeing to terms by an electronic transfer from your Swiss account to one of my operational accounts in Grand Cayman."

Pollard paused dramatically and gave Riley a quick glance.

"However, there will be a surcharge of one million seven hundred fifty thousand dollars because the original shipping instructions were FOB Odessa, Ukraine. So, are you ready to transfer funds?"

Riley laughed out loud.

"I came here ready to transfer the amount agreed upon by you and my principal. The FOB destination was always New Jersey. Please check our correspondence. It's there in black-and-white!"

Pollard smiled and snapped his fingers loudly. A white-jacketed servant appeared from the kitchen and recharged his beer mug; no one else was asked if they wanted anything. The atmosphere in the room dropped to ten below zero. After he had consumed half the mug, he glanced at Riley.

"There are only four hundred seventy-five kilos of this product available on the private market," Pollard said, pronouncing each syllable slowly and distinctly as if Riley needed a monosyllabic explanation. "I control over half the inventory, and the remainder is held by a mixed bag of Russian businessmen. You ordered two hundred kilos. We're not talking about fruit or frozen fish, Mr. Riley. If I have to carry the risk of loss all the way to New Jersey, then the price has to be adjusted, or it's no deal—no way. So it's your call, pal."

Pollard gave Riley a quick glance and picked up his cell phone from the table. The he turned to the side, busying himself with reviewing some messages that appeared on the cell phone's two-inch screen.

Riley summoned the inner strength that had allowed him to survive impossible situations in the past. It was the major gamble of his life.

"Well, my lad, it looks like you'll have to sell your *shit* elsewhere because we're not interested anymore."

He slid his chair back roughly over the marble floor and stood up. The two Colombians also stood, following Riley's lead.

Pollard did not acknowledge their pending departure and continued to thumb the cell phone's keyboard, staring at its screen. Then he placed the phone back on the ebony dining table and looked at Riley, who was packing his laptop and cell phone.

"Let's not be so hasty. You've come a long way. Maybe we can adjust the shipment to FOB Elizabeth at a cost of another million…just to keep the figures simple. I'll have to eat the remaining seven hundred fifty thousand."

Hamsa had warned Riley that the purchase price had been quoted low to draw them in and had allowed for another three million dollars as "cushion." Riley knew he had him now, but he didn't react immediately. He hesitated, looking down at his reflection in the table's highly polished surface.

"Larry, baby, this is not some dusty Arab bazaar, and I'm not here to haggle over the price of fruit or fish. You'll do me the *fucking* favor of playing it straight with me from now on, or this meeting is over!"

The look in Riley's eyes communicated something primitive and evil. And Pollard understood that he was not dealing with some nouveau-riche drug lord or rap-star gangster.

Riley sat down slowly, giving Pollard a second glance as if to put an exclamation mark on the nonverbal message he'd just delivered. He opened the laptop and connected it to the cellular phone. After energizing the computer, Riley waited for a minute and then entered the website of Hamsa's Swiss account. He typed in the account's security code, the amount to be transferred, and the destination codes. Then he pressed the enter key and looked over casually at the other party, who remained transfixed at the end of the table.

"It's in your account, Mr. Pollard. Please give your bank a call to confirm the transaction."

Pollard picked up his cell phone and punched in a text message. Within thirty seconds, the cell phone chirped, signaling that a reply had been received. He glanced at the cell phone's screen and then looked at Riley. This time, he smiled broadly.

"You are a man of your word. The money cleared. You'll take delivery in two weeks at the Port of Elizabeth. The vessel's ETA and all necessary documents will be faxed to you tomorrow. And now you'll have to excuse me," he said, glancing at his watch, "I'm expecting some dinner guests...and I never mix business with pleasure."

Riley and his two companions pushed their chairs back and stood. Pollard also stood and walked around the table, shaking Riley's hand vigorously. The four men then walked toward the entryway, chatting amicably. As they reached the round foyer entrance, Pollard stopped and turned toward Riley.

His smile reminded Riley of the expression on the face of a great white shark...just before it devours a full-grown sea lion.

"There is just one more question I have for you."

"Ask away," said Riley.

"How did the IRA get mixed up with the FARC in Colombia? The last time I checked, ninety-nine percent of the Colombians are Catholics. What happened…run out of people to blow up in Ireland?"

Riley answered without pause.

"Oh, I dunno, Larry. Maybe it's for the same reason that you sell arms to the ragheads or any other group with ready cash. It's the money, isn't it? It doesn't really matter if your clients are Christians, Muslims, or Jews—as long as their money's good. That's what it's all about, isn't it, Mr. Pollard? It's just an unemotional international monetary transaction for you. I'm fast approaching eight thousand victims; what's your body count look like?"

Pollard smiled bitterly and nodded his head.

"Touché, sir!" he replied.

Riley and his group turned and departed through the entryway, this time rudely waving off Pollard's security guards as they approached them.

• • •

Riley's two FARC companions, now seated comfortably in the Lincoln Town Car, began laughing hysterically after they'd cleared the main gate. Riley looked puzzled.

"What's so funny?" he asked.

"Jack, you stuck it so far up his ass that he'll never walk right again in his life."

Riley gave them a knowing smile.

"Well, lads, I didn't mean to insult the bugger, but what I told him is true. I have nothing against any man's religion. If it weren't for religion, the whole bloody world would be getting along just fine, and we'd be looking for honest work."

22

Fox Hunt

The next day
Quantico, Virginia
8:45 a.m.

The list of Hamsa's associates and acquaintances that had been requested finally arrived. It contained a total of thirty-eight people and represented all those who had any possible connection to Hamsa. ATF, DEA, and the FBI had submitted their information, but the CIA got wind of the request and called in legal counsel.

The delay in the list's receipt had been caused by CIA resistance and posturing. After losing the initial request for a temporary restraining order, the agency claimed that anyone, other than agency personnel, would have to undergo additional background checks before they would be allowed to review any of the documents. These normally took three to five months. Sabinson cured that problem with one phone call to the vice president, a former FBI special agent.

It was tedious work. None of the information had been updated in years, which meant tracking people down electronically. Failing that, Garcia and Montiel would have to rely on the same innovative techniques used by private investigators and bill collectors—guile and luck.

Eighteen people on the list were deceased, and three had vanished without a trace. They divided the remaining twenty in half and began making phone calls. Garcia called the fourth person on the list, Sean Lee.

• • •

The database information on Lee showed he'd served two years of a ten-year sentence for conspiracy to sell military explosives to an undercover ATF agent and a number of unindicted coconspirators. Hamsa, one of the coconspirators, had evaded arrest because, at the time, ATF had been told by one of their informants that he was a minor player and out of the country. The informant who made these assurances had never been identified in court documents. In any case, he wouldn't be providing any further information: Rashid al-Bakar was dead.

Lee was presently employed by a food-service company at Dulles International as their maintenance supervisor.

• • •

After Garcia introduced himself, Lee asked for his number, saying that he was in a meeting but would return the call. Garcia gave him one of the recorded lines as a call-back number and never expected to hear from him again. But no more than a minute passed before the phone on Garcia's desk rang. It was Lee.

"Sorry about brushing you off like that, but I had to get to my office. I've been waiting for months to have someone contact me. Can we meet in my office this afternoon?"

Garcia was surprised by Lee's eagerness but decided to accept the invitation. "How do I get there?" he asked.

• • •

Garcia had broken all existing traffic laws getting from Quantico to Olney; after parking his car, he quickly found Lee's office. The two sat down after Lee had locked the office's entry door.

"You're still on probation?" Garcia asked.

"For the rest of my life," replied Lee.

"No problem for you to talk to me?" he asked.

"My lawyer would kick my ass for talking to you, but for some crazy reason, I trust you. I'll play ball—just don't shove the bat up my ass."

Garcia grinned, remembering the number of times he'd conducted interrogations in the Coast Guard when he'd wanted to do exactly that.

"You attempted to sell explosives to a group of people that included Abdul Hamsa about six years ago?"

"Correction, Mr. Garcia: I arranged the deal with that bastard. But someone ratted us out to the ATF."

"What was it you were trying to sell?" asked Garcia.

"Hamsa wanted Semtex, like four hundred pounds of it. And he wanted it to be shipped to Colombia. I had a connection, but one of his IRA buddies grabbed my guy and squeezed me out of the deal. I was the only one who took a fall—the rest of them ran."

"Have you had any contact with him since then?"

"Hell no!" thundered Lee. "I hate that bastard for what he's done. If I had, you guys wouldn't have this problem now."

"Would you know of anyone who may have maintained contact with him?"

There was an ominous silence. Then Lee said, "There's only one person I can think of: that IRA prick. He and Hamsa were two of a kind. His name's Jack Riley. Now, there's someone who makes Charlie Manson look like a limp-wristed hairstylist. He had a scrapbook full of newspaper articles written about the jobs he'd done. He kept a ledger with two columns: one column showed the number of people killed in a particular event, and the other column contained a cumulative count of the dead. He liked to show it around."

"Any idea of where Riley is today?"

"He was always talking about Costa Rica because of their extradition laws. I think he said it was better than Brazil because he spoke a little Spanish."

"Do you know what Riley might be doing now?"

"He's an explosives expert, Mr. Garcia! He's a bomb maker for hire. Take it from there, and follow the trail of dead bodies. You'll find him where the trail ends. And hopefully, you'll find him before he finds you."

Garcia thanked him and set up an appointment with two FBI field agents, who would complete the debriefing.

● ● ●

After returning to the office, Garcia saw the seventh name on his list, Jackson Xavier Riley. The only data gathered on Riley during the computer search was an asterisk, meaning that Riley was a foreign national and had been on the agency's payroll. He had, for want of a better term, "conveniently vanished."

Garcia realized he was about to stick his hand into a hornets' nest and called Sabinson. The agency would be immediately defensive about anyone poking around in their Contra graveyard. Their use of Riley, al-Bakar, and their associates in the "Dirty War" in Nicaragua had been conveniently buried. It would take someone of Sabinson's stature and reputation to exhume this information, and he accepted the challenge.

Sabinson called the Bureau's liaison with the CIA to begin the process. And he also called the FBI's legal attaché at the US embassy in Costa Rica. He knew that the bureaucratic process within the agency would take time. He needed a shortcut in case he was stonewalled by Langley.

Sabinson asked the attaché to use his contacts with the Costa Rican National Police to locate Riley. It was a long shot, but it was all that they had.

Two weeks later
Port of Elizabeth, New Jersey
5:15 a.m.

The Liberian-flagged containership *Achilles* had moored an hour earlier, and the quayside gantry cranes were hurriedly offloading its mixed cargo of foodstuffs and imported ceramic tiles under the glare of banks of halogen lights. Five lanes of container transport trucks waiting to take on cargo extended a half mile from the vessel. *Achilles* was only one of seven containerships being offloaded at the same time in this busy port, and the flow of vehicles and personnel was a well-choreographed blur of activity. Blasts of frigid air that followed in the path of a two-day snowstorm made the offload even more hazardous.

The five US Customs agents assigned to the port decided to concentrate their inspection efforts on two containerships that had made stops in Colombian ports. Two forty-foot containers offloaded earlier from the *Achilles* made their way slowly to the port's final checkpoint on a tandem-trailer rig. Their bills of lading described the contents of each as bottled water and organic coffee beans. They were destined for the Nu-Path Natural Foods Company in Camden, New Jersey.

As always, time was of the essence in the container-shipping business. The gate attendant retrieved his copies of the shipping and clearance documents from the tandem's driver and, after a short review to ensure that all documentation matched the data in their computer database, waived the truck through the gate.

The truck driver pulled over just outside the port's exit gate and dialed a number that had been programmed into his cell phone. The conversation was quick, not lasting more than ten seconds.

"I just picked up the items you ordered. I'll keep them at my house until the weather gets warmer."

"Thanks," said Hamsa. "I'll let my friends know. They will be very happy."

23

UNINTENDED CONSEQUENCES

One week later
Chester, Nova Scotia
11:20 a.m.

The marked RCMP Jeep Cherokee pulled up slowly in front of the realty office and parked. The constable, dressed in his green work uniform, pulled up his fur-lined hood to protect himself against the chill Artic winds. It didn't help that the heavy cloud cover had blotted out the sun for almost a week. He trudged forward, clutching a briefcase in his left hand.

"Good morning, miss," he said, looking at the young receptionist. "Is Betty in?"

"You just missed her. She and the family are taking their first vacation in years. They're flying to Orlando for two weeks—going to visit Mickey and Donald," she laughed.

The constable returned her smile as he opened his briefcase, handing her a thin manila envelope. "When she gets back, have her take a look at these. The FBI's after someone they think might be in Canada. We're passing these out to all the businesses. I'll stop by again after she returns."

As the RCMP vehicle backed out of the parking space, the girl opened the bronze-colored metal clasp and withdrew the two sheets of paper, glancing at them.

"Oh my God," she said, "he looks like a fifty-year-old Eminem."

She pushed the documents back into the manila envelope and closed the metal clasp, placing the envelope in a wire basket with the rest of the mail she was holding for Betty Thompson, the realty company's owner.

• • •

Just four miles away, inside a weathered clapboard cottage, Hamsa was heating a bowl of barley soup in the microwave. He was thrilled at how well Riley's new e-mail system was working. The codebook Riley had given him allowed him to stay in continuous contact with his key agents.

But it was now early February. Hamsa had no time to lose.

Two weeks later
Chester, Nova Scotia
7:15 p.m.

Betty Thompson had returned to her small realty office after a glorious twelve days in the Florida sunshine. She, her husband, and two daughters had gone nonstop, not wanting to miss a minute of the attractions.

She'd arrived earlier in the afternoon on a direct flight from Orlando to Halifax and felt energized enough to slip into the office and catch up on her correspondence. At the bottom of the stack of magazines, bills, and junk mail, she came upon a manila envelope. She opened it and pulled out the two letter-sized sheets of paper.

Betty Thompson read the bold-face type at the top, under the prominent FBI shield of the first sheet, "WANTED FOR TERRORIST ACTS," and wondered how it had gotten into her mail basket.

But as she flipped to the second page, she froze. She looked at the first page again, reading the text carefully, and then at one of the computer-generated photos on the second page. She laughed out loud, thinking that the stress of the trip was making her imagine things.

As Betty Thompson stared at the photos, she decided it was worth a visit, just to put her mind at ease. After all, she reasoned, the cottage was on her way home. She placed her mail in a stack under her arm and walked toward the front of the office, where she turned out the lights and locked the door.

• • •

Hamsa was watching the evening news on the small TV in the kitchen when he noticed the glare of car lights shining through the curtains of the kitchen windows. He jumped up quickly, pulling on his down-filled jacket, and shoved the loaded Colt 9 mm semiautomatic in his waistband. He sprinted out the backdoor and circled around toward the cottage's front, waiting in the heavy brush to see who it was.

He saw the old Ford Escort roll to a stop next to his car. The driver was bundled up against the weather. He instinctively discounted a policeman, but he couldn't recognize the person. He started to step out from the thick stand of pines but hesitated. His security system was now on full alert. Betty Thompson pressed the car's overhead-light switch on and sat for a long moment, studying the photo. Then she got out of the car and began the forty-foot walk to the cottage's front door.

Hamsa, who had observed her sitting in the car, followed a short distance behind. As he passed the car's illuminated interior, he saw the pile of magazines and mail on the passenger's seat and stopped. On top of the stack was the FBI flyer. He opened the car door and took the flyer in his hand. He read it quickly in the light cast by the interior bulb and then shoved it into his jacket pocket. Hamsa began to jog, trying to catch up with the woman.

She peered into the dimly lit cabin and continued to tap on the glass panes of the entry door. As she turned to leave, she found herself facing Hamsa.

"Oh!" she yelled out. "Mr. Braswell, you gave me a fright."

"I'm sorry, Betty. I was out for a walk and saw the car lights."

She gazed directly into his face. She was now sure that Winslow Braswell was the man in the FBI flyer: John Thomas Cronin, alias Abdul Hamsa. Thompson tried to remain calm and think of a way to extricate herself from the situation she found herself in.

"Well, I'm back from vacation. I wanted to stop by on my way home and see that everything was OK with you."

Hamsa smiled and placed his hand on her shoulder.

"Are you sure you can't stay for a few minutes. I have some good hot soup I just made."

"I appreciate the offer, but I must be going. I was supposed to be home an hour ago and don't want my family worried about me. My husband has a bad habit of calling the police if I'm five minutes late."

Hamsa lowered his hand from her shoulder and moved to the side of the path to let her pass.

"Thanks, Betty. You're a great landlady," Hamsa said, smiling broadly, "and a fucking liar!"

He thrust his hands upward and clamped down hard on her throat. She tried to fight but was powerless against him. He squeezed hard for almost a minute until her body became limp and fell to the ground.

• • •

Hamsa drove Betty Thompson's Ford Escort toward the main road. Her lifeless body leaned to the right in the passenger's seat. He stopped and looked to see whether any cars were coming and then laughed at his overly cautious attitude. In this weather, everyone tried to stay inside.

He turned the car to the right, onto the paved road, and began heading southwest along the coast road. He smashed the accelerator to the floor, hoping that the scenic overlook he'd seen on his way from Yarmouth was close. In a little more than a minute, he saw the green entry-lane reflectors in the headlights and turned into the wide parking area just above the crashing Atlantic surf.

He placed the car's transmission in park and pulled her body into an upright position behind the steering wheel. Then he placed the car into drive and stepped back, slamming the driver's door hard as the vehicle inched away. The car gained speed on the slight decline and proceeded straight toward the edge of the promontory. The taillights rose into the air as the car smashed through the old split-rail fence and plummeted down the granite cliff into the pounding surf fifty feet below.

Hamsa turned and began walking back toward his cottage. His mind was racing ahead as he tried to consider why she had stopped at the cottage and, more importantly, why she'd had the FBI flyer with her. He concluded that she had decided to verify his identity before telling anyone. Otherwise, he reasoned, his secluded cottage would have been crawling with cops. He had to leave, but when, and how?

He crouched in a patch of thick shrubs near the cottage, listening for approaching vehicles. As the black sky turned gray, no vehicles entered the cabin's long driveway, but he had seen one police vehicle pass by slowly on the main road. The initial rush of adrenaline had passed. He was cold and tired and decided it was safe to return.

He entered the warmth of his house, took off his jacket, and pulled the 9 mm out of his waistband, placing it on the table next to his computer. After pouring himself half a glass of the Irish whiskey from the bottle Riley had left him, Hamsa sat on the edge of his chair, staring at his laptop's keyboard. Then he began typing an e-mail to Riley.

Two hours and six drinks later, he sat back feeling satisfied. Yes, he thought, this plan would guarantee his place in history.

24

ON THE RUN

One day later
Chester, Nova Scotia
2:35 p.m.

Betty Thompson's husband had reported her missing at ten the previous night, when she failed to return home. Although police units had been asked to look for her disabled car, no sightings had been made. After dawn that morning, an RCMP unit checking rest-stop areas noticed the broken split-rail fencing at the scenic overlook off the main coastal road. When the constable looked down the steep bluff, he saw the car submerged in fifteen feet of water.

Her husband blamed himself, thinking that he should never have allowed his wife to stop by the office after such a long trip. The police concluded that she had probably fallen asleep and crashed through the fence and then plummeted over the embankment.

The bruise marks on her neck had been hidden by the massive trauma she had suffered when her face and neck had struck the steering wheel during the car's entry into the water. The coroner determined that she'd been alive when the vehicle had plunged fifty feet into the ocean below.

The funeral at the old Episcopal church in Chester was packed with people from Betty Thompson's life. It was the same church she'd been married in.

• • •

A few days later, her husband was reviewing his wife's office files to finalize her estate when he came upon a thick envelope containing forty-three hundred dollars in one-hundred-dollar bills. Inside was a note in his wife's handwriting: "For telephone and Internet payments, Winslow Braswell cottage."

He turned to the young high-school girl who had helped his wife in the office and who was now assisting him with closing the business.

"What's this?" he asked.

She read the note and smiled.

"The renter gave that to Betty to pay his phone and Internet bills. I think he's a writer from the States and wanted Betty to start phone service for him because he had no credit here."

The man looked at the envelope for a moment and then handed it to the girl.

"Be a dear and take this to the gentleman, will you. Explain what happened, and let him know that he'll have to take care of his own phone bills in the future. His rent is paid up through the summer, so there's no problem there."

"I'll go straight away, Mr. Thompson."

• • •

She drove down the cottage's sandy entry lane and parked next to Hamsa's plain gray compact. She knocked on the cottage's front door, but no one answered. Then she knocked harder.

Hamsa had gone to bed about two hours before the girl's arrival. He'd been up all night, packing. As ideal as the cabin had been, he realized that the FBI flyers could cause trouble. His usual arrogance was being displaced by a growing concern that someone could recognize him. He startled awake, aware now that someone was pounding on the door, rolled out of bed, and pulled on some sweatpants. Then he took the Colt 9 mm from the bedside table, cocked the hammer, and held it at his side.

He tiptoed toward the entry door and peered through the sheer curtains that covered the door's glass panels. A young, blue-eyed blonde stood in front of the door, holding a thick envelope. But the sun was behind her, and this made it difficult for him to see clearly.

"Can I help you?" he asked.

The young girl continued to look straight ahead.

"Mr. Braswell, I'm Jennifer Zinc, from Betty Thompson's realty office."

"I'm sorry, Jennifer, you caught me napping. Writers keep odd hours. I'm still not dressed."

She could see his features through the flimsy curtain. The sun was in his eyes, forcing him to squint. His hair was tousled, and he had the look of someone who had just awakened.

"I apologize, Mr. Braswell. I'll just leave your package here."

She leaned over and laid the envelope against the door.

"What do you have there?" he asked.

"Mrs. Thompson was killed in a car accident, the same day she got back from her vacation. Her husband's settling her accounts and wanted you to have your telephone money. He's asked that you make the payments because he'll be selling the company."

"That's a shock," Hamsa said, voicing as much surprise that he could muster. "She was a wonderful lady."

The girl smiled and stepped away from the door, still staring straight ahead.

"I paid Betty until July. Do you think there will be any change in my lease?"

The young girl smiled.

"There'll be no change. Mr. Thompson told me that you're paid up. I forgot that part of it."

"No problem, Jennifer. You've been busy."

He placed his index finger through the trigger guard and brought the weapon up to waist level.

"Did you have a chance to talk to Betty after she got back from her vacation?"

"No, I didn't. I worked part-time for her. I was taking a university entrance exam that day and never got the chance to see her. I wish I had."

Hamsa watched her closely, noting that she hadn't shown any signs of nervousness. He relaxed his hold on the pistol.

"Thanks for your trouble, Jennifer."

She turned and walked to her car. Hamsa watched her from behind the sheer curtains until she had driven away.

• • •

As she drove back toward the office, she couldn't shake the feeling that she'd seen Braswell before. Even though he stood behind the sheer curtain, his face was illuminated by the sun. She tried to remember but finally gave up and concentrated on her driving.

When she returned to the office, she found a note from Betty Thompson's husband telling her to finish typing the letters he had started. As she reached into the wire basket for the first letter, she remembered where she'd seen Winslow Braswell before. She dug furiously in the stack of papers, looking for the manila envelope that the RCMP constable had dropped off weeks before. It wasn't there.

She decided to call the RCMP substation. However, she was told that the constable was in Halifax, testifying in an assault case. She started to hang up but hesitated and then asked, "Do you have one of those FBI flyers that the constable distributed a few weeks back?"

"Give me a minute...Yes. They're in the hallway display case."

"I'll be right there!"

• • •

At the cottage, Hamsa's survival instincts were setting off alarm bells in his head. The girl's visit seemed too opportune. He couldn't define it, but something was wrong. It was the same kind of feeling someone gets in the forest when the birds stop singing and the animals are still.

He walked to the living room, disconnected the laptop, and packed it in its case with the codebook. Then he rushed to the bedroom and threw his remaining clothes into the already jammed suitcase. He pulled on his down jacket and stuffed the envelope of cash Jennifer Zinc had delivered into one of its pockets. The last thing he did was to push the 9 mm semiautomatic into his waistband and turn all the lights on.

He locked the front door and threw the key into the woods.

• • •

Jennifer Zinc opened the RCMP substation's glass entry door and walked toward the receptionist's desk.

"I called about the FBI flyer."

The receptionist smiled and pointed to the wall behind her

"Over there in the case, dearie."

She walked to the display of wanted posters and stared at the two-page FBI flyer for a moment, concentrating on the computer-generated likeness of a clean-shaven Abdul Hamsa with short, sculpted blond hair. Then she turned and walked toward the receptionist.

"That man in the FBI flyer…Hamsa or Cronin…whatever his name is—he's living at one of Betty Thompson's rental cottages. He's there now! I delivered a package to him not more than an hour ago!"

The receptionist picked up the radio handset and called Halifax dispatch immediately.

• • •

The RCMP SWAT unit surrounded the cottage just before dusk. They'd tried calling the number that was listed to the property, but no one answered. The team leader had also noticed that the small, gray car described by Zinc was missing.

One of the officers, equipped with a thermal imager, crawled to a stand of pine trees near the backdoor and began sweeping the interior. Aside from the lights, he couldn't detect any other heat source. He crept around to the front of the cottage and got the same readings. The place appeared to be deserted.

The decision was made to storm the cottage. Within minutes, the RCMP had control of Abdul Hamsa's Canadian refuge, but their prey had vanished.

25

FLIGHT TO FREEDOM

Washington, DC
FBI Headquarters
8:05 p.m.

Colby Sabinson listened intently as the chief of the RCMP's Special Branch described the events that had transpired near Chester.

"Colby, we've sealed off all the main roads, and we have plain-clothes units scouring every ferry terminal, airport, train and bus stations. We're also featuring the photo identified by the eyewitness as Cronin or Hamsa on all TV stations. He'll have to pop up soon."

"Chief Inspector, you're closer to him than anyone has been, but I'm not as optimistic as you are. All we can do is hope he screws up again."

"Colby, that son of a bitch is going to have to come up with a miracle. He's on my turf now."

"We'll support you all the way."

After Sabinson hung up, he turned his chair slightly and placed his feet on the desktop. He leaned back, massaging his temples and wondering where Hamsa was, what he was doing, and what he was planning. He could almost see him, and the punk was laughing.

Near Windsor, Nova Scotia
8:15 p.m.

Hamsa was following the escape route he'd prepared in advance. He'd driven to Chester and turned left onto Rural Route 12, which would take him north toward Windsor. This was a sparsely inhabited area of small farms separated by thick forests and well off the main roads.

At dusk, he turned onto an old logging trail and drove two hundred yards into the dense forest until the thick brush prevented him from going any further. He got out of the car and pulled his small, black nylon suitcase and laptop case from the trunk. Then he began walking back to the main road and the brightly lit Irving gas station he'd passed that had a small restaurant attached to it. He made sure his ball cap was pulled down low and made his way directly to a bank of outdoor telephone booths.

Once inside the booth, he pulled out an international calling card and punched in the code for a number in Costa Rica.

"Hello," said Riley.

"I need some help."

"Where are you?"

"I'll give you the number…"

Within a minute, the pay phone rang, and Hamsa picked up the handset immediately.

"What can I do?" asked Riley.

"Remember the gas station I showed you when we took a drive one day?"

Riley hesitated, trying to recall the sites.

"Yes," said Riley, finally picturing the Irving station near Windsor.

"I need someone to pick me up there as soon as possible. I need to get out of here. Call me tomorrow at noon, my time, at this number."

"Consider it done," replied Riley.

Hamsa placed the handset into its cradle and opened the bifold door, raising the fur-lined hood over his head before exiting. As he neared the restaurant's front door, Hamsa glanced through the windows before entering; it was deserted. He also noticed that the small TV sitting on a shelf over the counter was off.

He entered and ordered two steak platters with the works and asked where the bathroom was. He locked the bathroom door and placed his bags on the rough concrete floor. He took his jacket, ball cap and shirt off and placed them on the hook extending from the wall.

In ten minutes, he exited the men's room and sat at a corner booth. The waitress, a thin, pale middle-aged woman, perked up as soon as she saw him. She was especially drawn to his brown eyes, which were offset by his prematurely gray hair. She placed his order in front of him, and Hamsa began to devour the food as if he hadn't eaten in days.

When she brought him the check, he glanced at her nametag.

"Beth, you wouldn't know an inexpensive motel close by?"

"There's a nice motel near Wolfville, but that's about thirty minutes away."

"That's a problem. My car broke down, and I was hoping to be able to walk. I have to be back here tomorrow at noon to take a call from the mechanic."

"I'll be right back," she said and walked toward the kitchen. In a few minutes, she returned. "The owner has a small cabin right behind the station. It's nothing fancy, but he rents it out every so often. It's got heat, hot water, and a TV. He says it would be thirty-five dollars for the night."

Hamsa reached inside his wallet and withdrew forty.

"Tell him he's a saint."

He picked up his bags and followed her to the rear door.

• • •

After showering, he turned on the TV, an older model complete with a set of flimsy, aluminum rabbit ears. He sat on the edge of the bed, flipping through the local channels; he was featured on each one. He watched as reporter after reporter linked him with the killings of Rashid al-Bakar and Betty Thompson. Jennifer Zinc provided the connection for the Thompson murder by describing the FBI flyer she'd seen before Betty Thompson's return. This pleased him immensely. It verified that his internal radar was working.

He smiled when he saw the FBI composites being shown; not one was close to what he looked like now. But the FBI had surprised him with their aggressiveness. He lay back on the bed and wondered who these people were and what they were doing at that instant. "Probably cursing their bad luck in frustration," he thought.

His thoughts returned to the two challenges he faced: escaping the dragnet that had been set for him and maintaining his schedule.

The next day
12:10 p.m.

Hamsa stood in the phone booth's entrance and picked up the phone after the first ring.

"You OK?" Riley asked.

"I will be once I'm out of here."

"Then get ready to feel better. At two, your time, a red Caprice will pull in front of the restaurant. He'll take you home."

"I owe you a big one," Hamsa murmured.

• • •

At exactly two in the afternoon, the red Caprice pulled in front of the restaurant. The driver, a boyhood friend of Riley's, had been a member of the same IRA unit that Riley belonged to.

164

After almost being captured by British troops, he decided that immigration to Canada was the best option for him.

He'd been successful in the paving business and became one of the IRA's top financial supporters. He was also a skilled pilot. His Beechcraft Queen Air was fueled and ready at his private airstrip, forty miles away in Kentville. He'd filed a flight plan for Manchester, New Hampshire.

However, he planned to land at a small private strip near Keene, New Hampshire, drop Hamsa off, and then return immediately to Kentville, Nova Scotia. He'd be on the ground for less than a minute. After taking off again, he'd call the FAA station in Manchester and report he was returning to Canada because of a landing-gear malfunction. Hamsa would be picked up and driven to an isolated safe house in Delaware.

● ● ●

As the aircraft lifted off, Hamsa bade the beautiful Maritimes and the frustrated RCMP adieu.

26

DON'T BET ON IT

The next day
Washington, DC
FBI Headquarters
11:45 a.m.

Garcia, Khamis, and Montiel lounged outside of Colby Sabinson's office, waiting to enter for their noon luncheon invitation. Even though the RCMP search for Hamsa had so far failed to produce results, it had been their concept of issuing a revised circular that had unmasked Hamsa in Canada. At the least, Sabinson thought that Hamsa might have used up eight of his nine lives.

Colby Sabinson ushered them into his office and got right to the point.

"The NSA's stumbled onto something that might get us into Hamsa's e-mail network. Our technicians are working out the kinks as we speak, but NSA wants you guys working with them. One intercept clearly shows that Hamsa's come up with a plan that was personally approved by bin Laden—something so secret that all planning is now being passed only in face-to-face meetings, nothing in writing and definitely no phone calls. We're sure of only one fact: it's going to happen this year. I know you haven't had much downtime, but I need you three to find a way to nail this bastard—and soon!"

One day later
West of Milford, Delaware
4:45 p.m.

The man who'd met Hamsa at the small airstrip in New Hampshire had driven south on I-95 all night, stopping only for gas. The large, white conversion van was stocked with sandwiches, soft drinks, and coffee.

The driver, Randall Campana, was a self-taught bomb maker who had worked with Riley for years. He was overweight and balding, and he wore heavy, framed glasses with thick lenses, looking more like a studious chemistry professor than an anarchist. But his appearance belied the fact that Campana was the most dangerous type of criminal—a loner. And unlike Riley, he was not gregarious and strictly business. Hamsa liked the change.

• • •

Campana continued driving past miles of open farmland, populated by an occasional two-story clapboard house. Without saying anything, he slowed and turned off the paved rural road onto a sandy lane. A sturdy, white board fence identified the property's perimeters. In front of them, blocking their path was a steel swing-arm gate. Beyond it was a single mobile home, surrounded by scrub pines. And beyond the mobile home was a thick stand of hardwood and pine trees. Hamsa noticed that he hadn't seen one person since they had turned west off of Route 13 in Milford.

Campana reached upward and pressed a button on a small RF remote that was clipped to the visor. The gate swung open, and Campana accelerated over a tubular metal cattle guard.

"No one lives there. It's just for show," he said dryly, as they continued to drive down the sandy road.

They drove past the mobile home and entered a wooded area that was so thick with mature hardwoods and conifers that the sun's rays had difficulty penetrating its leafy canopy. After a minute or so, they entered a clearing. Campana slowed the van and pointed forward. Hamsa looked but saw nothing more than another broad grove of hardwood trees.

"There's your new home."

If Campana hadn't mentioned it, Hamsa would never have seen it. A single-story log house had been built under a stand of older hardwoods. Its weathered earth tones blended in perfectly with its surroundings.

"You have a hardwired phone and two prepaid cell phones; that's what Riley ordered. The closed-circuit television monitors are in the kitchen and bedroom; one camera covers the gate we passed through, and the other covers this entry road. The refrigerator's stocked. You have a loaded M-16 in the closet with five full sixty-round clips. Your Internet connection is by a cable that's laid out on the kitchen table. Call me if you need anything; my number is on a card next to the phone on the kitchen table. I'll be in touch."

Hamsa thanked him and picked up his two bags, weaving toward the front door. In the last three days, he'd slept a total of five hours, and he was finally feeling the effects of exhaustion.

At six o'clock, after a hot shower and warm meal, he collapsed on the king-size bed. He woke up twenty hours later. It was two in the afternoon.

Two days later
Greenbelt, Maryland
NSA Headquarters
1:30 a.m.

One of the electronic-intelligence analysts glanced at her monitor, intrigued by a pattern that was being produced by one of the installed applications. Their computers had been scanning e-mails being sent and received in the northeast United States. A common IP server code began to show up with greater frequency. This was the same IP code the program had identified as belonging to three members of the Hamsa group. The encryption key for each user was stored on the server and was encrypted with a password, but the password had to be transmitted to the server every time one of the users wanted to read an e-mail. The NSA program had intercepted the passwords and was now reading cipher text in plain text. Riley's super secure server was hacked.

The analyst also noticed that faulty signature files pointed directly to the owner of a food manufacturer located in Michigan. She gathered all the pattern information from the Fantasy Baseball e-mails and others and routed the message to the FBI's Quantico Intelligence Center.

The NSA program had also discovered a fatal error made by the rogue programmer. The signature file, or "sig file," as it was called in the trade, had not been completely deleted. The sig file identified the sender. This allowed them to determine the sender's true identity.

The analysts then began to search for similarities and patterns in the other five billion e-mails that had been transmitted through that particular system. It had identified eighteen. One group of three emails from the CEO of a food company in Michigan was tagged because the encryption fuction had totally failed.

The initial pattern it developed pertained to similar subject lines contained in the eighteen e-mails: "Fantasy Baseball All-Star Game, Home Run Derby." But NSA had discovered another aspect of the encryption that was causing problems.

The text in some of the messages was written using a onetime pad cipher. Plain text was converted into cipher text using the random key. So far, the cipher text had proven to be unbreakable; there had been no repetitions that would permit a comparative analysis.

But for some inexplicable reason, some of the senders had failed to encrypt the subject lines and text. The trail might have ended here if it weren't for that vague, unscientific principle called "Chance."

One of the senior NSA analysts had written a doctoral dissertation entitled "Development of Random Encryption Keys by the East German STASI." This may not have made the *New York Times* bestseller list, but it would prove to be much more valuable than that honor. She recognized a similarity in the key's characteristics to those produced by the STASI for the IRA. With this information, NSA redoubled it efforts.

Quantico, Virginia
10:10 a.m.

Montiel printed the message-traffic summary received overnight from NSA. He placed the stack on top of a legal-size clipboard and began his morning ritual. Montiel would read the message aloud, and then he and Garcia would vote on whether to keep it for analysis or shred it. They usually retained about 1 percent of all the message traffic.

The ninth message in the stack caught their attention. NSA analysts had identified a pattern from eighteen messages sent through a system used by one of the Hamsa groups. The subject line in each one read, "Fantasy Baseball All-Star Game, Home Run Derby." NSA was still attempting to decipher the code that had been used in the text portion of each message.

"Chris, what was the controversy about the all-star game this year? Remember, we saw a show on ESPN, and you were laughing because everyone was so upset?"

"The Major League Baseball commissioner changed the dates for the all-star game and the home run derby to coincide with the president's visit to Philadelphia...," Garcia paused, looking at the message on Montiel's clipboard, and continued, "from July nineteenth to the Fourth of July. Leo, that's got to be it! A day of national significance in a place of national significance; the Declaration of Independence was signed there. Remember what Mrs. Beltran told us at the embassy in Guatemala. It all makes sense now. And the president will be in attendance!"

"You wouldn't be making one of those inferential leaps that we're famous for?" Montiel said as he glared at Garcia.

"We'll know soon enough," Garcia replied as he typed out an IIR, Intelligence Information Report, identifying the significance of the home run derby's date, the location, and the president's presence. He also requested that Terrorism Task Force agents interview the food company's CEO in Michigan as soon as possible.

• • •

But there were conflicting views. The Defense Intelligence Agency had submitted a rebuttal to Garcia's premise. It argued that their analysts had pinpointed the attack on the president to August 14, the date he was to dedicate the new Defense Department Intelligence Center near the Pentagon. They cited some vague informant information and the fact that their terrorism unit would be located there as supporting evidence. But the report went further than a rebuttal. It attacked the competence of the FBI's Terrorism Intelligence group, stating that they had "lost" Hamsa and were trying to fabricate the Fourth of July scenario to justify their existence.

Garcia knew that he was dealing with interagency politics, a losing situation without powerful allies. He'd spoken about the issue with Montiel but, so far, had been unable to come up with a solution.

"Chris, do we have any news about the DIA's challenge?" Montiel asked as he entered their cubicle.

Garcia looked at him with an evil smile.

"The day I arrived here, Colby Sabinson invited me to dinner. I'm calling him now and accepting! It's called bypassing the DIA. We don't have the time to waste fighting over dates now. And I'm absolutely convinced that we're right. The information that you received from the DOD Intelligence Center's architect seals it. The DIA is trying to create something from nothing."

Montiel laughed and patted Garcia on the shoulder.

"You are a brilliant man, Christopher Garcia...devious, but brilliant!"

27

Obstacle Removal

One day later
Great Falls, Virginia
7:45 p.m.

Sabinson's modest two-story home was filled with the aromas of roast turkey and baked ham. His wife, Peggy, had been waiting for an excuse to use the new convection ovens she had installed in their remodeled kitchen. As usual, she'd outdone herself. She'd also invited their next-door neighbor, Priscilla Barnes, a recently divorced lieutenant commander in the US Navy Nurse Corps, to join them.

Garcia arrived fifteen minutes late after fighting his way through I-95 traffic and I-495 congestion. As he was introduced to Barnes, he almost forgot his reason for coming.

She was petite, no more than five feet two. Her auburn hair was cut short. She had smiling brown eyes and expressive full lips. And Garcia found himself unable to stop staring at her. After she caught him twice during cocktails, he forced himself to concentrate on looking only at Sabinson.

During dinner, the conversation was lighthearted and fast moving. Barnes described her childhood growing up on a farm in the mountains in southwestern Virginia. When Garcia mentioned that he had graduated from Rice University, Barnes almost fell off her chair. She'd graduated from Rice University's nursing program in Houston the same year.

Garcia began to feel completely at ease with her and slowly dropped the defensive walls that he'd constructed over the past years. The two of them almost monopolized the conversation for the remainder of the dinner. He talked about the Coast Guard, and she listened, entranced.

This did not go unnoticed by Peggy Sabinson, who felt that her dinner-guest idea might have been the best thing for both of them. And in the midst of the rambling dinner conversation, Colby Sabinson remembered another story about Garcia's father.

A CBS news crew, headed by a young Dan Rather, had arrived at the Da Nang Marine Corps Air Station to interview pilots who were returning from their missions. Rather found out that Chris Garcia Sr. was a Texan, like himself. As soon as Garcia's A-6 had landed from a mission, Rather ran over to the aircraft with his camera crew. As the canopy rose, he thrust a microphone into Garcia's face.

"So Rather says, 'I understand you hold the record for SAM site kills, Captain Garcia. How was it up north today?' Then your dad said, 'Let me tell you something! Those SAM's are killing pilots every day! We know where they are, but we can't go after them unless the targets are approved by some *REMF* in Washington DC! If we're not here to win, we should get the hell out of this place!'" Sabinson could barely sit up in his seat from laughter.

"Rather couldn't use the footage, but he sure got the message! Just after that, Walter Cronkite paraphrased your dad's sentiments in his famous opinion on the war. After hearing Cronkite's broadcast to millions, President Johnson knew that his continuing war could not be supported."

• • •

After dinner, Peggy steered the two men into the den for coffee while she and Priscilla retired to the kitchen.

Sabinson motioned Garcia to a large overstuffed chair while he closed the den door.

"Priscilla is a great girl," he said nonchalantly, "but she was married to a real asshole! They were both career navy: he was a staff puke, the kind of officer who seeks the shelter of a headquarters' assignment, and she was a nurse. He'd secretly requested a transfer to the West Coast, where he's from, and one day while Priscilla was working, the bastard just packed up and left. It really destroyed her for a while…but it looks as if she's come out of her shell," he said with a smirk. "But I don't think you came all this way just to gorge yourself on my wife's cooking," Sabinson said, staring hard at Garcia. "What's up?"

"I'm here to make my case for the Fourth of July as al-Qaeda's target date for their attack."

"You're talking about the DIA rebuttal report?" asked Sabinson.

"Sure am," replied Garcia.

"So where is DIA wrong?" Sabinson asked, realizing that Garcia had arrived armed for battle.

"First, the president is not going to speak at the dedication of the Defense Department's Intelligence Center. He was only penciled in and has rescheduled that week in August for his summer house in Nantucket."

"Where did you get that information?" Sabinson asked warily.

"From your secretary," Garcia said and smiled. "I called you yesterday morning, and you were in a meeting. I asked her to verify the schedule."

"Christ!" moaned Sabinson. "You're just like your father. Are there any other reasons?"

"The building won't be ready for occupancy until next year, sometime in March. Leo Montiel drove to the site this morning and spoke with the project architect, a man by the name of Juan Entrecanales, from Madrid. Entrecanales has been a friend of Leo's family for over thirty years. The contractors poured the foundation too shallow on the east end of the building. They will have to dig it out and repour it. But there's more," said Garcia with the air of a lawyer who'd just caught an adversarial witness in a lie.

"Don't hold back now—let's have it all," Sabinson said, sensing that the cherry atop the cake was about to arrive.

"Leo was told by Entrecanales that the date for the dedication of the DOD Intelligence Center was never August 14. It was September 11, the fiftieth anniversary of the Pentagon's groundbreaking ceremony. They were blowing smoke from the beginning."

Sabinson interlaced his fingers and looked at Garcia for a long moment. Then he shook his head and chuckled.

"I'll have a personal chat with DIA's director tomorrow morning," Sabinson said as he glanced at his watch. "And speaking of morning, I have a six o'clock meeting with the task force. Two of our agents will be flying down to Guatemala to interview some additional witnesses, so I'll have to call it a night."

Garcia thanked him and walked slowly toward the kitchen. As he turned the corner leading into the pantry, he saw Peggy Sabinson and Priscilla Barnes seated at the large center island, sipping brandy. He thanked Peggy and was about to say goodbye to Priscilla when he noticed that she was slipping her jacket on.

"I have to be going too," she said. "Chris, it was great to meet you!"

"Same here, Pris," he said. "I enjoyed my evening—maybe dinner sometime?"

Barnes looked him directly in the eyes. "I'd like that very much!" she said with her soft southwestern Virginia accent.

They both departed the Sabinson's house, and Garcia suggested he walk her to her door, which she gladly accepted. As they approached the threshold of her two-story brick colonial, he reached over to kiss her good night, but she stopped him, holding his face in her hands.

At first, Garcia thought he'd made a mistake. But she looked into his eyes and brought his face toward hers, kissing him deeply.

Garcia hugged her tightly, feeling her body pressing against his. Then she drew her head back slightly, breathing hard.

"Christopher Garcia," she said, her soft, brown eyes twinkling, "Colby told me that you had been working too damn hard. So you are not driving back to Quantico tonight. It's not safe. Plus, I make an outstanding breakfast!"

Garcia looked at her and smiled as he felt her fingers clutching his belt. "This is the kind of medicine I've needed for a long time, Pris."

She pulled away slowly. "That makes two of us, Chris," she murmured, as her hand reached inside his waistband and plunged downward.

• • •

At about four thirty the next morning, Garcia kissed her good-bye and walked silently toward his old MG-B. He'd tried to leave an hour earlier, but both decided they were in need of one more round. As he opened the car door, he turned and saw her on the porch steps. He waved slowly, and she did the same.

Quantico, Virginia
11:40 a.m.

Garcia felt strangely energized. Although he hadn't slept very much, he had thrown off years of emotional baggage that he'd carried around with him. He'd told Montiel about his meeting with Sabinson, and they were looking forward to the results of Sabinson's meeting with the DIA director.

The STU-IV secure phone rang, and Montiel answered it. Garcia was initially puzzled by Montiel's formal tone.

"Yes, sir," Montiel said. "Well…it's about time. No, sir, he's right here. I'll put him on."

Montiel handed Garcia the phone with a grin the size of Texas.

"I don't want you guys to gloat," Sabinson said, "but DIA has officially accepted your Fourth of July theory. They've also buried the hatchet—in their chief of intelligence's head. He's been transferred to a job that clearly suits his qualifications—assistant chief of statistics. Oh, one more thing," Sabinson said, "you should call Triple-A the next time something like that happens!"

Garcia was lost.

"Triple-A?" he asked.

"Yes," Sabinson said, laughing hilariously, "I saw your car was still there when I left this morning! I thought you might have had an *ignition* problem!"

Garcia could feel his face turning crimson.

"Next time, I'll park around the corner!" he shouted and placed the handset back in its cradle.

He turned quickly to Montiel. "Leo, we're back on track. DIA is with the program. Now let's find that son of a bitch Hamsa."

Montiel stood up and let out a victory yell that froze everybody on the first floor in their seats.

28

NEVER TRUST A SMILING DOG

Two days later
Detroit, Michigan
Jasmine Tea Company
7:45 a.m.

The two FBI agents who'd been waiting in the lobby to interview the company's CEO stood as he approached the door to his office. They introduced themselves and asked to speak with him.

The CEO, Edward Hazbali, shook hands with each man, smiling broadly as if he were welcoming new members of his board of directors. Hazbali was in his midfifties, tall and fit with short black hair and deep olive skin. He was dressed in the business-casual fashion that was typical for the area.

• • •

The background check that the agents had conducted revealed nothing out of the ordinary. Hazbali's parents had emigrated from Guyana; he'd been born in Detroit, one of five children. He'd graduated from Michigan State University with honors, had no criminal record, and was a very successful businessman. He was married, had two children, and served on the boards of a number of charitable organizations that provided medicine and food for refugees in the Middle East. In plain terms, his life resembled a page out of the "American Dream."

The agents began the interview by asking where he'd been the preceding week and whether he had sent any e-mails from the computer in his office.

Without questions or hesitation, he calmly denied using the computer at all, stating that he'd been in Chicago the entire week. Hazbali described in detail the meetings he'd had with his construction contractor, reviewing plans for the installation of industrial water filters in one of the company's new food-processing plants. As further proof, he opened a file folder on his desk and offered the agents receipts from the hotel: his room charge, room service fees, and telephone record, all accompanied by his corporate American Express card receipts. He handed the file to the agent sitting closest to him.

"I'll have some copies made for you," Hazbali said.

After reviewing the receipts and making some notes, the agent handed the file back to Hazbali.

"Copies won't be necessary at this time, Mr. Hazbali. Did anyone use your computer or have access to it while you were in Chicago?" he asked.

Hazbali thought for a moment, and then his face brightened. "My office manager should know the answer to that question. I'll be right back."

As Hazbali stood to leave the office, so did the two agents.

"We'll walk with you, Mr. Hazbali," the senior agent said. "We'd like to hear your office manager's answers."

The two FBI agents accompanied him as he exited his office and walked toward the office manager's desk. As they approached the desk, an older bald man looked up, smiling pleasantly.

"Good morning, Mr. Hazbali. How was your weekend?"

Hazbali didn't appear to hear the question.

"Karl, these gentlemen are from—oh yes, my weekend was too short after my Chicago trip last week. These gentlemen are from the FBI. They're here investigating some e-mails that may have been sent from my computer. Did anyone use my office or my computer last week?"

The office manager looked directly at Hazbali for a long moment.

"The only people in here last week were the electrical contractors. They had to run three new lines into your office and to the CFO's office, but that's about it. I was with them almost all of the time. I didn't see anybody touch your computer. Is there a problem?"

"No," replied Hazbali, "just trying to solve a mystery."

"I can contact the electricians if that would help, Mr. Hazbali. I think I still have their business card somewhere."

The office manager opened the top drawer of his rosewood desk and pulled out a stack of business cards secured with a thick rubber band. He thumbed through the stack and finally looked up at the agent closest to him.

"Their card's not in this stack, but I can contact our purchasing department and get that information for you," he said pleasantly. "I must have put it in the billing file."

"We'll be back," the agent replied. "Thanks anyway."

They returned to the CEO's office, where Hazbali had coffee ready for them. After some small talk about the company's history, the agents continued their interview.

"How long has Karl been with you?" the agent asked dryly.

"About a century," Hazbali replied, laughing. "Karl was here when I arrived as a newly hired salesman, fresh out of Michigan State, so that should tell you something!"

One of the agents reached into his pocket, pulling out a small notepad.

"What is Karl's full name?" he asked.

"Karl Muller," responded Hazbali.

"Does Karl have a middle name?"

"Yes," replied Hazbali, "Karl Bernard Muller. I think he immigrated to the United States from someplace in South America."

"Do you know his date of birth and place of birth?" the agent asked.

"Not by memory," laughed Hazbali, "but I will look it up for you in our employee database."

Hazbali pulled the touch-screen monitor closer to him and began his search. In a few minutes, he pushed the screen away and turned toward the agents.

"That's odd," he murmured. "I can't find the data. I'll ask our human resources manager to get that information for you."

Hazbali hesitated for a moment and then leaned toward the agents, lowering his voice to a conspiratorial whisper.

"You don't think that Karl's involved in this…uh…this?"

The agent taking the notes looked up and stared at Hazbali.

"*This*, Mr. Hazbali, what do you mean by *this*?"

"This…this investigation," replied Hazbali, stumbling over his words. "That is the reason why you are here, correct?"

"I don't think we actually explained why we were here, but thank you for your time."

The two FBI agents stood, handing their business cards to Hazbali in silence, and walked toward the office's door.

• • •

As the agents drove out of the company's parking area, the senior agent turned to the other.

"Hazbali and his buddy, Karl, are lying through their teeth! He led his office manager through that conversation. And he never asked about the content of the e-mails. He's too damn nonchalant. That prick knows that he's in trouble, but he doesn't know how deep those intel guys in Quantico have gone."

The other agent thought for a minute and then reached into his pocket, retrieving his notepad. He pulled off the road and took his cellular phone from his belt, punching in the numbers of the FBI's Intelligence Center in Washington.

Ten minutes later, he lowered the cell phone from his ear.

"Our boy Karl Muller immigrated to the United States in 1992 from Guyana. 'Karl Bernard Muller' is an alias. His real name is

Khalid al-Mihdhar, and his sponsor for his work visa was none other than Hazbali, who is presently suffering from short and long-term memory loss. Khalid was arrested for interstate wire fraud in 1995, but the case was dropped after the witnesses disappeared.

"Hazbali was too damn eager to give us those receipts. Screw those people! I think we better take a drive to Chicago. I want to start with that hotel."

• • •

After the agents had left, Hazbali called Karl into his office.

"I don't understand any of this!" Karl said as he entered.

"Close the door and have a seat," Hazbali said.

The man did as he was asked and sat in a chair directly in front of the CEO's desk.

"I thought you told me the system was foolproof—that no one could determine where a message originated, that all the text would be encrypted. *Unbreakable* was the term you used," Hazbali barked.

The man grew pale, but he sat still like a schoolboy being disciplined by the principal.

"That's what the technician—that smiling dog—told me," pleaded Karl. "He said the system had been used by the IRA to communicate with their contacts in Cuba and Colombia without any problems."

"Obviously there are problems!" Hazbali shouted, shaking with anger. "We have been duped by these people!"

"I can stall the FBI for a while, but they will be back," replied Karl. "You saw how they acted so arrogantly."

"But this visit has certainly changed things, hasn't it? I don't like it a damn bit," Hazbali said, scowling. "I think it's time for you to travel."

"You aren't coming with me? These FBI people may stumble onto more information. We cannot risk being apprehended. You know that those are orders from the top."

"From the top…of a dung heap is a better description. All of this is coming apart because of Hamsa and his friends. He's surrounded himself with fools. He has become the king of fools."

"Those are harsh words for Sheik Osama's chosen one," Karl said with a sarcastic smile.

"Karl, both you and I know that Hamsa is a novelty. He is incapable of delivering on his promise. May God help us all."

"God is great," said Karl as he stood and walked out of the office.

29

Damage Control

The two FBI agents entered the plush lobby of one of Chicago's most expensive hotels and asked to see the manager. They identified themselves and asked to see her previous week's records pertaining to Edward Hazbali.

"We normally require a court order or warrant for such a request," she said with a wry smile.

"Then let's make it an unofficial request to look at the records. This has to do with the terrorist, Abdul Hamsa—the bomber and his friends. However, if you truly need a court order or warrant, I can get it. Of course, your noncooperation will be duly noted and might even leak out to the media. Not a good thing for your hotel's image."

"Give me a minute, please" the manager said, "I'll clear this up for you now. I'll be right back."

The manager walked into the accounting office and returned in a few minutes with a four-page printout of charges.

As the senior agent checked the dates of the stay, the younger agent began a conversation with the attractive hotel manager.

"How did Mr. Hazbali pay for his bill?" he asked.

"With his corporate AMEX card, as he always does," she said politely.

"Sounds like he's one of your best customers," the young agent said as his partner reached the final page of the hotel bill.

"Only when Madonna is in town," she replied. "Otherwise, his father is our best customer."

The agent looked incredulous, and the senior agent raised his head from his review of Hazbali's bill.

"Madonna?" the agent blurted out. "Are you sure we're talking about the same man? How old is Mr. Hazbali?"

She scrunched up her lips, agonizing a bit.

"You know," she said, "I have a hard time with that age, but I would say…midtwenties. Edward Hazbali Jr., his son, was here last week. Mr. Hazbali Sr. is in his fifties, but he didn't make the trip this time. Only his son! Young Edward has permission to use his father's corporate card. That's why it shows the father's name in the billing. Both sign as Edward Hazbali."

The senior agent thanked the manager as calmly as he could and left with a very happy partner. They got into their car and immediately called Sabinson.

Hollywood, Florida
4:30 p.m.

The man pulled a chirping cell phone from his shirt pocket and glanced at the calling number before he answered it. He was one of five young men seated at a patio table in front of one of Hollywood's many low-rent beer joints. They'd been nursing cheap draft beers all afternoon, watching the bikini-clad women passing by and speaking in whispers. The young men appeared to be average tourists dressed in the typical uniform: t-shirts, shorts, and sandals. The caller was the CEO of the Jasmine Tea Company. The conversation was conducted in coded Arabic slang.

The tension in Edward Hazbali's voice was evident. The listener nodded a few times but spoke little. He didn't have to. The message was clear. Hazbali was in trouble. After a short minute, the young man quickly snapped the flip-top phone closed and leaned toward the others.

"Do not send any more e-mails. Go back to the motel and pack. We are leaving in an hour."

After the four departed, he opened the phone again and dialed a number from memory.

Abdul Hamsa answered after the third ring. The young man passed on Hazbali's message and cell number. The call took all of ten seconds.

Grosse Pointe, Michigan
6:25 p.m.

Hazbali reached for the prepaid cellular phone that he'd placed on a nearby table. He answered the call as he looked out at Lake Michigan from the twentieth-floor balcony of his condo.

"Where are you?" Hamsa asked.

"It doesn't matter!" Hazbali replied impatiently. "The FBI knows about the bets—the e-mails!" he blurted out.

There was a long silence as Hazbali waited for a reply.

"Stay away from specifics," growled Hamsa.

"Oh...I forgot," said Hazbali sarcastically. "We are always to think about security."

"Did they say anything else?" Hamsa asked, ignoring Hazbali's attitude.

"No, they didn't have to. I saw it in their faces. It's just a matter of time before they connect all the dots!"

"You give them too much credit," Hamsa said. "They are fishing. They know nothing. Otherwise, they would have arrested you."

"Are you deaf?" he screamed. "Your e-mail scheme is worthless; they know all about it. I have helped you to get this far, but I will do no more. You have become a tyrant, no better than they are. It is not God's will to go any further. What can be accomplished by the spilling of more blood?"

Hamsa's reaction was immediate.

"Who are you to tell me about God's will? You finance our operations; that's all you have to be concerned about. You are weak and a coward. You cry like a woman, blasphemer!"

Hazbali threw the phone as hard as he could. He watched it as it arced against the sky and then fell to the parking lot below, smashing into small pieces of black plastic and microchips.

• • •

Hamsa had doubts about Hazbali's loyalty before he called him, but now he was sure that his biggest financier was more than a disciplinary problem—he was dangerous.

His next call was to another prepaid cell phone in the Detroit area.

Near Milford, Delaware
11:15 p.m.

The white sedan pulled up in the small clearing by Hamsa's cabin. He'd watched the vehicle's entry on the CCTV monitors and walked to the front door to let the man in.

Hamsa's face was uncharacteristically tense. As soon as the man entered, Hamsa motioned for him to sit at the small kitchen table. This was no social call. The visitor was a Pakistani agent who worked directly for al-Qaeda's senior members.

"We have to remove someone from our group," Hamsa said with an edge of fury in his voice as he handed the man a piece of paper with Hazbali's name and other data printed on it. Hamsa also handed him a color photograph of Hazbali.

The man sat silently, looking briefly at the paper and the photograph, and then nodded his head affirmatively.

"You're sure he hasn't spoken to anyone?"

"Not yet!" Hamsa replied coldly. "But his office manager called me and said that if the FBI visits Hazbali again, he will come apart. He's one of our financiers, not a warrior."

The man nodded without saying anything as Hamsa passed him a thick envelope containing fifty thousand dollars.

"You know what to do!" Hamsa said.

"I'll see to it," the man said as he stood and walked through the front door quickly toward his car.

The next day
Detroit, Michigan
7:05 a.m.

The four FBI agents waited patiently for the arrival of Edward Hazbali. They had purposefully parked in front of the Jasmine Tea Company, in view of all who entered; it was called *intimidation*.

They'd spent several hours on conference calls the previous evening with Sabinson and the US attorney's staff in Detroit, trying to agree on the next step in their investigative plan. The majority of the agents had wanted to arrest Hazbali immediately. They reasoned that he could be isolated and would "flip" on his associates, becoming an invaluable witness. However, the US attorney prevailed, arguing that their case was dangerously circumstantial and that Hazbali, almost certainly one of Hamsa's associates, could be physically and electronically surveilled, leading the government to Hamsa. The agents had reluctantly agreed to proceed with the US attorney's plan.

Hazbali, known to be an early-rising workaholic, didn't disappoint them. He pulled into his reserved space near the front door at the exact time predicted. When he got out of the car, he found four federal agents facing him.

"Good morning, Mr. Hazbali," the senior agent said. "I'd like to continue our conversation about those e-mails. Would you like to chat in your office or ours?"

Hazbali jerked backward as if he'd been slapped in the face. "Well…well," he stammered, "how about my office?"

The five men walked slowly through the building's entry doors. The unsmiling group entered the elevator, going directly to the penthouse.

After they were all seated, Hazbali instructed his secretary to hold all his calls.

The senior agent, seated closest to Hazbali, leaned forward in his chair, looking directly at him. The look on the agent's face was totally different from the friendly face he'd worn during his first visit.

"I didn't see Karl, your office manager, when we came in. Is he available?"

"No," replied Hazbali, "he's on annual leave."

The agent smirked and mumbled a long and sarcastic, "O…K," before continuing.

"And where is your son, Edward Jr.?" the agent asked.

For the first time, Hazbali exhibited some concern by shifting nervously in his chair, but he tried to answer as calmly as possible.

"My son is visiting some university friends in Arizona," he said finally.

The agent smiled broadly and uttered another sarcastic and slow, "O…K, where in Arizona is your son?"

"In Phoenix, but I don't have his address!" Hazbali shot back. "He'll be there for a week."

"Do you have his cell phone number?"

"No, he lost his cell and hasn't gotten a replacement yet."

"How convenient," the agent remarked, as he made a few quick notes in a small spiral binder. Then he raised his head, glaring at Hazbali.

"You weren't in Chicago last week, Mr. Hazbali; your son was. Is there something you may want to correct in the statement you gave us last week?"

Hazbali hesitated, realizing that he had truly misjudged these men's capabilities. He exhaled loudly.

"I lied to you because I was scared. I knew I shouldn't have participated in that betting pool—it's against federal law. I've never been in trouble before! I just panicked."

"Then you wouldn't mind explaining the betting pool—the fantasy all-star game, the home run derby!" the agent said.

Hazbali felt them tightening the noose around his neck but tried not to show his concern.

"They're just a bunch of people I met on the Internet," Hazbali said quickly. "We finished the fantasy football Super Bowl, and now we're into baseball!"

The agent stared at Hazbali, not saying anything. Then he stood and looked at his notes, glancing at something he'd written down.

"Then you wouldn't mind explaining why, in your e-mail, you said you were not—and I repeat, *not*—going to bet on the home run derby?"

Hazbali looked stricken, but fought to remain calm, to think of a plausible excuse.

"I didn't know enough about the players to place a bet...I didn't want to be involved—"

"Involved in what?" the agent demanded. "What was the basis for the bet, Hazbali? You don't know shit about baseball, and yet, you're part of a baseball betting pool! That doesn't make any sense. You are either in or out. What was it that made you stay away from participating in the scheme?"

Hazbali looked straight ahead and remained silent.

"How long have you known John Thomas Cronin?" the agent continued.

"Who?" Hazbali asked weakly.

"Abdul Hamsa!" the agent shot back. "What is Hamsa planning that you don't want to be involved in? Where and when is it going to happen?"

The agent waited for the questions to sink in, but Hazbali refused to take the bait.

"I have nothing to do with that man! He's hijacked our religion, committed atrocities in the name of God. He's not a true believer! He wants to..." Hazbali stopped short.

"I think it's time to speak with my attorney," he said softly.

"OK, Mr. Hazbali," the senior agent said as the three others stood up. "It's your decision. But remember this!" the man said forcefully, "We're very close to arresting all those involved with Hamsa; the next stop will be a maximum-security federal prison. And in this case, violation of the Espionage Act carries the death penalty with it. First in gets a break. Just think about it," the agent said as the others began leaving the office.

Hazbali watched the men depart his company's parking lot and walked back to his credenza, where he picked up an innocuous-looking daily planner that sat on the edge of his desk. He began to flip through its pages, stopping at an entry for the month of March. Then he picked up his cellular phone and punched in eleven numbers as he sat heavily in his leather chair.

His son answered. He was driving toward Philadelphia to attend the wedding of a classmate.

"Go the bank and withdraw your emergency funds," Hazbali said. "The time has come to disappear. Tell your brother to do the same."

His next call was to his attorney. He began a rambling explanation of the FBI visit and the criminal statutes that he could be charged under. But his meandering monologue caused his attorney to take charge of the conversation.

"Edward, I've been your attorney for fifteen years. I have managed all of your contracts and defended you successfully in the civil suits brought by your competitors. I have never liked the subject of criminal law, not even in law school. But I remember one thing from my criminal law professor: always call your lawyer and get his advice—*before* you fuck up, not *after*! I'll schedule an appointment for you with the firm's criminal litigator at eight o'clock sharp tomorrow morning. And if you didn't know it already, you are in some serious trouble, my friend. Shalom!"

• • •

Hazbali had not been able to concentrate after the agents departed. His aborted conversation with his lawyer merely added to his agony. Time dragged on. He checked his watch a hundred times, waiting for the end of the workday to arrive. He felt paralyzed by the thought of spending the rest of his life in a federal prison.

Finally, at six o'clock, he placed all of his offshore bank information in a brown leather attaché case and called his attorney again. The man was in conference, so he left a message that he would call him after he arrived at his condo. He checked to make sure that his computer terminals were turned off and finally made his way to the elevator.

After exiting on the ground floor, he strode through the glass entry doors and walked toward his car.

A short fifty yards away, a man—pencil thin and dressed like one of the many homeless people who roamed the streets—watched Hazbali closely from the inside of an abandoned building. He glanced at the color photo that had been faxed to him the night before and then crumpled it into a small ball. He brought the stock of the silenced AR-15 firmly into his shoulder and rested it on the windowsill of the building that faced the driver's side of Hazbali's silver Lexus. He looked through the telescopic sight as Hazbali stopped and faced the rear of the car, pressing the vehicle's remote control to unlock the trunk.

The subsonic hollow-point .223 round hit Hazbali squarely in the head, just above his right ear. The man disassembled the telescope, barrel, and stock, placing them in the padded portions of his small nylon sport bag. He then slung the bag over his shoulder and walked through the old newspapers and fast-food wrappers that littered the abandoned structure's first floor.

He exited through an open doorway into a waiting older-model Ford Bronco. The vehicle began to roll forward, heading for the I-94 interchange.

"It's done," he said to the driver.

The driver, an older bald man, accelerated steadily while glancing in the rearview mirror. "What a waste of talent," Karl said, "but he never would have survived the FBI's questioning. Sheik Abdul Hamsa was correct; he was weak."

Soon they were on I-94 North, heading for Karl's summer house outside of St. Clair Shores. They planned to celebrate.

• • •

Karl handed the fluted glass of Taittinger Brut to the man who had hours earlier ended Edward Hazbali's life and raised his own glass in a toast.

"To the end of the infidel's world; may their suffering last for centuries."

As he drew the glass toward his lips, the man raised a small Walther .380 pistol and shot Khalid al-Mihdhar, alias Karl Muller, twice in the face. Abdul Hamsa's orders had been clear: leave no witnesses.

• • •

About thirty minutes after Hazbali had left his office, one of the security guards discovered his crumpled body as it lay next to his car in a pool of blood. He called 911.

One of the first units to arrive included two infuriated FBI agents.

30

THE FERRET AND THE RAT

The next day
FBI Headquarters
10:30 a.m.

Sabinson had been on the phone with the agents in Detroit for more than an hour. The US attorney had spent most of the morning defending his failed strategy. But it did no good. Sabinson's task force realized they were no closer to Hamsa than they had been before Hazbali's murder. He decided to call Garcia.

Without telling him in so many words, Sabinson made it clear that time was running out. He asked Garcia for a miracle.

The next day
Quantico, Virginia
11:45 a.m.

As they were about to leave for lunch, Garcia and Montiel heard the chime of an incoming e-mail. Garcia saw the sender's name: US embassy, San Jose, Costa Rica, and opened it. The embassy was requesting an immediate conference call.

One day later
US Embassy
San Jose, Costa Rica
9:10 a.m.

Special Agent Carlos Graham eased his six-foot-five-inch frame into the embassy's Toyota Land Cruiser and began the short drive to Costa Rica's National Police Headquarters.

Graham knew Costa Rica well. His grandparents emigrated from the island of Barbados and had worked on Costa Rica's first railway construction project. He'd grown up in San Jose, where his parents taught in the Anthropology Department at the National University. He had received a basketball scholarship from Boston College and, after graduation, had served in the US Army as an infantry officer, reaching the rank of captain.

His local informant network had been unable to provide any information on Riley. His sole remaining contact, Major Arturo Blanco, had been out of the country for two weeks, participating in an international pistol competition. Blanco was the chief of intelligence for the National Police and Costa Rica's silver medalist in pistol competition in the last Pan American Games.

"The major will see you now," the receptionist said.

Graham stood and walked into the sparsely furnished office on the fifth floor of the National Police Headquarters Building.

Standing in front of his desk to greet him was Major Arturo Blanco. He was a trim five feet seven. His blond hair, green eyes, and unaccented English, thanks to a bilingual prep school he'd attended, often caused people to do a double take. His family had emigrated from the north of Spain. He was born in San Jose—100 percent Tico and proud of it.

"Carlos, let me guess: another small favor."

"It may be a little more than that—just a simple miracle this time, Arturo," Graham responded as he gave Blanco a hearty abrazo.

"Arturo, my request has to be handled on a personal basis. We don't have time to go through official diplomatic channels."

"OK, that's fine," Blanco answered, eager to hear the details.

"I need to locate a man: Jackson Xavier Riley, probably born in Ireland. I have no photograph and no date of birth; he's about fifty-five years old. He may not be in Costa Rica at all. And I needed the information yesterday. Can you do it?"

"I like solving these puzzles you bring me. If we can find your Irish friend, I'll call you."

Graham thanked him and returned to the embassy, through the building lunch-hour traffic. As he walked into his office, his secretary handed him a sheaf of phone messages. The one on top was marked "URGENT" and was from Blanco. It said simply, "Lunch at Las Palmas, 1:30, you're buying."

Graham stuffed the remaining messages into his suit jacket and passed his secretary's desk on the run.

• • •

He found Blanco seated in the rear of the restaurant's patio area, at an isolated table near a grove of mango and avocado trees. Immediately he noticed the thick file that was placed to his right.

The waiter, dressed in a crisp white shirt and black bowtie, approached them and took their order. As the waiter returned to the restaurant, Blanco began speaking.

"Can you tell me what your real interest is in this man?"

"He may be connected to a group of terrorists in the United States. We need to find him fast."

Blanco nodded pensively and then looked at Graham.

"I think we both may have an interest in him. He's been a Costa Rican citizen for twenty years. He's been married four times, all to Ticas and all...in descending order of age. Wife number four turned seventeen two months ago. But it's not his sexual prowess that concerns me. He arrived here immediately after that Contra mess. I have his entire file with me."

Blanco motioned toward the thick file on the table next to him.

"You will see an Interpol request from 1986 for information on Riley because he'd been involved in the bombing a British Army barracks. And you will also see a cable sent from a member of the National Security Advisor's Office in the White House. That cable arrived after we had arrested him on the Interpol warrant. Basically, this man had the full protection of the United States government. And so my friend, what has changed since then? Will this result in another cable from the White House?"

Graham knew that this was not the time for excuses. He'd gotten to know Blanco very well and realized that he was observing righteous anger. He allowed Blanco to continue without comment.

"I will help you in any way I can, Carlos, but only because it is *you* who has asked for help. This man Riley is a psychopathic monster, not a national hero."

Blanco pushed the file toward Graham.

"You are thorough, as always, Arturo," Graham said as he flipped through the first file, noticing that Blanco had clipped copies of Riley's most recent phone bill to the front of the folder. And as the brilliant sunlight broke through the overcast sky, Graham could feel its intense heat, along with that produced by Blanco's words.

After they were served the main course, Graham explained in detail what he was going to need: twenty-four-hour surveillance, phone taps, and banking information. Blanco nodded affirmatively as he attacked the tender churrasco.

After finishing their lunch, a caramel flan and two cups of steaming coffee put both men at ease. Graham paid the check and rose to leave. Blanco looked squarely at the towering FBI agent.

"We will get this terrorist, Carlos. Just remember our agreement."

Graham returned to his office and ordered a pot of coffee. He was intending to call Sabinson after he had reviewed the file, but one of Riley's phone calls jumped off the page. He called Sabinson immediately.

• • •

Sabinson made him repeat the entry three times.

On February 23 and 24, Riley had made international calls to Windsor, Nova Scotia, two hours away from Chester. These calls were made at the same time that Hamsa was evading the RCMP's dragnet. Now there was no doubt that Riley was involved. Sabinson's task force was back on track. After spending an hour reviewing the documents that Graham had e-mailed, Sabinson called Christopher Garcia to bring him up to date.

Later the same afternoon, Blanco authorized the surveillance that Graham had requested. For Blanco, it was time to settle a long-standing debt.

31

A Message to Garcia

Two days later
Near Milford, Delaware
8:15 p.m.

Hamsa was furious. He'd been glued to the TV as accounts of the documents found after Hazbali's murder surged through the media. Most painful was the revelation of the amount of money spent on secular, nonreligious items, such as prostitutes, liquor, and international-business-class seats for the religious faithful. One reporter had even speculated that the FBI had hacked into the terrorists' computer system, gathering inside information.

Hamsa was stunned. Riley's system had totally failed. Hamsa was now cut off and had to resolve the communications problem or risk the entire operation.

As he looked away from the television, he reached for the telephone's handset. Campana was his only source left.

Campana reviewed the caller-ID window before answering.

"How can I help you?"

The next day
San Jose, Costa Rica
8:45 a.m.

The florist's truck, painted in giant red and yellow hibiscus blossoms, pulled slowly to a stop in front of the tall, iron entry gate. The driver leaned out of the open window and pushed the buzzer mounted on a polished-aluminum gooseneck post. The two wrought iron gates swept inward, and he drove into the estate's beautifully manicured grounds.

One of the National Police officers parked in a wooded area near Riley's entrance noted the time of entry and license number of the truck. The other man confirmed that the video camera had captured the entire scene.

Within five minutes, the gates opened again, and the florist's truck exited the property, speeding off in the direction of downtown San Jose.

● ● ●

Riley opened the square box of orchids and read the enclosed card: "Let's meet at Burt's house—noon," the card said.

Riley, who was fighting a terminal hangover, suddenly stiffened.

Burt Shapiro was a young, thirty-something Californian who had cashed in his dot-com stock at its peak and opted for early retirement. He lived on a sixty-five-foot Hatteras motor yacht in Puntarenas, on Costa Rica's Pacific Coast. He was as naïve as he was rich.

Shapiro had met Riley at a beachfront bar in Puntarenas and loved socializing with him. Riley regaled him with outrageous tales of spy craft, hinting at associations with "the dark side." Shapiro became more disciple than friend. He offered Riley the use of his yacht, including its marine telephone, and became an important financial contributor to Riley's imaginary causes.

Hamsa had selected Shapiro's yacht as an alternative communications site after Riley had told him about it during his visit to Canada. It was to be used, in Hamsa's words, "only in case of extreme emergency."

Riley checked his watch and stumbled painfully toward the shower. Puntarenas was two hours away, and he would not survive the trip in his present state.

● ● ●

With fifteen minutes to spare, Riley wheeled his red BMW 701 into the private dock's parking space and was relieved to see Shapiro's heavily chromed Harley-Davidson Softail parked in front of the luxurious yacht.

However, Riley hadn't noticed the older-model dark-green Honda Civic that had just parked near the crowded seafood restaurant fifty feet away. Blanco's agents had followed him from San Jose, not once losing sight of Riley's BMW.

The other surveillance team had followed the florist's delivery truck back to the center of San Jose to await instructions.

When all the units had reported in, Blanco called Graham at the embassy. Graham emphasized the instructions Sabinson had given him: all surveillance actions were to be covert; no contact would be made until the agents knew what role Riley might be playing.

● ● ●

At exactly noon, the marine telephone on the yacht's bridge began ringing. Riley had explained to Shapiro that he would be receiving a call from one of his old CIA contacts, regarding some undercover work he had to do in Jamaica. This appeared to satiate Shapiro's curiosity, and he excused himself, going below to take a shower in his stateroom.

"Your system crashed. Haven't you been watching the news?"

"No," replied Riley.

"Someone's been reading our mail."

"Impossible!" Riley screamed.

"Watch the news. See if you can figure out how it happened."

"OK. I understand."

"I've decided to go with the plan we discussed in Canada. It requires fewer people."

"That'll work," Riley murmured.

"I'm going to have everything ready in two weeks."

"OK," replied Riley, "but if necessary, how do we—"

"Flowers!"

"Understood," Riley replied.

• • •

In the surveillance car near the pier in Puntarenas, one of the agents lowered the small digital-video camera and raised the handheld radio. "He's been talking on a radio or telephone from a large yacht, the *Poseidon*. Now he's leaving, walking back toward his car."

"Stay with him. Remember: covert!"

• • •

Riley's conversation with Hamsa had set off alarms inside him far beyond the Internet failure. He began looking for the slightest nuance, anything that signaled danger. Although he controlled his breathing, his mind was racing forward. He glanced about the pier and restaurant while pretending to fumble with his keys. All he saw were the comings and goings of the restaurant crowd: couples, children, and groups of businessmen.

As he exited the parking area and began to drive up the road that would take him back to San Jose, the traffic became snarled. Riley glanced in the rearview mirror for signs of a tail, but all he could make out were three older-model cars that had left the restaurant parking area. The car immediately behind him contained a couple and three young children.

The line of cars leaving the pier area grew in length. A minor accident on the main road had been cleared, but still there was no movement. Everyone seemed to be using their horns in an effort to move the stalled traffic.

Riley swerved the red BMW out of the line of traffic and doubled back toward the wharf. But halfway down the hill, he cut between two cars and across a rutted path that led him directly to the paved roadway above.

The agents, five cars behind him, were trapped in the group of cars and had no choice but to sit and watch. They saw Riley's BMW cut through the brush and onto the main road, away from the accident scene and toward the empty San Jose highway and radioed their headquarters immediately.

• • •

Graham listened as Blanco described the agent's observations in detail. Then Blanco made a request of his own.

The covert surveillance was demanding more agents than Blanco had in his inventory. He had no time to make a formal request through diplomatic channels. He asked Graham for at least ten more people.

As Blanco was about to hang up, he remembered another critical discovery his agents had made. "We visited the florist who delivered the orchids to Riley. The order was placed from a florist shop in Baltimore, Maryland, prepaid in cash. We also got a copy of the note that was inside the order. It said, 'Let's meet at Burt's house—noon.' I hope that helps."

After Graham finished speaking with Blanco, Sabinson was his next call. There was no doubt in his mind now: this was going to be a labor-intensive operation.

The next day
Greenbelt, Maryland
NSA Headquarters
3:45 p.m.

Garcia had requested intercept information from the NSA. It arrived in a message marked "Priority." Blanco's agents had determined that Riley's call had been made by high-frequency (HF) radio or by the marine-telephone channels.

After a few hours, the HF traffic had been reviewed and disregarded. However, the marine-telephone data was immense and sorting through it was a time-consuming process. Then, one of the analysts suggested looking for outgoing calls from Baltimore, citing the fact that no one really knew whether Riley had been placing or receiving the call. Within twenty minutes, they'd gotten a hit from one of the mainframes.

At 2:00 p.m., eastern standard time (twelve noon in Costa Rica), a call had been placed through the marine operator in Baltimore to a marine-telephone number registered to Burton Shapiro. The FCC license information showed the set was aboard a US-registered yacht, the *Posiden*. The call to the marine operator had been made from a pay phone near the Lexington Street Market, in center-city Baltimore. The call had been paid for with an international calling card. And most importantly, NSA's electronic tentacles had captured the text of the Hamsa-Riley conversation. The information was sent by urgent message to Sabinson and the Quantico Intelligence Unit.

The next day
Baltimore Police Headquarters
8:55 a.m.

The FBI agent sat in front of a bank of CCTV monitors that showed real-time views of different locations in Baltimore. Accompanying him was a console operator from Baltimore's

Street Crimes Unit, who had located the segment the FBI had requested. The archived images that had been stored on a two-terabyte hard disk began to play on the agent's monitor. The color and focus were perfectly balanced. A date/time function flashed on the bottom right of the monitor.

At 1:58 p.m. on the sixth of June, a gray-haired man wearing a New York Yankees baseball cap and dark glasses stepped into the public phone booth on Lexington Avenue and pushed its bifold doors shut. He pulled out a small card from his shirt pocket as he raised the handset and deposited some coins.

As he finished the conversation, the time function read 2:03 p.m. He opened the bifold doors and stepped out, glancing up and down the pedestrian walkways. As he did, he looked directly into one of the camouflaged cameras mounted about twenty-five yards from him. Then, he walked across the street and out of camera range.

The scene was replayed, but this time as the figure looked into the camera, the console operator froze the crisp digital image and zoomed in. Abdul Hamsa's face filled the screen.

The Street Crimes Unit entered Hamsa's face in their facial-recognition database, which analyzed the relative position, size, and shape of the eyes, nose, cheekbones, and jaw, hoping to locate him on another camera. All camera images located in or near bus stations, airports, maritime terminals, parking garages, and vehicles entering and leaving the city were reviewed, but no other match was found.

The FBI agent shook the console operator's hand. "Great work. How long will it take to burn a copy for me on a disk?"

"We'll have it for you in five minutes. We want this guy as much as you do!"

32

THE PALE RIDER ENSNARED

One week later
Washington, DC
FBI Headquarters
9:05 a.m.

It was one of the most difficult decisions Sabinson ever had to make. They were running out of leads and time. If they moved against Riley, the Costa Rican government could refuse to extradite him. The resulting publicity would notify the entire terrorist cell. Hamsa would slip away again and could be more dangerous.

The president was adamant about not changing his schedule for the Fourth of July festivities. He planned to speak at the dedication of Philadelphia's historic Harbor Park at noon. Afterward, he planned to attend the MLB All-Star Game Home Run Derby. The president's philosophy was simple and direct: he wasn't going to allow any group the unprecedented role of limiting the president's freedom of movement in his own country. To do otherwise, he argued, would be to surrender to the terrorists.

The director of the Secret Service had exhausted himself, at first trying to convince the president by using logic and, afterward, by begging him to modify his plans. The president smiled politely and told him that if he heard one more plea, he'd place him on the early-retirement list.

Sabinson called Garcia and asked for his opinion of the Riley matter. Should they arrest or continue surveillance?

Garcia's answer surprised Sabinson and the Department of Justice.

"We're running out of time. Take Riley down; use the same notification system that Hamsa used to trap him. Riley won't talk under any condition, but his arrest may force Hamsa to make a mistake. Hamsa's always been the master strategist when he's had time to plan. He's a rookie quarterback. Force him out of the pocket. Let's see how good he is under pressure."

"What about Riley's status?" Sabinson asked. "The Costa Rican government will never allow the extradition of one of its citizens, terrorist suspect or not."

"Alex, Leo, and I have been through that maze. Forget extradition; move for expulsion."

"How can you do that? He's a damn citizen," Sabinson said, raising his voice.

"Not if he lied about his criminal record on his citizenship application. It's called fraud, Colby, and it cancels out his citizenship status. Then they can expel him as an undesirable. The Costa Rican government preserves its sovereignty, and we provide them an easy out. It's a win-win for us!"

"Son of a bitch," Sabinson screamed, "you're right! I'll call Graham right away…and thank you, Chris."

Garcia turned to Montiel and Khamis, who were turning blue from anxiety. "He bought it!" he yelled out, as high fives were exchanged in their workspace.

The next day
San Jose, Costa Rica
9:00 a.m.

The brightly painted florist delivery truck pulled to a stop in front of the high wrought-iron gate. The driver leaned out of the truck's cab and pressed the call button. The twin gates opened, and the truck entered. About thirty minutes later, Riley's red BMW blew out of the gates, heading west at high speed.

• • •

He checked his watch constantly during the drive to Puntarenas and only relaxed when he reached the entry to the dockside parking area. The message in the flowers was the same as he'd received a week before, but this one contained the word *urgent* at the end. He locked the car door and ran to the private wharf where Shapiro's yacht was moored, quickly climbing the inclined boarding ramp.

He opened the cabin door and froze. Four armed men pointed their 9 mm automatics at him. Behind them sat Burt Shapiro—handcuffed, gagged, and pale.

"I don't have any money!" Riley shouted as he raised his hands into the air.

"Don't move!" yelled a tall man wearing a dark-blue golf shirt with an FBI insignia on it. He walked toward Riley and ordered him to turn around.

Riley complied and immediately felt his hands being brought down forcefully as cold metal cuffs were tightened around his wrists.

Then the man turned him around and glared at him.

"Jackson Xavier Riley, I'm Special Agent Carlos Graham of the Federal Bureau of Investigation. You are under arrest for violations of the Espionage Act."

It took Riley about two nanoseconds to understand what Graham had said.

"Bugger off, you FBI prick," Riley laughed. "You're not dealing with an American here. I'm a Costa Rican citizen. We have no extradition treaty with you bastards."

At this point, another man stepped toward Riley. He was dressed in the pressed khaki uniform of a Costa Rican National Police officer and was smiling broadly.

"Mr. Riley. I'm Major Arturo Blanco, chief of intelligence for the Costa Rican National Police. You are quite correct that we do not permit the extradition of Costa Rican citizens. However, I have in my hand an order of expulsion, signed by our president last night. We found that you lied on your citizenship application where it asked about your criminal history. You failed to mention the matter of the army barracks in Ulster, your membership in the IRA, and your association with the FARC in Colombia. Therefore, you are *not* a Costa Rican citizen. And as an international terrorist, you are not welcome in our country."

Blanco's friendly demeanor changed to an icy stare.

"You are hereby expelled from Costa Rica, effective immediately. These gentlemen with Special Agent Graham have been kind enough to offer the services of their Cessna Citation jet, on which they arrived earlier this morning, to take you out of our country. Our president accepted their offer. Have a pleasant trip to the United States, Mr. Riley."

Having said that, Blanco forced a folded copy of the expulsion order into Riley's shirt pocket and returned to the group of FBI agents.

As Riley was being led down the yacht's ramp, he decided to exact a little revenge. He would head butt Blanco as a "going-away present." At the base of the ramp, Blanco was standing about five feet from him, speaking with one of the FBI agents. But as Riley sprang at his target, he stumbled in the loose gravel, losing his footing. He recovered and flung himself headfirst at Blanco, who arched backward, avoiding the airborne Riley.

Graham's brick-hard fist caught Riley squarely on the bridge of the nose, and he landed on his back in a heap. In addition to some instantaneous blood loss, Riley's right eye shut immediately, making him look more like Quasimodo than a feared IRA terrorist.

• • •

As the jet passed over Costa Rica's Caribbean coastline near Puerto Limon, one of the FBI agents approached Riley. He read the statement on his Miranda card and asked if Riley understood his rights.

Riley's response was immediate.

"Piss off, asshole," he growled.

"I'll take that as a yes," the man said.

"Do you want an attorney present, or are you willing to speak to us without an attorney present?"

"Fuck you and your mother! This arrest is illegal!" yelled Riley, twisting against his waist and arm restraints.

"I'll take that as a negative response, Mr. Riley. We will not ask you anymore questions and will allow you to remain silent," the agent replied.

"What's your name, asshole?" growled Riley as he finally stopped struggling.

"Special Agent Jimmy Fannon, and the big guy in front of you is Special Agent Aedan O'Hara. He played defensive tackle at the University of Alabama. His grandfather was killed in Dublin by an IRA bomb. He was a good Catholic on his way to Mass. Any further questions, Jackie my lad?" Fannon asked, glaring at Riley.

"Yeah, Fannon, I've got another question," smirked Riley. "Do any of you pricks have the slightest idea of the bloody nightmare that's heading your way? You and your families—"

Special Agent Aedan O'Hara stood and spun around so quickly that Riley was taken completely by surprise. O'Hara had torn a twelve-inch length of silver duct tape from the roll he carried in his travel kit. He pressed the strip of tape hard against Riley's mouth, silencing his outbursts.

"He said he wanted to remain silent, Jimmy. I'm just ensuring that his rights are protected."

As the FBI's Cessna Citation landed in the dusk at Dulles International, Riley had formulated a plan.

• • •

Sabinson called Garcia and described Riley's arrest.

"You were correct about using the same method of contact with Riley; he walked right into the trap."

"He'll make mistakes, Colby. We just have to watch him closely. He may not contact Hamsa directly, but contact will be made. Riley's been lucky, but luck only takes you so far."

"His arraignment is scheduled for tomorrow morning. The US attorney has asked the media to keep this quiet for a week. That should buy us some time."

33

The Corruptors Gather

Lorton, Virginia
Lorton Federal Detention Center
4:15 p.m.

The federal public defender assigned to Jack Riley's case, Katherine Lacey, found him to be a personable and interesting man. She was appalled by the purple-and-black swelling on his face. He looked like he'd survived a bad traffic accident.

"How did you get that nasty black eye, Mr. Riley?"

"The FBI agents beat me while my hands were cuffed behind my back," Riley said with a whimper. "Then they threatened to throw me out of the airplane if I didn't talk."

"Did they question you after your arrest?"

"During the entire bloody flight, those two agents never shut up. They made me walk from the front of the plane to the back. Then they'd push me into an empty seat and tell me that I had to talk to save my life."

"Didn't they read your rights to you?"

"Yeah," said Riley, laughing sarcastically, "they told me I had the right to medical treatment as soon as we landed in the States."

"Did they inform you that you had the right to remain silent?"

"Yes they did…after an hour of questions about what I did for the CIA in the 1980s. They kept yelling at me, accusing me of being a terrorist and helping some guy named Hamster… Hamsa…or something like that. I told them I'd never heard of that person. The big guy, O'Hara, put duct tape over my nose and mouth so I couldn't breathe. And then we landed, thank the dear Lord!"

She began writing furiously on her yellow legal pad, asking more questions about the arrest.

At twenty-six, she'd practiced law for three years after graduating first in her class from the University of Pennsylvania's law school. She held the record for wins in the office and saw no reason why this case would be any different.

For hours, Riley discussed his past, conveniently editing the facts and emphasizing the importance of his work with the CIA. He made sure to stay away from his connections with Hamsa and the FARC.

She immediately saw that their defense could be based on the highly classified work Riley had been involved with. She called it her "Ollie North Special," a reference to the infamous defense used by the Reagan White House's "Contra Patriots," whereby they would be unable to properly defend themselves unless they used classified documents.

As she got up to leave, Riley asked for a favor. He had watched her carefully during the interview and felt she was the perfect combination of idealism and naiveté; she could be manipulated. "Miss Lacey," he said, looking down sadly, "am I allowed visitors?"

"Of course you are, Mr. Riley! You're in the United States, not some third-world country."

He grinned sheepishly.

"Could you contact a friend of mine and see if he would like to visit me...without going through official channels?"

"Of course!" she exclaimed. "Give me his name and number."

Milford, Delaware
8:50 p.m.

The phone rang in the small ranch-style house that was nestled among other modest homes along the residential street.

Campana noticed that the caller ID's window was showing, "Federal Public Defender, Leesburg, Virginia." He decided to take the call.

The female caller asked for Randall Campana.

"He's not in right now. Can I take a message? This is his brother."

"I'm Katherine Lacey, an attorney with the Federal Public Defender's Office in Leesburg, Virginia. I represent Jack Riley. He was arrested in Costa Rica and flown back here two days ago. He'd like your brother to visit him. He's being held at the Lorton Virginia Federal Detention Center. And make sure your brother brings a photo ID. They won't let him in without it. Do you know Mr. Riley?"

Campana hesitated for a few seconds.

"No, Miss Lacy, I don't, but the visit may be a problem. Randy's moved to Florida and works on a fishing boat out of Pompano Beach. It may be a few weeks before he's back, but he might call in. If he does, I'll give him the message."

"I think your brother's visit would cheer up my client. The federal agents who arrested Mr. Riley really did a number on his face. Tell your brother that he'll probably still be in the facility hospital for a few weeks. He's a mess."

"That sounds serious, Miss Lacey," Nichols fawned. "This person's in a federal detention center and wants to talk to my brother. What did this guy do to get locked up by the feds?"

"Mr. Campana, Mr. Riley's done nothing to warrant the arrest or the brutal treatment that he's received. But the federal government has charged him with violations of the Espionage Act; go figure."

Campana winced, remembering that the Espionage Act carried the death penalty for certain violations.

"Wow," exhaled Campana, "I'll do my best to get a message to Randall right away!"

Campana locked the front door and walked toward his white Chevrolet conversion van. He was going to deliver this message personally.

• • •

Hamsa was stunned. Riley was immortal—the last person in the world who would fall into a trap. He had no idea how the FBI had located him. At least Riley had gotten word out that he'd been burned. Hamsa knew that Riley would never talk. But how had the FBI tracked him? The question began to bother Hamsa.

He reached into his laptop bag and withdrew two thick-banded stacks of hundred-dollar bills.

"Here's twenty thousand. I need a rental car, something plain, and I need you to contact a man in Wilmington. His name is Michael Simpson."

He picked up a sealed envelope from the table and handed it to Campana.

"Call him from a pay phone at the number written on the envelope. Tell him you're interested in buying his piano; he'll understand. Give him fifteen thousand up front. He needs to read the document in the envelope. It's our operations order; guard it with your life. I want to meet with him here in two days, ten in the morning. And make sure you bring the car by tomorrow noon. I need some mobility."

Two days later
Lorton, Virginia
9:30 a.m.

As Katherine Lacy entered the prison's administrative area, she decided to fill out a visitor's request for Jack Riley ahead of time. This was a standard practice. She was being overwhelmed by new cases and knew that if she didn't do it now, it might be forgotten altogether. She carefully printed the man's name, "Randall Campana," and his phone number in the spaces provided, and handed the card to the bored clerk, who was busy admiring her curved three-inch airbrushed acrylic nails.

The clerk tossed the card into a stack of other visitor requests that were pending approval and returned to more pressing work, gluing the blue and silver glitter on her nails. Then Lacey placed her attaché case onto the X-ray machine's conveyor belt and told the guard she was there to see Jack Riley.

Near Milford, Delaware
10:00 a.m.

Hamsa watched the CCTV monitors as the white conversion van entered the gate and slowly wound its way toward his cabin.

As Campana and his passenger entered the kitchen, Hamsa stood by the small, round table.

"God be praised, Michael Simpson," Hamsa said as he walked toward the visitor and embraced him tightly, kissing him on both cheeks. "It has been seven years since I have seen you and still you have not aged a month."

The man, Hamsa's height with short, black hair and dark-brown eyes, smiled broadly as he returned Hamsa's embrace.

"Abdul Hamsa, I bring greetings from all our brothers who have followed your successes. May God always protect you."

The men sat down at the table, where Hamsa had prepared three tall glasses of steaming tea.

• • •

Simpson had been one of Hamsa's classmates in Pakistan, where both had completed their early religious and military training. He had been born in East London to a Jamaican father and British mother. But Simpson had never fit in with his family's work ethic, choosing instead petty crime and drug dealing as alternate careers. In the midst of his tumultuous adolescence, he'd been drawn toward a group of disaffected Muslim youth who were spellbound by a charismatic Saudi leader and promises of a better life after the jihad. The group's religious justification for increasing violence in the Middle East gave Simpson an ideological home.

He'd excelled in both his religious and military training, being selected just behind Hamsa as an honor graduate, a true "Sword of Retribution." Simpson was schooled as a mechanical engineer in the United States after his terrorist training in Pakistan and put to sea as an assistant engineer on one of the many supertankers carrying crude oil to the thirsty US refineries.

● ● ●

"Can you do what's necessary?" asked Hamsa.

"Abdul, the procedures you laid out in the plan are crystal clear. It should be no problem. As the senior engineer, I have total authority over the loading of the vessel."

"Excellent, Michael, do you have any questions?"

"I have just one. How did you conceive of such a brilliant plan?"

Hamsa sat back in the small kitchen chair.

"Actually, I must give that credit to a dear friend of mine, an Irishman who had a vision while drinking whiskey in Canada."

Simpson burst out laughing, shaking his head in disbelief.

"And they say that alcohol is evil."

"But not when it is used as a lubricant for brilliance," replied Hamsa.

Even the usually reserved Campana laughed heartily.

"Randy," Hamsa said, turning to Campana, "I need you to deliver the spare-parts boxes to Michael on July first. Are we clear about the schedule?"

Both Campana and Simpson nodded silently. Hamsa smiled broadly as he rose from his chair.

"From here on in, we will discuss the details of the plan only when we're face-to-face—no more phones. Randy, if I need to speak to you, I'll use the cellular that you got me. Now let's move forward."

"I'm ready," Simpson said, now more upbeat than before, "This is worth every day we spent in training."

"One last thing—and this is critical that you both follow these instructions, without exception. The rendezvous point will be the northwest corner of the Cherry Hill Mall. Randy will park his van there at exactly eleven forty-five…"

Simpson would arrive earlier and was instructed to make some purchases and blend in with the crowd. At noon, he was to walk to Campana's van and wait for Hamsa, who would arrive at exactly 12:15. Then the three would drive away from the Philadelphia area to the hunting lodge in western Pennsylvania.

"There will be a lot of confusion and panic. We will join the five million others driving to their holiday celebrations in upstate Pennsylvania. Do either of you have any questions?"

Both answered with a gruff no.

"Randy, you are the key to our success. If we, Michael or I, are not on time, leave the area and drive back to Delaware. Both of you know that there will be no arrests made if you are captured. They will torture us, and then kill us. We will be the three most hated people in this country."

• • •

As the conversion van approached the shopping mall in Milford where Simpson had parked his car, he wrote something on a notepad he'd taken from his backpack and pulled off the top sheet, handing it to Campana.

"If we have to go separately, just drive to the port area and ask for the vessel by name; it's on this sticky note. Tell the security guards you're there to deliver a bag I forgot, and they'll let you in. The pier security is the worst I've ever seen—which is good for us. See you on the first of July."

"OK, Mike. See you soon," Campana shouted as he drove away.

• • •

After parking the van and waving to the neighbors, Randy Campana entered his front door with the yellow note stuck to his right index finger. He walked directly to the wall-mounted phone and attached the three-by-three-inch paper to its side, noting Simpson's neat printing: *MARAVI.*

34

SMALL DETAIL—BIG IMPACT

Two weeks later
FBI Headquarters
8:45 a.m.

Sabinson was meeting with the task force, trying to pick up Hamsa's trail again. The Fourth of July was a short two weeks away. Since Riley's arrest, the trail had grown ice-cold.

But Riley's arrogance had caused him to overlook a small detail. He'd assumed that his attorney would merely contact Campana as he asked her to do. He hadn't considered the possibility that she would follow the rules. No one in his world did.

• • •

Sabinson took the call on his direct line. He immediately recognized the voice of the supervisor of the four agents assigned to the Riley investigation.

"Riley's public defender submitted a visitor's request for him two weeks ago. Somehow, it only surfaced today in the Administration Section. We have a name and phone number. I ran a reverse check on the phone number and have an address in Milford, Delaware. His name is Randall Campana. He has two prior convictions for possession of unlicensed weapons and one for distribution of methamphetamines. The convictions took place about fifteen years ago, but Riley knew him well enough to list his current contact information. I want permission to set up on this guy and see if anything shakes loose. I'll take care of the search warrant applications."

"You've got it! And I want two units on him twenty-four-seven."

• • •

Shortly before noon, Sabinson called Garcia.

"How goes the war?"

"We're wading through rivers of documents—cross-checking every lead, not very exciting, but necessary," Garcia replied.

"Chris, I'd like for you, Alex, and Leo to be my liaison officers in Philadelphia. You'll be coordinating our security plan with the Coast Guard for the president's visit on the Fourth. They're installing the same data links you have at Quantico. I just thought it would be a natural fit; you speak the same language, and you served as a Coast Guard officer. The kickoff is scheduled for noon on the thirtieth of June."

The following day
Milford, Delaware
4:30 a.m.

The gray Chevrolet sedan drove down the dark suburban street. It slowed as it passed a white conversion van parked next to a modest ranch-style house. The two FBI agents inside the vehicle were familiarizing themselves with the area and, most importantly, looking for the best cover available to surveil Campana. They drove through the sleeping neighborhood and returned to a small strip mall, where they pulled up alongside two other agents in another vehicle.

"I think we're in luck. He lives on a short residential block: one way in and one way out. The white van is there now—no side street exits to worry about. There's a ballpark across from one entrance to his street and a convenience store at the other end.

You'll be able to look down the street directly at the house from either site."

"OK, we'll set up at the convenience store."

"Good, I'll notify the other units to return to the motel and get some sleep before tonight."

Throughout the day, the unrelenting sun beat down on the surveillance teams. The combination of high heat and humidity was taxing the cars' A/C units to their max. Campana had not left the house. He was busy in his basement workshop.

• • •

He lifted the latches and opened the metal box's top. Each one was the size of a large attaché case. His next step was to secure the dull, white ten-pound block of Semtex explosive to the inside of each box with a quick-drying epoxy. Then, he inserted a small cylindrical detonator in the core of the Semtex block and joined its male pigtail of red and blue wires into the female base of a set of photocells powered by two hearing-aid batteries. He attached the unit to a digital timer. After a pause, he glued the digital timer and photocells into place. The timer had been preset to the date and time Hamsa had requested, the fourth of July at twelve noon, Eastern Standard Time. The photocells guaranteed that if their light source was interrupted before the time set, the bomb's circuit would close, and detonation would occur.

The next step had Riley's signature all over it. Campana drilled a one-eighth-inch hole in the box's side, the side that would face the container when it was finally mounted. He placed a six-inch-diameter magnetic disk containing a small eyehook on the tip of its thin raised nipple through the case's side panel, so the disk was flush with the outside, and the eyehook protruded into the box itself.

The final step was to attach a short piece of ten-pound-test monofilament line to the eyehook and to a smaller pressure switch connected to the detonator. This gave him certainty that if anyone attempted to remove the boxes from the containers before the set detonation time, the bomb would explode.

Campana turned the box on its side on the wooden worktable's surface and glued a microantenna and transmitter into each box, making sure that the antenna was pushed into the Semtex block.

He tack welded the latches shut to prohibit anyone from opening the box accidentally. After sanding and repainting the welds, Campana checked his watch. He'd totally lost track of time, and his stomach demanded satisfaction. He returned to the kitchen and fixed dinner: two pounds of roast beef on rye, washed down with three cold Heinekens. Then he returned to the basement to clean up his workshop.

It had taken him all day, but he had completed the assembly of the two "spare-parts boxes," matching Riley's specifications exactly. The boxes sat upright and were painted a glossy white with the words "EMERGENCY SPARE PARTS—KEEP LOCKED" stenciled in bright red letters.

• • •

The phone on his shop wall began ringing. He glanced at the caller ID window It was Hamsa's prepaid cell phone. He picked up the handset.

"Did you finish packing the two boxes?"

"All done and gift wrapped."

"There's a slight change in plans. You'll be picking up Michael and another person. The third person will have to borrow your van while you and Michael finish what you have to do on the ship. But don't worry. We'll get you back to the motel."

"No problem at all," said Campana as he hung up.

But it was a problem. Campana, the loner, didn't like changes that he hadn't initiated. He was the polar opposite of a team player. And he started to wonder about other things that could go wrong. Something called *doubt* began to creep into his subconscious mind.

• • •

The other man Hamsa had spoken of was not part of the original mission. He was a Brazilian street thug who had immigrated to the United States using a student visa. He'd been brought in by the al-Qaeda leadership to silence a bothersome Islamic cleric who headed a small mosque near Cherry Hill, New Jersey.

The imam had committed an unpardonable sin. He had spoken out publicly against the Taliban terrorists for killing school children in Afghanistan, calling them "infidels." Vengeance had been dispatched.

• • •

Meanwhile, the agents went through gallons of Gatorade, dozens of donuts, and more than a few cups of coffee while they waited for something to happen. Just before they were going to be relieved by the other teams, the senior agent walked to a public phone. He wanted to make sure Campana was in the house. He dropped some coins in the slot of a pay phone outside of a convenience store and punched in Campana' phone number.

"Hey, Tony, you're late. It's five-card stud...you snooze, you lose."

"You've got the wrong number," Campana said coldly as he glanced at the caller ID. It showed the call was coming from a local pay phone.

"Sorry," said the agent as he hung up, having confirmed that their target was still in the house.

The following day
Milford, Delaware
11:30 a.m.

The surveillance team almost lost Campana during a trip he made to a nearby mall. Another van, identical to Campana's, exited the underground parking garage at high speed just after Campana entered. After following the van for a few miles, the surveillance team discovered that it wasn't Campana and radioed the news to the backup unit.

The second surveillance team located Campana just as he entered a sports bar in the mall. He was seated at a table by himself. Clearly, he was there to watch the baseball game that had just started. And judging from the way he was ordering pitchers of beer, Campana would be there for hours. The team leader called Sabinson with an update.

"I'm going to put a tracker on his vehicle. I've got two in the trunk. If he stays in that bar for twenty more minutes, we're in business."

The tracker he mentioned was a powerful transmitter, the size of a carton of cigarettes. It sent out a signal that was carried by the same microwave relays as a cell phone's. The location was fed through GPS software and appeared as a small, blinking red dot on a digital street map. The map could be acquired through a private Internet site, and the target could then be followed on a standard laptop.

The team leader grabbed the tracker and three nylon cable ties. Two agents from another team sat in the sports bar sipping iced teas, keeping an eye on Campana, and enjoying the air-conditioned surroundings. He slid under the van and pushed the tracker into a channel in the vehicle's frame, pulling the restraining nylon ties tight. Then he clipped off the loose ends. The last thing they wanted was Campana making a chance discovery of the device.

For more than two hours, two teams of agents—one group parked inside the mall's garage and the other outside—waited patiently while Campana guzzled beer and ate pizza. The team leader drove back to an area close to Campana's house while his passenger watched the laptop's screen. The tracker's thirty-day battery powered the transmitter flawlessly, and the blinking red dot representing Campana's van showed up clearly on the screen, still parked in the mall's underground garage.

Finally Campana departed the bar, listing heavily. He entered the white van and began his trip home, followed by two teams of agents. In a short ten minutes, the relieved agents watched Campana turn into his street and stop, backing the van into his driveway. The last thing they needed was Campana being arrested for DUI.

"He should be right in front of his house," said the team leader over the radio.

"Confirmed; looks like we're in business. It works!"

● ● ●

For the next two days and nights, Campana remained indoors. He began to make preparations for a trip to Wilmington. Tomorrow was the thirtieth of June.

June 30
Philadelphia
US Coast Guard—Captain of the Port Offices
9:10 a.m.

Garcia, Montiel, and Khamis entered the broad expanse of offices located on the tenth floor of the federal building. The view encompassed part of the old Navy Yard and the broad expanses of the busy Delaware River. Even though it was a full four days before the president's arrival, the office was busy. The conversations among groups of people were punctuated by the sounds of ringing phones.

A young ensign walked toward the three, glancing at her clipboard. "You must be Mr. Garcia. They wanted to put the FBI out there in the middle," she said, looking perturbed, "but... Lieutenant Garcia, the captain of the port changed the seating, nothing but the best for you." She added proudly, "The Coast Guard takes care of its own."

"I'm glad I didn't come by myself," Montiel shot back, as the three analysts and their escort began making their way toward the east side of the building.

"Just like home," Khamis laughed as they entered the area where three desks had been pushed together, encircled by heavy, blue, acoustically padded dividers.

"Briefings will be held at zero seven daily from the platform in the center of the room," the ensign said, pointing over one of the dividers. "Coffee and donuts are just to the left of the entrance, and we had a phone and three computers installed for you, the same net you're on in Quantico."

As she turned to walk away, Garcia called out to her, "Thanks for everything. It's good to see the uniform again."

She stopped and turned toward the three. "My uncle served in *Isla Grande*," she said. "Mr. Garcia, you are worshiped in our house. It's the least we could do for you."

Lorton, Virginia
Lorton Federal Detention Center
11:30 a.m.

Riley fit in well with the prison population in his restricted wing. And as always, he made friends easily. It had not taken long for his fame and inflated resume to spread throughout the cell block. One group in particular, the jihadists, had become his unofficial protectors and guardians. Riley was especially impressed with their leader, Orion Jones, a West Indian who had been involved in gun running and drug dealing. As it turned out, they shared a common enemy, the late Rashid al-Bakar.

• • •

Jones had purchased five hundred AK-47s and two thousand hand grenades from al-Bakar for resale to a violent drug cartel in Mexico. After the initial tests and acceptance by Jones, al-Bakar had substituted inferior Pakastani knockoffs for the original Russian AKs. He'd also switched the hand grenades, substituting training grenades instead of the fragmentation grenades that had been agreed upon. The cartel head was furious, but instead of demanding his money back, he called the ATF's anonymous informant line.

• • •

Orion Jones could make prison hooch better than anyone, and Riley became one of his best customers. Jones worked in the commissary. Ten-pound bags of sugar and five-gallon tins of peaches and cherries were his for the taking.

One night, Riley had surpassed his old record of two liters of the strong liquor and was working on his third. He'd developed a liking for the young West Indian and decided to share something with him.

"Remember the thing that came down about a year ago, the attack on the White House?" whispered Riley.

"I do," replied Jones. "Was that your thing?"

"That fucking al-Bakar fucked us and slipped some cheap Chinese detonators into the deal. That's why the shit never went off. They failed!"

"Wow," exclaimed Jones, "and nobody knew."

"Bullshit," growled Riley. "I begged Abdul Hamsa to stop dealing with that fuck. I told him that they wouldn't work, but he kept it on the down low and made believe that our conversation never took place."

"Hamsa knew about it before it happened?"

"He sure as hell did," slurred Riley. "But no one listens to old Jackie Boy until it's too fucking late! I had a battle with al-Bakar in front of the whole group—two bloody weeks before the operation. But nobody listens to old Jackie Boy until it's too late! Pour me another, my brother."

• • •

Two days later, Jones stood in line with the others to make a telephone call. When his turn came, he handed the prison operator a slip with a 412 area code and the number. The operator punched in the numbers as Jones picked up the handset.

"I have a collect call from Orion Jones in the Lorton Federal Detention Center. Will you accept the charges?"

"Yes."

"He knew about it," said Jones.

"Before the event," the woman's voice asked.

"Two weeks before."

"Thank you," the woman replied, and the connection was broken.

Milford, Delaware
3:10 p.m.

"He's moving," said the voice on the radio. "looks like he's carrying a large duffel bag and a suitcase."

One of the agents leaned forward, looking through his ten-by-fifty binoculars.

"That prick's packed to go someplace. Call the motel, and get the other teams out here. Tell them to pick up the search warrant and stop by the state police troop. Let's see what we can find. If Campana decides to come back, I'll call you."

The two FBI surveillance cars followed Campana out of Milford at a safe distance. The tracker was performing flawlessly.

The backup teams arrived in twenty minutes, accompanied by two Delaware State Police detectives and the state police K-9

Unit. The bomb dog had been specifically requested by Garcia, based on Riley's association with Campana.

They walked around the property but saw nothing out of the ordinary, other than a large pile of ashes in Campana's incinerator. However, as the group passed the house's entry door nearest the garage, the dog alerted, barking and scratching on the door's glass storm panes. The FBI agents stood to the side of the door with the K-9 officer as the detectives walked to their car to retrieve a steel battering ram from the trunk.

As the group entered, the dog continued barking and pulled its handler down the steps into the basement. A heavy, wooden worktable and a full tool rack were the only items they saw, but the dog refused to leave the table, barking and snapping at it. The K-9 handler had to physically carry the dog upstairs and out to his vehicle.

Their search of the remainder of Campana's house revealed that the refrigerator had been cleaned out and turned off. The spartan furnishings consisted of a sofa, TV, bed, and small kitchen table with two cheap plastic chairs.

The only physical evidence found was a small, yellow gummed note, stuck to the side of the telephone with one word neatly printed on it: *MARAVI*.

They called Sabinson, describing the results of the search. He wasn't surprised at the lack of physical clues, but the dog's reaction concerned him. And he couldn't make sense of the word, *MARAVI*. It sounded Spanish. He dialed a number in Philadelphia.

"So how's your new office?" Sabinson asked.

"It's so good, we're not coming back," replied Garcia.

"We hit the house belonging to Randall Campana. You were right: the bomb dog went nuts, but that's another story. The agents found a piece of notepaper with one word written on it. I need you, Leo, and Alex to see if you can tell me what it means."

"Sure, go ahead."

"It's spelled m-a-r-a-v-i, written in all-caps. *Ma-ra-vee?*" said Sabinson, sounding more like a third-grade phonics teacher than an assistant director for the FBI.

Garcia thought for a moment.

"It could be a shortened form of the word *maravilla*. It means 'a wonder,' something fantastic. Could also be a flower—the marigold. But *maravi*...It just doesn't make any sense. I'll run it past Leo and Alex."

"Well, we're going to send the document to the lab for prints. Maybe NSA has some history of the word's use. I'll check in with you tomorrow."

Garcia wrote the word down as Sabinson had spelled it. He looked at it but was unable to get any further. Montiel was also stumped. Their hopes were dashed after Alex Khamis admitted defeat.

Wilmington, Delaware
5:50 p.m.

The FBI's two surveillance cars had followed Campana from southern Delaware into center-city Wilmington without incident. The only problem they'd encountered was his unexpected stop at a McDonald's and a twenty-minute respite in a public park, where he polished off two Big Macs and the three super-sized fries, washed down by two super-sized drinks.

As Campana neared an area just south of the Delaware Memorial Bridge, he turned off the roadway and pulled into the visitor's lane of a very upscale and exclusive townhouse development. After speaking with the uniformed security guard, the gate's barrier arm rose, and Campana drove through the tall brick entryway.

The gate was the development's only entrance and exit. But the security was thorough and presented a problem for the surveillance team. Strict covert surveillance was to be maintained.

Both trailing cars pulled forward next to the twelve-foot-high brick wall that surrounded the entire development, and the team leader was called.

"Try to get in! Try to see where he's going, but for God's sake, be cool about it!" yelled the team leader into the radio.

The agents approached the guardhouse through the visitor's lane, and the driver lowered the window, smiling politely.

"Good afternoon, sir," he said to the eighteen-year-old security guard, "I'd like to speak to the manager about renting one of the units."

The young security guard smiled back at the two agents.

"They're closed for the day. You'll have to come back tomorrow at nine."

"Gosh!" replied the agent, feigning sorrow, "Don't guess there's any chance of taking a short tour to look at the units from the outside? We've driven a couple hours to get here."

The young man looked at the agent coldly.

"Not until nine tomorrow!" he repeated.

The agent thanked him and made a quick U-turn back onto the street.

Another agent dashed into the Bank of Delaware Tower, one of the tallest buildings bordering the development, and spoke with the security director, a retired FBI agent. He explained that he needed a high observation point, and the security director approved his request, no questions asked. He took the elevator to the top floor, which was deserted and undergoing a remodeling. Through the broad windows, he saw the van parked in an area marked with bright yellow letters on the pavement: "Visitors Only." The group of agents requested an additional surveillance unit and began the most common action connected with surveillance work—waiting for something to happen.

• • •

Inside Simpson's condo, the atmosphere was anything but tedious. Campana and Simpson reviewed their procedures, leaving no room for error. The third man—the Brazilian thug—remained asleep in one of the guest bedrooms.

Two forty-foot refrigerated containers would be delivered to the vessel late the next day. They would be loaded under Simpson's supervision on the most forward portion of the foredeck and locked into place. There, they'd sit side by side in the open—no others to the left or right.

Then Campana would install the metal boxes just below the refrigeration units, fitting them into prewelded racks. Their stenciled markings, "EMERGENCY SPARE PARTS—KEEP LOCKED," masked their true purpose.

• • •

At midnight, a fresh team of agents arrived from the Baltimore office and relieved the other teams. The only item of interest that occurred during the night was a ferocious electrical storm that had swept in from the north.

35

SNIPE HUNT

July 1
Philadelphia
US Coast Guard—Captain of the Port Offices
7:00 a.m.

The morning briefing began on time as the various federal agents and Coast Guard personnel stood around the raised platform in the room's center. Discussions of security zones and patrol-boat placement took up the majority of the thirty minutes allotted.

After the briefing ended, Garcia, Khamis, and Montiel huddled in their cubicle, reviewing the latest intercepts from NSA. The secure phone rang, and Garcia answered it. It was Sabinson.

"Chris, I just fought off the director's request for us to pick up Campana now. I need your input. Do you see any alternatives to tailing him?"

"If you take this guy down now and he refuses to cooperate, you'll lose the only sure lead we have. I'd go with the covert surveillance. All the evidence points to something happening in three days. Other than Riley, Campana is our only known connection. Hamsa has to surface soon; this is his show."

Wilmington, Delaware
11:45 a.m.

The agent stationed on the top floor of the Bank of Delaware Tower saw the three figures as they came around the side of one of the brick townhouses. They were walking directly toward Campana's white van parked in the visitor's area. He grabbed the ten-by-fifty binoculars from the windowsill and saw Campana and two other men as they entered the vehicle.

"Campana is in the van, driving toward the guardhouse," the agent's voice crackled over the radio. "He's got two passengers: white males, light-brown hair, slightly taller than Campana. One is wearing light-blue overalls and is carrying a yellow hard hat. The other one's carrying a small, black nylon bag. Looks like a name tag on the overalls, but I can't make it out from here. Campana is wearing khaki pants and a red polo shirt. Neither of the passengers is Hamsa."

"We'll take him," the team leader replied. "We have the tracker active on the laptop. Units one and two will back us up. Let's roll."

• • •

Campana exited the condominium's entry gate and merged into traffic at a leisurely pace. He continued at the same speed as he turned onto the entry ramp for I-95 North. At that point, he accelerated, leaving the FBI cars six vehicle lengths behind him.

"He's trying to shake us," radioed one of the agents.

"No," replied the team leader, "he's clueless, just involved in an animated conversation with the front-seat passenger. Keep some vehicles in front of you, but not too far back. This traffic's tricky. We'll decide who takes the lead once we clear the construction."

The closest surveillance car was still three vehicles behind Campana when the traffic was funneled into a single lane bordered by concrete barriers. All they could do was watch as a traffic signal-man directed Campana's van to proceed and then stood in front of the remaining column, holding them for almost five minutes.

The agent rolled down the window and honked his horn to get the young signalman's attention. He held his badge case out, pointing to it.

"FBI—we have to get onto I-95; it's an emergency!" he shouted.

The young man, wearing a set of earbuds, glanced ahead of the line of traffic, bobbing his head rhythmically and swaying to the music blaring in his ears. He held the red stop sign high over his head, oblivious to the pleas of the agent.

"We're jammed in a construction site—three cars in front of us and concrete barriers on each side," radioed the frustrated agent.

The team leader responded immediately.

"I've got him on the tracker. He's still proceeding north on I-95. Go when you can. I'll vector you in if he leaves the road. I'll see what Philadelphia can do."

The team leader immediately called the Philadelphia office and requested aircraft support. He was informed that the heli-copter was being refueled and would be in the air in another forty minutes. He chose to go with what he had.

Campana's initial five-minute advantage widened as addi-tional traffic was diverted onto the already congested I-95.

The team leader watched the laptop as the tracker's flash-ing red dot passed the Walt Whitman and Ben Franklin Bridges, continuing north on I-95. The closest Bureau car was still twenty minutes behind him. Just before Campana reached the Betsy Ross Bridge, he exited I-95 and proceeded directly to the entrance of Philadelphia's commercial shipping docks.

"Tracker shows he's off on the Delaware Avenue exit. He's heading parallel to the river."

"Roger," the trailing agent replied. "We're still fifteen min-utes behind the asshole."

• • •

Campana was waved through the security gate after Simpson displayed his entry badge and drove directly to the vessel's berth. They exited and walked to the rear of the van, where Campana unlocked the twin doors. The passenger, who had remained silent throughout the trip, moved into the driver's seat. Simpson took one of the black nylon bags, and Campana picked up the other and his small gym bag.

"I'll let the first mate know that you're the refrigeration repair guy for the two containers we're expecting this evening," Simpson said. "You'll stay in my office until it gets dark. Then we'll get to work."

"Pretty impressive," said Campana as he gazed up at rows of containers rising from the deck of the thousand-foot-long ship.

They heard the van start up, and the driver departed through the unattended security gate. Campana instinctively checked his pockets for the spare set of keys; they were there.

• • •

At this same time, the agents in the trailing car had finally exited I-95 and were speeding toward the location given to them by the team leader.

"He's coming back at you!" the team leader shouted, now watching the blinking red dot as it reversed its path, backtracking toward the west.

"Shit!" yelled the driver. "We're on a one-way street going toward him. Hang on. I'm going to cut through that opening. We're not going to lose him again."

His passenger, a twenty-year veteran with the FBI, watched in terror as the driver swerved left in front of three lanes of traffic. The only entrance to the other street was through a busy carwash that suddenly appeared in front of their hood. The driver accelerated through one of its open bays, scattering a group of men waiting to wipe down the cars as they exited. Upon clearing the scattering group of men, he accelerated into an open space in the traffic, now just five vehicles behind Campana's white conversion van.

"Jesus!" yelled the passenger as the driver brought the car under control.

The driver looked over quickly at him with a smile on his face.

"I haven't done that since I was sixteen," he laughed.

"And I hope it's sixteen more years before you try it again!" the other agent blurted out.

"You guys have him?" the team leader's voice crackled over the radio.

"Piece of cake," the passenger replied calmly as the microphone shook uncontrollably in his hand.

"He's getting on the Betsy Ross. We're heading for New Jersey."

"Roger," the team leader replied. "Are the passengers still with him?"

The pursing agent hesitated before answering, trying to see through the van's curtained rear windows.

"The van has its curtains pulled down. We'll try to ease up on him for a look as soon as we can."

"Negative!" the supervisor shouted instantly. "Just stay with him. Covert!"

• • •

One mile outside of Cherry Hill, New Jersey, the van made a sharp right turn into an alleyway in a run-down industrial area.

The agents slowed and parked thirty feet from where the van had pulled off the street.

"Stay where you are," the team leader radioed. "The van's parked down the alley. The map shows it's a dead end. I'll let you know when there's some movement."

Five minutes later, the team leader's voice came over the radio.

"He's coming back toward the street. Get ready."

● ● ●

The man had done his job well. He'd walked into the rear entrance of the makeshift mosque and shot the cleric, his wife, and two children, emptying the nineteen-round clip of his 9 mm Glock. After calmly checking to make sure that all were dead, he tossed the weapon into a trash can as he left.

● ● ●

The white van came out of the alley and turned right, merging into the flow of traffic without stopping. It continued toward Cherry Hill with the FBI surveillance teams following closely. It finally pulled into the parking area of a low-end two-story motel whose most prominent feature was a multicolored neon sign that read, "Flamingo Cay Motel." The vehicle pulled through the tall portico into a nearby parking space, and the driver exited, carrying a small, black canvass bag. He walked through the motel's front door.

The agents in the trailing car watched the van from about fifty yards across the empty parking area. Immediately they noted that the man who exited the vehicle was not Campana, and worse, he was alone.

One agent picked up the microphone.

"Unit One. Campana and the other passenger did not return in the vehicle. Did the van stop someplace before we picked it up again?"

"Stand by," replied the team leader. "Yes, it was less than a minute. The map shows a small public park and the entrance to the Tioga Street Shipping Piers, where the target stopped. The accuracy of the vehicle's position is plus or minus twenty feet."

"Can you send another unit to Tioga Street to see whether Campana is there?"

"Roger," the team leader replied.

The agent turned to the driver.

"We'll give him fifteen minutes; then we're going inside for a look. I'm losing my patience with these assholes!"

• • •

The two casually dressed agents walked into the motel's lobby and approached the young, blond female sitting at the receptionist's desk.

She glared at the two men.

"Are you cops?" she demanded.

"No," the agent replied with a smile, "do we look like cops?"

"You can never find one when you need one," she said sarcastically.

"What happened?" one of the agents asked.

"The man who came in here just before you guys was carrying a black bag and asked to use the bathroom. He said he was checking in. Then he comes out of the men's room dressed in a different T-shirt and walks out the backdoor, gets into a small, blue car, and drives away. He just disappeared. I should have called 911 when he came in. His shirt looked like it was spattered with blood."

The agents looked toward the backdoor.

"You sure it was blood?" one asked.

She looked at the man, trying to visualize the scene.

"Yes, I'm sure it was blood. But he's gone now. How can I help you?"

"You already did," the agent said as both ran toward the bathroom.

Inside, they found a blood-spattered T-shirt that had been tossed into the trash can and covered with paper towels. They called the group supervisor immediately, reporting what they'd found, and requested the presence of a local police unit.

"They'll need a plainclothes unit and unmarked vehicles. Remember: we don't want to spook Campana if and when he ever shows up. We'll bag the T-shirt with one of the extra black bags we found in the bathroom. I'll leave it at the front desk. All they have to do is retrieve it and interview the receptionist."

36

GOOD TO GO

Washington, DC
FBI Headquarters
3:55 p.m.

Sabinson was furious—not so much with his agents as with the series of bad breaks that had plagued the surveillance teams. Although he wanted to grab Campana, Sabinson realized that they would have to continue the nerve-racking covert surveillance. There were no new leads, and Hamsa had disappeared. He ordered his teams not to touch the van, hoping that Campana would reappear. He authorized both rotary and fixed-wing coverage. They may not have been able to observe his every move, but Campana had confirmed one critical point. He was connected to Hamsa's network through Riley, and his presence in Philadelphia was not a coincidence.

Sabinson called the senior Secret Service agent in charge of the White House security detail and requested that he try again to dissuade the president from making his Fourth of July trip. Although the president listened more attentively than before, he still rejected the agent's pleas. Instead of threatening the agent with early retirement, the president merely handed him an AARP brochure, showing a group of smiling, gray-haired couples playing volleyball on a beach in Florida.

Later that day
Philadelphia
5:00 p.m.

The squad of four FBI agents had set up a surveillance of the neat, brick row homes along Tioga Street. Another car had parked near the public park, but there was no trace of Campana or his other passenger.

The team leader parked his vehicle to the side of the entry gate for the Tioga Cargo Terminal. He identified himself and asked the guard whether he kept records of vehicles that entered the pier facilities.

"Yeah," the old man replied, "what can I do for you?"

"Need to check on a vehicle that may have entered here around one forty-five this afternoon—one forty-seven to be exact."

The guard reached for a clipboard that hung from a rusty nail on the guardhouse wall and handed it to the agent. The agent studied the information for a moment and then shook his head.

"There're only seven entries, and nothing from one to four; half of them don't have plates listed."

The old man nodded knowingly and smiled.

"The kid I relieved is nineteen years old; he can barely read or write. The company pays us the royal sum of five fifty an hour. You were expecting maybe J. Edgar Hoover?"

He took the clipboard from the agent and placed it back on the rusty nail.

Philadelphia
US Coast Guard—Captain of the Port Offices
8:50 p.m.

Garcia, Khamis, and Montiel were reviewing the most recent message traffic on Hamsa's group, trying to fit together the last pieces of the puzzle. From their area, they could see the city of

Philadelphia lit up. Hamsa was somewhere out there, and they had to find him.

Sabinson's agents had finally obtained the name of the person who rented the townhouse where Campana had spent the night through a connection with the development's security company in Wilmington. The man, Michael Simpson, had rented the three-thousand-dollar-a-month townhouse from the owner for two years. He'd listed his occupation as "engineer" and always paid his rent in cash and on time. He'd left the "EMPLOYER" block empty.

The security company also reported that Simpson would sometimes be gone for months. None of the neighbors knew him; he stayed to himself and never socialized.

A check of Simpson's past revealed that his social security number was fictitious, and he didn't appear in any credit database. He joined Campana in the suspect pool.

Philadelphia
Tioga Street Container Terminal
10:15 p.m.

The two containers that Campana and Simpson had been waiting for cleared the terminal's main gate. The loading evolution finished without incident, and the containers were locked down onto the ship's deck. Both were listed as consignments from the Jasmine Seafood Company, Portland, Maine, destined for San Juan, Puerto Rico—the vessel's next port of call.

Simpson had notified the first mate that he'd detected an ammonia leak in one of the container's refrigeration systems. He'd submitted the names of Campana and two others as repair technicians, so their presence aboard would be authorized. The two other men arrived in a rental car and boarded the ship, carrying heavy, canvass equipment bags.

Simpson knew that the first mate feared ammonia leaks, having survived a tragedy when he had first sailed in the merchant fleet, some twenty-five years before. Three of his shipmates had been overcome by ammonia vapor and had died. He'd been the sole survivor of the incident. They wouldn't be bothered by him until they finished what they had to do.

• • •

Campana attached the spare-parts boxes just below the refrigeration units of each container, connecting a power source lead to the detonator cord that had been run through the container wall. He removed the heavy silicone cup that covered the magnetic trip-wire disk, and the boxes were now firmly attached to the outer container wall.

As he reached inside his black nylon bag for the anti-tilt switches, the first mate appeared near the bow. He had come up to the weather deck from one deck below with three US Customs agents. He saw Simpson and the three men standing by the container.

"Just an orientation tour—keep on about your work!" he shouted to Simpson.

Simpson could hear the first mate explaining the problem of the ammonia leak to the Customs agents. They were standing in one of the ship's designated smoking areas, casually sipping their coffee. Although the sun had set, it was still hot and humid, typical July weather for Philadelphia.

Campana froze, noticing the group was watching the activity. Their constant gaze in the containers' direction began to make him nervous. He leaned toward Simpson and whispered, "Where did they come from?"

"Customs uses our vessels for orientation; they're new agents," Simpson whispered back.

"How long will they be here?"

"Sometimes they stay for their entire shift. This was supposed to take place tomorrow. Someone changed the date."

Campana thought for a moment.

"I can't install the anti-tilt switches; it will take too much time—it's too risky."

"Will it work without them?" Simpson asked.

"Hell yes," replied Campana. "It would take a miracle to get past the two layers of protection; the anti-tilt switches prevent someone from tilting the boxes to remove them. We'll have to go with what we have. Can you get them away from here for about an hour?"

"Watch me," said Simpson. "The minute we leave, put your two guys to work."

Campana smiled.

"You'll have your thirty minutes plus," Simpson said, patting Campana on the back.

Then he turned away, walking toward the group that had formed around the bow's weather-deck hatch.

"Anyone interested in seeing our new computer-based container-loading software in action? It's on my laptop in my air-conditioned office, two decks down. It's not much of a place, but I do have donuts and coffee, and you can smoke there."

The entire group, including the first mate, opted to leave immediately and accept Simpson's invitation. Watching anything from the comfort of an air-conditioned office took immediate precedence over sweating in the humid night air and breathing the foul vapors drifting in from a nearby refinery's sour gas stacks.

Campana waited for about five minutes and then gave a thumbs-up signal.

One man cut the seals on the container doors while the other opened his equipment bag and took out a commercial cordless drill fitted with a large cylindrical socket where the drill bit would have been. This connection would mate with the flange bolt on top of the heavy, lead-lined, steel cylinders inside the container and allow quick removal of the safety plugs.

Campana glanced around and then motioned for them to begin. Each man donned a one-piece white suit and hood and adjusted the hood's attached fiber-optic light headpiece. He held up ten fingers, ten minutes in each container would be their time limit. They both nodded and entered the first container. Campana walked toward the second container, pretending to check the tubing connected to the refrigeration unit. He had a clear view of all approaches from this position.

July 2
1:35 a.m.

It had taken them two hours over the time allotted, but they had done it. Simpson glanced at Campana, who was bleary-eyed but happy.

"Now we can get some rest. I'll have someone take you to the motel."

Campana smiled and shook his head.

"Not necessary: my guys will do that. I'll see you in a few days under better circumstances."

• • •

The trip to Cherry Hill was quick, and the traffic was light. About a mile from the motel, all traffic stopped and began to crawl ahead slowly. Four marked police units were parked alongside the road with their red and blue strobes flashing. As they passed by an alleyway to the right, Campana could see two more marked units.

"Another drug killing," remarked one of the men. "This god-less country's going to hell."

Two blocks from the motel, Campana motioned for the driver to pull over to the shoulder. He would walk the rest of the way.

• • •

As Campana walked under the brightly lit motel portico, an FBI agent seated in the driver's seat of one of the surveillance vehicles nudged his slumbering partner. They were parked about fifty feet from the hotel's entrance.

"Campana is back. He just walked into the motel. No car: the asshole just appeared. Call Sabinson. This will make his day!"

• • •

Campana walked up to the reception clerk.

"I made a reservation yesterday; name's Randall Campana."

He slid a stack of twenty-dollar bills toward the night clerk, five hundred dollars in cash.

The old man quickly checked him in and passed a key card to him along with a cash receipt.

"Room two twenty-five in the corner as you requested. Have a good stay, Mr. Campana. Do you need a wake-up call?"

Campana gave the man an incredulous look.

"Anyone who calls me before noon is dead!"

37

Newton's First Law of Motion

July 3
West of Milford, Delaware
6:15 a.m.

The two teenage boys had spent the warm summer night drinking beer and smoking crystal meth. They'd broken into a Honda motorcycle shop earlier that morning and stolen two ATVs that now sat half in and half out of the Chevrolet Silverado's bed. Each carried a .357 magnum pistol, stolen from the driver's grandfather.

Shortly after they'd stolen the ATVs, a Milford PD unit had spotted them and was in pursuit when the one of the boys leaned out of the pickup and shot out the police car's windshield. The officer called for backup from State Police Troop 3 in Dover.

The teens sped west on one of the rural roads, trying to escape with their new ATVs. They had enough crystal meth in them to make them bulletproof and drove on at speeds of over 100 mph until their front tire blew out.

The driver over steered and lost control. The Silverado veered toward the pavement's edge and went airborne, cartwheeling over a white board fence and ejecting the teens and the two stolen ATVs.

By some miracle, the boys survived. Although dazed by the accident, they realized that the two Delaware State Police cars screeching to a halt by the heavy metal gate were after them. They stood and began running down a sandy lane toward a thick patch of woods.

• • •

Hamsa was eating breakfast when heard the faint chirping sounds of the perimeter alarm system and looked at the kitchen's video console. Two Delaware State Police cars were nose to tail at the entry gate. One of the troopers in the lead car got out of his vehicle and pulled down the gate's override handle, allowing him to push the gate open. The troopers were heavily armed and wore their tactical web gear.

Hamsa was stunned, taken completely by surprise. One vehicle tore down the sandy lane, and the other drove across the open field toward the tree line.

He ran to the bedroom and grabbed the M-16 from the closet, pulling back hard on the T-shaped charging handle, driving a round into the chamber. He checked to make sure the twenty-round clip was full. Then he returned to the kitchen's video console, but there was no sign of the police cars.

• • •

"Stop! Get on the ground!" shouted the pursing trooper as he aimed his service weapon at one of the teens. The boy had twisted his ankle in the accident and was able to do no more than a fast hobble. Even with amount of meth he'd smoked, the pain forced him to fall to the ground. However, the other teen looked like an Olympic sprinter as he entered the tree line at full speed.

The two troopers cuffed and searched the first boy and soon had him walking toward their vehicle. The second vehicle, containing the shift sergeant, circled back to where the teen was being placed in the backseat.

"Call for a tow truck, and then take him back to the troop." the sergeant said. "Start the booking sheet on this clown. Then call the duty deputy attorney general and proceed from there. What charges do you have on this one?"

"We've got evading, attempted murder of a police officer, reckless driving, first-degree burglary, possession of a firearm during the commission of a felony, pollution of a protected wetland area, and possession of a controlled substance. You want us to add any more?" asked the young trooper, with a sarcastic grin.

The stone-faced sergeant looked at the rookie. "You can add underage consumption of alcohol and littering, for starters," he replied. "We're going to drive around that wooded area and see if we can find Speedy Gonzalez. There used to be an old log cabin about a quarter of a mile down that lane. We'll check out the area."

As the sergeant wheeled the pursuit vehicle out of the field and onto the sandy lane, he called their headquarters.

"Troop Three, nine-four-four—we'll be ten-seven at the old Smith house. Nine-two-five has one suspect in custody, en route to Troop Three."

"Ten-four, nine-four-four," the dispatcher replied. "We'll show you ten-seven at the old Smith house."

• • •

Hamsa saw the state police car coming down the lane at high speed. He ducked behind the sill of the kitchen window and peered out from behind the curtains. The car pulled up beside his rental vehicle, and Hamsa backed away from the window.

• • •

"Must be the caretaker's car," the sergeant said. "Run that tag before we go in. I want to know who we're talking to."

The Troop 3 dispatcher contacted them in less than a minute. The vehicle was a rental. Thomas North Toscano was the name of the person who'd rented the car, using a Delaware driver's license as identification.

"This place hasn't changed in years," the sergeant grumbled. "It still looks like shit, but first things first. Let's see if Mr. Toscano has seen that kid."

The troopers exited the vehicle and looked around before walking toward the front door.

The sergeant knocked on the glass-paneled front door.

"Mr. Toscano, Delaware State Police!"

• • •

Hamsa brought the M-16 to his shoulder and backed away toward the darkened bedroom.

After not getting a response, the sergeant knocked harder.

"State police, Mr. Toscano!" shouted the sergeant. "We're looking for a fugitive."

Hamsa peered around the side of the bedroom door, hoping that the two would drive away, but they stood near the front door with their weapons drawn. He switched the M-16 to fully automatic.

• • •

"Sarge," said the trooper, "I just saw some movement inside."

"Fuck it," the sergeant growled, "that little punk is armed, Toscano's not answering, we're going in!"

Within seconds, the troopers had broken through the door in a shower of glass and splintered wood. Hamsa was no more than twenty feet away. The first trooper couldn't see him because his eyes hadn't adjusted to the darkness inside the house. The sergeant was directly behind the trooper; both were standing completely exposed in the middle of the room. Hamsa jumped up and fired two quick bursts. Both troopers went down.

Hamsa quickly checked both: one trooper lay on his side, and the other was face-down. Neither moved or showed any signs of life. He kicked them hard to be sure and got no response.

• • •

The intrusion by the state police had destroyed his carefully planned schedule. He moved quickly from room to room, throwing clothes, cash, and his 9 mm into his nylon traveling bag. Instead of a controlled exit, Hamsa was overcome by raw panic. He knew he had little time and ran past the bodies of the troopers and toward the open entryway, which was littered with the remains of the front door. Then he came to a complete stop. He'd forgotten his car keys and only now remembered that they were on the countertop by the door.

As Hamsa reached out for the keys, he saw a bright flash of light and then heard a loud explosion. He was spun around and stumbled outside toward his car. He heard a second explosion and felt a jolt rip into his bag, almost knocking it out of his hands.

He realized someone was shooting at him. His left arm burned like fire, and he looked down to see that a bullet had torn through his shirt; everything below his elbow was soaked in blood.

He didn't know how, but one of the troopers was still alive

• • •

Hamsa accelerated at high speed out the property's sandy lane and onto the hard surface of the paved rural road. He headed west, now fully alert to the possibility that the police could set up roadblocks. But he had to take care of more pressing matters—his arm.

He found a small rest stop with a picnic area along the side of the road that contained bathrooms, and he pulled in. It was deserted.

• • •

Hamsa grabbed his sports bag and spent the next ten minutes in the public bathroom, getting rid of his bloody clothing and cleaning up. He tied off the wound with an ace bandage he'd found in the first-aid kit he carried. The bullet had torn a two-inch chunk of flesh from his left elbow.

As he left the bathroom, his thoughts turned to transportation. He had to get rid of his vehicle, and opportunity graced him with a way out when he saw an older-model Volkswagen pull into a parking space. The driver, a man in his early seventies, walked into the bathroom, and Hamsa followed him in.

• • •

After making sure that the man's body was well hidden in the rest stop's thick foliage, Hamsa placed his bag in the backseat of the Volkswagen and started the car. Within a few hours, he reached a small motel near the outskirts of Philadelphia.

The motel was situated next to a series of abandoned strip malls and liquor stores, the domain of drug dealers and prostitutes. All appeared to be doing a thriving business. He pulled off the road and out of harm's way. He decided to contact Campana later in the day.

Hamsa turned on the room's small TV and was mesmerized by the news coverage. It was then that he realized he'd driven out of a trap that had locked down most of the state of Delaware. The only positive note was that, once again, his blond, blue-eyed photo was being shown.

• • •

A group of Delaware State Troopers and FBI agents swarmed the property where Hamsa had hidden out. The sergeant and the other trooper had been transported to the hospital and would survive. Their Kevlar vests had been reinforced with ballistic panels that had saved their lives. One had been grazed in the neck and head, and the other had been hit in the shoulder and thigh, where the round had just missed the femoral artery.

The sergeant had regained consciousness as Hamsa had stopped at the front door for his keys. Although his vision was blurred by blood loss, he'd gotten off two shots. He was certain that he had hit Hamsa because he saw him spin around, but he couldn't say where he was hit. The blood trail that led outside to where Hamsa's car had been parked confirmed that he'd been wounded.

This information hit the news just as the superintendent of the state police was briefing Sabinson. As soon as Sabinson's briefing was over, he called Garcia in Philadelphia.

• • •

"I remember you telling me that Hamsa may not do well under pressure. Well, Chris, looks like you got the opportunity to prove that theory out. But where the hell is he now?"

"He's here, Colby, in the Philadelphia area. His luck held. Somehow he was just ahead of the roadblocks. The Delaware State Police found his rental car abandoned at a rural rest stop. The inside looked like a slaughterhouse, so we know he's bleeding badly. But Hamsa's not going to miss the show he has planned for us. His ego wouldn't tolerate it. Just keep a tight rein on Campana. He's Hamsa's center of gravity right now."

• • •

All clinics, hospitals, and pharmacies within a sixty-five-mile radius of Philadelphia had been contacted to be on the lookout for Hamsa, or anyone attempting to purchase medical supplies that could be used to repair a gunshot wound, including strong pain killers.

During the search of the house, one of the agents found a down-filled parka that had been neatly folded and placed in the rear of the bedroom closet's top shelf, out of view. In his rush to leave, Hamsa had missed it. In one of the jacket's pockets, they found a crumpled FBI wanted poster and seven Canadian pennies in another pocket. Hamsa had been positively identified by both troopers as their assailant.

The FBI agents realized how close they had come. Now, the full force of the FBI's surveillance fell upon Campana.

• • •

Campana continued to maintain his low profile. He'd left the room only once, at 2:17 p.m. to buy a newspaper; he'd made no phone calls and had no visitors. He'd ordered a sandwich and a six-pack of beer from room service. That was it.

The FBI's surveillance team dedicated to him had grown to fourteen agents, including two female agents who now assisted at the front desk. But waiting for something to happen was taking its toll. Sabinson was receiving more pressure from other agencies to take Campana down, but he resisted it. He was betting his career on Campana leading him to Hamsa. There were no other options.

• • •

Sabinson had tried one last time to dissuade the president from making the trip to Philadelphia but had failed. Air Force One was scheduled to depart Andrews at nine the next day. The president was to speak at the dedication of a new historical park at Penn's Landing on the Delaware River at noon. After that, he would attend a barbecue on the waterfront and the MLB All-Star

Game Home Run Derby scheduled to begin at three. Then it was back to Washington for fireworks on the Capitol Mall.

The president refused to change his schedule.

• • •

Hamsa had used all the toilet paper and every towel in his motel room, but the bleeding continued. He'd taken five extra towels from the maid's cart that had been left near his entry door while she was cleaning another room. The pain was excruciating, and he'd developed a high fever. He decided to contact one of the many drug dealers who were plying their trade in the motel's parking lot.

"I'm looking to find something to help me relax…oxies…ten milligrams. Can you help me out?"

The young man looked hard at Hamsa.

"You a cop?" he asked.

Abdul Hamsa grabbed the left sleeve of his windbreaker and pulled it up fast, revealing torn flesh and the blood-soaked rags that covered his forearm.

"Does this look like a cop to you, motherfucker!"

Twenty minutes later the young dealer knocked on his door and handed him a small brown paper bag.

• • •

The pain had subsided long enough for Hamsa to think about his predicament. His first call was to Campana.

"I won't be making the trip with you, but I'll be listening to the news," Hamsa said, his voice barely audible.

"Why?" asked Campana.

"Watch the news."

"OK, but where are you?"

"Traveling," was Hamsa's muted reply.

• • •

261

"Campana just received a call from a blocked cellular number. The male subject could be Hamsa, but we'll have to have the voice analyzed," the FBI agent said.

"OK, let me call Sabinson. He may want to pop this shit bird now," the FBI Supervisor replied

• • •

Hamsa's next call was to Mahmud Fayad. The procedure he was about to initiate had been discussed during a planning session a year before and was to be used in case he had to be extracted.

"I am in need of your services, Mahmud," Hamsa said. "I have been wounded but have escaped the infidel's trap."

"It is on the news, Abdul. Where are you? We need to bring you to safety."

Hamsa gave Fayad the address and room number. Fayad's voice was caring and reassuring. Fayad himself and a doctor would arrive in two hours and drive Hamsa to their lodge in northwestern Pennsylvania, where surgeons would be standing by. Hamsa could finally relax.

• • •

At about ten o'clock that evening, a light tapping on the door alerted Hamsa to the arrival of his rescue team. He looked through the side curtain and saw three males, one carrying a medical bag. He recognized Fayad and opened the door.

Fayad glanced around before entering, ensuring that they had not been followed.

"God is great, my brother," said Fayad, as he kissed Hamsa on each cheek.

The two other men stepped forward to embrace him but, instead, grabbed Hamsa by his arms and pinned him on top of the bed. In seconds, the men had his mouth taped and legs and feet bound together with nylon cord. His hands were pulled roughly behind him and taped together. Hamsa's screams were barely audible as they sat him upright on the bed, facing Fayad. His eyes darted back and forth. The drugs he'd taken earlier had done more than numb the pain. They had dulled his senses. He needed to think his way out of this trap but couldn't.

Fayad sat in a chair, directly in front of Hamsa, so he could see his eyes.

"You have forgotten who you served. This operation became *your* plan, not *our* plan. The operation's successes became *your* successes, not *our* successes, but the defeats and failures were *ours*, never *yours*. You drew apart from us."

Hamsa attempted to speak, but his words were muffled by the heavy tape. He began struggling against the hold the two men had on him but was punched into submission. Fayad moved closer to him.

"I gave you an opportunity to cleanse your soul, to tell me the truth. But you piled one lie on top of another. You deceived me, and I, in turn, deceived my lord, Sheik Osama bin Laden. I repeated your lies about al-Bakar and the detonators. You converted to the one true faith in name only. Your spirit never accepted God's will. Your ego, false prophecy, blasphemy, and deceit have reached such depths that it is impossible to tell you apart from those who we have marked for death. In reality, you are no better than they are. You are now and always have been an infidel."

Fayad turned and removed the video camera from the hard plastic case that Hamsa had thought was a medical bag. The two men flipped him over, face-down on the bed. One straddled him, holding his face toward the camera.

Fayad pushed the power button and zoomed in on Hamsa while the man straddling him pulled a black hood over his own head. Hamsa attempted to move, to escape, but he lacked the energy to fight.

"Abdul Hamsa," Fayad said in a clam voice, "the Supreme Council has found you guilty of blasphemy and deceit. These

charges were confirmed by your friend Jack Riley when he con-
fessed to our trusted informant. You were asked if you had prior
knowledge of the negligence of Khalid al-Bakar. You swore to
God and the Prophet that you did not. This was a lethal lie and
an unpardonable sin against the Almighty. You shall remain in
the bottomless pit for eternity. You will seek death but will not
find it; you will long to die, but death will flee from you. God is
great!"

With this said, the hooded man straddling Hamsa pulled
up hard on his forehead with his left hand while bringing the
twelve-inch knife toward his neck with his right.

Hamsa's muffled screams were cut short by the man's sawing
motion. But he could not separate the head on the first attempt.
After a few more thrusts, he held Hamsa's head in front of the
camera.

"This is the price for blasphemy," continued Fayad as the
man straddling Hamsa's body moved the severed head closer to
the camera. "Let it be known by all that our sacred law applies
to believers and nonbelievers alike. Justice has been done. God
is great!"

38

HIDING IN PLAIN SIGHT

July 4
Tioga Street Pier
5:15 a.m.

Michael Simpson stumbled into the ship's medical office. He was pale and writhing in pain. Twice while the physician's assistant had attempted to take his blood pressure, he'd vomited. The medical officer called the first mate.

"You'd better arrange for a replacement for Simpson—looks like appendicitis. He's going to have to be hospitalized."

Even though the ship was not due to get underway until 11:30 a.m., the doctor knew from his experience that this man could not be permitted to sail. He began to call for an ambulance, but Simpson reached out, grabbing his arm, and stopped him.

"No, I'll take one of the cabs by the gate," he groaned. "I want to get to the hospital in one piece. Which hospital is it?"

"Our contract's with the Cityside Medical Center, but I think you should wait and let me call the ambulance, Mike."

"Negative," replied Simpson, "I'm taking a damn cab. I can make it to the ER without lights and sirens."

The doctor glared at Simpson for a minute and then shook his head as he reached into one of the desk drawer files, withdrawing a preprinted medical form with the hospital's address on it.

"OK, Simpson, have it your way. But have the ER physician call me immediately. All the information they need is on this sheet. Make sure you give the intake people your medical insurance card."

Simpson nodded dutifully.

"Thanks, Doc," he said weakly as he turned and walked out of the office toward the engineer's station.

One of the assistant engineers carried Simpson's small overnight bag to the gate and waited as Simpson entered the cab. He waved good-bye and was gone.

"Where to, buddy?" asked the driver, noticing Simpson's pallid complexion.

"Cherry Hill Mall—I think this will get me there."

The driver smiled as he fingered the two one-hundred-dollar bills that Simpson had handed him.

"Buddy, that will get you to New York and back," he laughed.

Simpson leaned back in the rear seat and felt relieved that he'd been able to convince the parochial medical officer to let him bend the rules. But he was especially proud of the ruse that he had used.

An hour before reporting to the doctor, he'd swallowed four ounces of Ipecac, a drug that was sometimes used to induce vomiting. Its side effects were the lowering of blood pressure and a clammy, pale appearance of the skin.

He was looking forward to arriving at the Cherry Hill Mall and breakfast at one of the fast-food restaurants. At noon, he would meet Hamsa and Campana in the parking lot next to Sears. From there, the three would drive to the safe house in the hills of western Pennsylvania.

He already knew how he would spend the money earned from this job. He'd invest five hundred thousand dollars in the Taliban's heroin distribution business and make over a million in a few months. Then it was off to Jamaica, where he would build a mansion in the Blue Mountains, smoke a little ganja on his balcony, and wait for the United States to become the next Islamic republic.

Philadelphia
US Coast Guard—Captain of the Port Office
6:00 a.m.

Garcia, Khamis, and Montiel had gotten little sleep. They'd reviewed every document in the task force's Hamsa file: every tip, intelligence report, sighting, field report, criminal history, and informant report. There was nothing they had not analyzed or discussed. But they had found nothing new. The only certainties remained the day and the target. There were few people in the office at this hour; the three proceeded toward their cubicle, armed with twenty-ounce foam cups of coffee.

Khamis propelled his chair in high gear toward the elevators. He'd spend the day with the linguists on the next floor up, reviewing the documents that had arrived overnight and translating any last-minute intercepts.

As Garcia and Montiel passed the Coast Guard area, Garcia stopped in midstride, spilling coffee on his shirt and pants. He stood transfixed, staring at the large whiteboard affixed to the wall.

"Damn, Chris," said Montiel, shaking his head, "you need to take a vacation after this is over."

Garcia continued to stare at the eight-by-ten-foot whiteboard. It listed Coast Guard vessel assignments and security-zone designations, printed neatly in large, blue letters. Garcia looked at Montiel and smiled as if he'd just won the lottery.

"Leo, it's there!"

"What's there? Chris, are you feeling OK?"

Garcia grabbed Montiel by the shoulder and spun him around, facing the board. Finally, Montiel saw what had gotten Garcia's attention.

In one of the columns, marked "MOVING SECURITY ZONES," was the designation "VESSEL NAME." The words *M/V Mara VI* were printed under that heading.

The two read the information contained in the block: "Under way at 1130 from Tioga Container Pier, LOA 320 meters, containership, nonhazardous cargo, must pass Penn's Landing NLT 1145."

"Leo, it's Sabinson's *ma-ra-vee*—it's a ship's name! That's what was written on that sticky note. Where's the captain of the port?" Garcia yelled to a passing petty officer.

"Right behind me, sir," replied the surprised man.

The captain soon appeared, balancing a stack of messages and a large coffee.

"Hey, Chris, Leo…Don't you guys ever sleep?" he laughed. "I realize we have a lot—"

"Captain," Garcia interrupted, "please have someone start contacting every law-enforcement resource you can lay your hands on. I'm going to call the FBI's Terrorism Task Force director now. I'll explain it all in detail as soon as I've finished the call, but we found the platform Hamsa will use. It's the *Mara VI*…on your Moving Security Zone board," Garcia said as he and Montiel ran to their cubicle.

• • •

Garcia punched in Sabinson's office number on the secure phone.

"Colby, I have the answer to the Spanish question you asked about a week ago. Remember: you asked me what the word *maravi* meant!"

Sabinson thought for a long moment.

"Yes, something about 'a wonder' or a flower."

"That's right. Your agent found a yellow sticky note in Campana's house. The word m-a-r-a-v-i was written out."

"Hell yes, now I remember!" hollered Sabinson, "What have you got, Chris?"

"It's not *maravi*. It's the word *Mara*, m-a-r-a, followed by the roman numeral six, a *v* and an *i*. It's a ship, not a flower!" Garcia said, trying to remain calm.

Sabinson hesitated as he wrote the letters out. "OK, Chris, I'll buy that. But what's the significance of the *Mara* Six?"

"She's a container vessel, three hundred twenty meters long. It's got to be the platform Hamsa will use! She's due to pass the Penn's Landing site within fifteen minutes of the president's opening remarks. The vessel's moored at the Tioga Container Pier, the same place where the surveillance units lost Campana and his passenger. The answer's got to be on that vessel."

"You have a game plan?" Sabinson asked.

"Yes, I do. You can't move the president, and we can't move Philadelphia, but the captain of the port sure as hell can move the ship! We'll haul ass down river into the Delaware Bay. The area's unpopulated. If anything goes boom, we've lessened the chances of a major tragedy."

There was a pause before Sabinson answered.

"I'll start the ball rolling from my end and call the Secret Service's director. This should give him the leverage he needs. Keep me in the loop."

Garcia spun out of his chair and walked quickly toward the port captain, with Montiel close behind.

"Tell me what you need, Chris?" the captain asked.

Garcia and Montiel had discussed a hundred different contingency scenarios with the captain of the port. But these paled in comparison to what they were facing now.

"First, I'll need an order from you to get that vessel under way. Next, we have to place some cutters out front of the containership to run interference and clear all other traffic out of the channel; issue a 'Notice to Mariners' and have it broadcast every five minutes. If the master or the pilot decides against the trip, we'll need some qualified people to replace them. And finally, we'll need an EOD team aboard ASAP!"

"You'll have everything you need. Two navy EOD teams are staging at Penn's Landing right now. They're fully NBC equipped. I'll send one team to the Tioga Pier immediately. The *Mara VI* is at berth seventeen. The ready helo is out front. They'll take you guys directly to the site."

"Excellent, Captain, Leo and I need to get over there like yesterday."

"Give me five minutes, and I'll have the underway order in your hands," the captain said as he motioned for his staff to meet him on the platform.

The large room now began to buzz with telephone conversations and the occasional shouted order. Garcia received the captain of the port order he'd requested, and he and Montiel took the elevator down to the ground floor. Even before exiting the building's large glass doors, they could hear the HH-60's turbines whining loudly.

39

LABYRINTH

Tioga Street Container Pier
7:15 a.m.

Mara VI's master, river pilot, first mate, and ship's agent were standing at the bottom of the gangway when Garcia and Montiel exited the HH-60 in the vast parking area. They were followed by three uniformed Coast Guard officers from the captain of the port's office.

In front of them was the *Mara VI*, 320 meters (1,050 feet) in length and loaded to its capacity. Its freshly painted red hull reflected the sun's rays with dazzling efficiency. The stacks of multicolored containers that ran from bow to stern enhanced the vessel's behemoth-like qualities.

The master was given a copy of the Coast Guard order as Garcia explained the law supporting it. The grizzled master, in his midsixties, glanced at Garcia.

"I understand the law, but why the urgency?"

"If we're right, your ship was going to be used as a platform to attack the president just as you passed Penn's Landing. Every piece of evidence we've gathered over the past six months points to today and to your vessel. My guess would be a massive explosive device. Do you need any more information?"

The master raised his eyebrows and slowly looked at his ship.

"So why are we wasting time? Let's get the tugs underway, and we'll be slipping lines in ten minutes. Mr. Garcia, the first mate will be your direct liaison."

Both the master and pilot turned and hurried up the steep gangway.

"Have you had any recent personnel changes?" Garcia asked the first mate.

The man thought for a moment.

"We hired three new ABs; they're all on board now. And our second mate transferred to another vessel about a month ago. That's it."

Garcia began to ask another question but was interrupted by a man dressed in light-green surgical scrubs.

"I don't know what's going on with Simpson, but he's not at the hospital. We checked with the cab company that picked him up at the gate, and the dispatcher says he never took him to the hospital—dropped him off at the Cherry Hill Mall."

"Who's Simpson?" Garcia asked the first mate.

"Michael Simpson is one of our engineers. He reported in sick after getting off watch. The medical officer thought he may have had appendicitis, but Simpson refused an ambulance and took a cab."

Garcia narrowed his eyes in concentration and looked at Montiel.

"Leo, he must be the same person that Sabinson's people have been tracking for the last two days."

"Your right!" shouted Montiel. "That's the guy that Campana picked up."

"Campana…," said the first mate. "Why does that name ring a bell with me? I've got name overload. It'll come to me in a minute."

Garcia turned slowly, looking upward at the vessel and then at the first mate.

"Did you have a chance to get the container documentation together?"

"Sure did, Mr. Garcia. Follow me, gentlemen; my assistant is waiting for us near the bow. He has the loading diagram you asked for. We'll start with that."

The first mate took the lead on the gangway with Garcia and Montiel in tow. The two continued looking upward, like some country tourists in the big city for the first time. Within a few minutes, the trio had reached the bow's weather deck. Garcia phoned Sabinson to update him on the Simpson's disappearance.

"One last thing, Colby, the cab took him to the Cherry Hill Mall. It doesn't make sense, unless he's got a car stashed there. I'd put some SWAT units there now. Maybe he's gone there to meet somebody."

"They're on their way, Chris. Keep your head down."

As Garcia turned to face the wall of containers stacked four high, the first mate reached out to Garcia, grabbing him by the arm.

"Of course!" he yelled out. "Campana—the technician Simpson brought aboard to repair an ammonia leak in the last two containers he loaded. That's where I heard that name before."

"Where are the containers?" Garcia asked.

"Those!" the first mate said as he pointed to two forty-foot containers sitting side by side on the deck in front of them.

"What's the ETA for the EOD team?" Garcia asked as he gazed at the containers.

"Looks like them now," the first mate said as leaned over the deck railing, looking down at a group of five men and two women dressed in the dark-blue tactical fatigues of the navy's EOD Team-6. They were hurriedly unpacking heavy equipment bags from a steel-gray Chevrolet Suburban at the base of the gangway.

"Excuse me!" one of the men called out. "I'm Chief Petty Officer Macpherson, EOD team leader. We're looking for a Mr. Garcia and a Mr. Montiel."

"Come on up!" yelled the first mate. "They're waiting for you."

• • •

The group gathered on the bow's weather deck as introductions were made. Garcia couldn't help but stare at the variety of specialized tools and sensors that were hooked onto each EOD team member's belt loops by nonmetallic D rings. He and Chief Macpherson discussed the possible scenarios as the team unpacked their heavy ballistic search suits and communications equipment.

The first mate arrived with the bills of lading for the two containers that had been loaded with Campana present. Garcia scanned the shipper information block: Jasmine Seafood Company, Portland, Maine, and the shipment description, ten thousand cases of chunk white tuna in thirty-ounce cans. He turned toward Montiel, handing him the document.

"Why would you refrigerate canned tuna?"

The first mate glanced at Garcia.

"The cooling units were never energized. But it's rare that a refrigerated container would be used for nonperishable cargo. Simpson was responsible for verifying the bills of lading."

Montiel was already one step ahead.

"Chris, I'll call the Jasmine Seafood Company and confirm the bills of lading."

Montiel took the documents from Garcia and walked toward the series of ladders that led upward to the bridge.

Garcia turned back toward the EOD team leader.

"Chief, we're working on a hunch that these two containers belong to our subjects. We're going to get underway soon, but if you agree, I suggest that your team inspect these two first. We don't have much time."

"I agree, Mr. Garcia. Let me set up our shop, and we'll get to work. If there is anything on this vessel, we'll find it."

"We need to find it before noon, Chief," Garcia said.

"Affirmative, we've been briefed," the chief replied.

Ten minutes later, Montiel returned from the bridge at full sprint.

"The number was disconnected two years ago. It belonged to an auto repair shop. There is no such listing for a company by the name of Jasmine Seafood in Maine, so I called Quantico. They ran the name and number through our databases. Jasmine Seafood was one of the shell companies created by Rashid al-Bakar."

Garcia was still processing the information when he noticed the EOD team's chief reach down toward a small cylinder attached to his belt loop; it was chirping loudly. The chief pressed two small, red buttons located midway along its metal shaft. Then a second instrument began to emit a short series of high-pitched beeps. He disconnected the first device from his belt and stared at the numbers that were flashing in its LCD window. He pointed to three of his team members and raised his index finger.

They nodded without saying a word and unzipped their heavy equipment bags, retrieving their ballistic disposal suits and other equipment.

The chief was unsmiling as he turned toward Garcia and Montiel.

"This," he said, holding the metallic cylinder out toward them, "is called a *dosimeter*. It's telling me that we have a gamma-ray source nearby; the reading is above the safe level. That means no more than ten minutes of unprotected exposure. After that, it's lethal."

He'd gotten their attention.

"The second instrument that alarmed is called an *explosives trace detector*. It's set up to sense PETN, RDX, TNT, dynamite, and C-4. It's telling me that one of those five is present in this area."

The chief looked at the first mate.

"Are you carrying any nuclear material or explosives on this voyage?"

"Our company prohibits both. The insurance premiums would put us out of business!"

Chief Macpherson looked at the three men and smiled weakly.

"We're going to get real busy here. Whatever is causing our sensors to be set off is damn close and probably inside one or both of those containers. We'll need the entire area forward of the bridge to be declared off-limits to the crew."

"Consider it done!" replied the first mate as he turned and walked toward the ladders leading to the bridge.

"Is there anything we can do?" Garcia asked.

"Well...there is one thing."

He reached into one of the large cargo pockets on his pants and pulled out a small, green nylon case.

"This is an extra headset with a mike attached. I'll need to have comms with someone away from the search area, just in case we run into problems."

Garcia took the nylon case and gave him a reassuring smile.

"I'll be your contact, Chief...just in case you run into any problems."

The true meaning of the words wasn't lost on either man.

"Yes sir, that's *exactly* what I meant," the chief emphasized.

"Chief," said Garcia, "my name's Chris, and this is Leo. We're way past the formalities stage."

The EOD chief smiled and nodded.

"Chris and Leo it is. We'll be working on two-eight-zero megahertz for comms."

• • •

The lines were singled up and released as the two tugs arrived to assist the massive vessel into the main shipping channel. Garcia could see the EOD team members pulling their bright yellow NBC suits over their ballistic search gear.

Ten minutes later, Chief MacPherson came out from behind the container stacks and motioned to Garcia to put his headset on. Garcia adjusted the padded earphones and adjusted the volume controls.

"Chris?"

"Good copy, Chief."

"Chris, everything said on this circuit is being recorded in Philadelphia. I'll try not to get too technical. Ready?"

"Ready."

"OK, here goes. Both forty-foot containers are hot—highly radioactive. My initial readings show about five hundred forty-five rads. I scanned the containers with the portable backscatter X-ray equipment—it *ain't* canned tuna! I've drilled an opening in the first container's right side behind its fifth column support, about fifty inches from the base, and I'm inserting the endoscope now."

Garcia waited for the next transmission and then jumped as he heard a load groan.

"Chief?"

"It's OK, Chris. I was just twisting a little to get a better look."

Garcia and Montiel sat at a chart table on the bridge near the ship's master and river pilot. Garcia began giving a play-by-play of the chief's actions, like a radio announcer at a sporting event. Montiel was in direct contact with Sabinson by satellite relay from the ship.

Within five minutes, the *Mara VI* had released the tugs and was making her way down river at twenty knots. All inbound traffic had been held in the lower Delaware Bay by Coast Guard order. *Mara VI* was now by herself, making a desperate run away from the populated areas of the upper Delaware River.

• • •

"Houston, we have a problem," said Chief Macpherson, breathing heavily inside the protective suit.

"Chris, I'm sending one of my team up to you. She has a wireless video monitor. You'll be able to see what I'm seeing."

In a few minutes, the petty officer entered the bridge area and placed a small four-inch color LCD monitor on the chart table where Garcia was sitting. It resembled a handheld video game, but what Garcia saw was anything but fun.

• • •

The sunlight filtered through the overhead opaque plastic roof panels illuminating the container's interior. Four light-brown fiberglass spheres had been placed along the container's centerline. Each was about ten feet in diameter and sat in a heavy, steel tubular ring with four stubby feet. A thick bundle of cables exited from an opening in each of the spheres' tops like umbilical cords, joining the four spheres together. A thick, sixteen-mil, clear plastic bag that contained about thirty pounds of a luminous blue powder was suspended from a ceiling hook above each sphere. Four large, metal cylinders, about three feet tall, sat along the container's sidewall. The fiber-optic tube and lens were slowly pulled out of the container and walked to the spare-parts box.

The chief switched to the handheld backscatter X-ray unit and placed the sensor head close to the metal box that Campana had installed. The flat-screen monitor showed a three-dimensional X-ray picture that was filled with circuitry and solid objects.

"OK, Chris, here's what we have."

A crowd formed around Garcia and the LCD screen.

"You're looking at what's inside the spare-parts boxes. I'll start with the least serious problem and make my way up the risk ladder."

The chief put the handheld X-ray device on the deck and picked up the fiber-optic camera lead, placing it again inside the container wall. He continued with his description.

"The explosive vapor detector has identified the spheres' contents as Composition C, also known as C-4. It's a military-grade plastic high explosive. From the volume tables I have for spheres, there's enough C-4 in both containers to have flattened the Port of Philadelphia. The detonation velocity or blast-wave speed, is clocked at about seventy-nine hundred meters a second, or about twenty-six thousand feet per second. The kill zone would be about three miles in diameter. To put this into perspective: the Hiroshima bomb was rated at thirteen kilotons; this is about a ten-kiloton yield."

Garcia cleared his throat slightly, visualizing the chief's description.

"And my radiation detection gear is really pegging out to the max," the chief continued. "The gamma-ray readings I'm getting from the material suspended in the bags positively identify it as cesium-137, probably enriched. It's sending out about twenty-five hundred curies through the steel walls. The safe limit for an hour is around nine hundred curies—then you begin to glow! The metal cylinders you saw against the container walls are how they got the stuff aboard without being fried in the process. That's not such a bad thing. In the other container, my team has already started to load the cesium into the same cylinders it came in. What we have here is called a 'dirty bomb.' The explosion would have spread this stuff into three states. And there's one more surprise."

Garcia noticed that the chief had shifted the fiber-optic lens closer to the backscatter X-ray's flat-panel screen.

"This guy is good—very, very good. He's installed the bomb's triggers in the spare-parts boxes complete with a nasty, unforgiving trip wire. There are a few ways around it, but all involve high risk. This is a textbook IRA device with a twist. But he's missed something, or he wants me to think that he missed something. I'll contact you when I have a solution."

Garcia reached for the ship's satellite telephone to call Sabinson. The crowd surrounding the chart table began to disperse, preferring instead to watch the passing scenery.

As he replaced the handset, Garcia noticed Montiel staring at him and smiling.

"Chris, I just wanted you to know that this is the only time since we started working together that I'm *not* happy that you were right about something."

Garcia studied Montiel for a few seconds. "Leo, don't worry. I already made arrangements for Alex Khamis to have your guitar and collection of Joaquin Sabina CDs if anything goes wrong today."

Montiel looked at him in disbelief and then smiled broadly.

"I know we'll make it through OK. God protects the insane, and he has big plans for you, my friend."

40

So Many Traps—So
Little Time

Outside of Cherry Hill
Flamingo Cay Motel
9:50 a.m.

Campana had spent a restless night. He'd watched the news as Hamsa had told him to and was angry that he'd done so. It was clear that he could never return to Delaware. The media had connected him to Hamsa. His anonymity was gone, and he was beginning to lose trust in the group. He packed quickly and walked to the front desk.

"How was your stay, sir?" the bright-faced young man asked as he tendered the remaining forty-five dollars of Campana's change.

"Oh, it was just great. I'll recommend this place to all my boring friends."

He passed through the motel's entry doors and walked quickly toward his white van.

• • •

"He just left through the front door," the young FBI agent said, speaking into the small handheld radio he'd pulled from beneath the reception desk.

"We've got him," said one of the Bureau agents watching Campana from his car about fifty yards away on the other side of the street.

• • •

Fifteen minutes into the trip, a news report caused Campana to pull over to the shoulder and listen.

"...Riley had been arrested earlier this year in Costa Rica after his ties with IRA terrorism had surfaced. Again, we're reporting that Jackson Xavier Riley, the former IRA and CIA contractor, was found dead in his cell this morning at the Lorton Federal Detention Center. Authorities at the prison stated that the cause of death may have been linked to alcohol poisoning but have requested additional toxicology tests. And now on to other news..."

He turned off the radio and thought about Riley. He didn't like it. He was no longer suspicious; he was sure. The jihadists were eliminating all witnesses. It was a cultural thing. Although he'd agreed to pick up Simpson at the Cherry Hill Mall, he was going to be prepared for any problems. He reached under the seat and placed the 10 mm semiautomatic in his armrest's storage space, within easy reach. Then he eased the conversion van into the flow of traffic, heading for the Cherry Hill Mall.

South of Chester, Pennsylvania
Delaware River
10:45 a.m.

The two Coast Guard 110-foot cutters, followed by two smaller 41-foot utility boats, swept the vessel traffic from the river as *Mara VI* increased her speed.

"Chris," the chief's voice crackled in Garcia's headphones, "I can see it better now—a digital timer with a photocell guard. The timer's set for noon. There's a magnetic disk connected to the back of the box. It has a pull-away trip wire connected by monofilament line to the trigger. Two trip wires—I'm impressed. Somebody's been to school."

The chief stopped and thought for a moment, trying to come up with a solution to what he'd discovered inside the metal box. After a few minutes, he reached into his tool kit and removed a small cordless drill. He placed a diamond-tipped half-inch brass cutting disk into its chock and tightened it. Then he turned toward his two team members.

"You're welcome to stay. But if I encounter a problem, there's not much room to hide."

Both men nodded affirmatively and remained where they were.

He placed the cutting disk against the center of the spare-parts box's lid and pulled lightly on the drill's trigger. The diamond-toothed cutting head turned slowly as small pieces of metal shavings fell on the deck around his boots. Within seconds, the cutting head had done its job, and he pulled the drill back from the box with the circular piece of steel he'd cut attached to it. He fed the fiber-optic cable's tip inside the box while he studied the LCD screen.

"Chris, I was wrong when I said the person had gone to school. Whoever made this taught the class. I can cut the mono-filament line and bypass the trip wire. But there's no way around the timer. The jerk set up a series of switches that are going to make it interesting to bypass. I can get it off the wall, but after that, it's anybody's guess."

"What do you recommend?" asked Garcia.

The chief glanced toward his equipment bag and then at the metal box.

"I can freeze the trip wire with the liquid nitrogen I have. That'll shatter the nylon line and won't put any tension on it. Then it's a matter of snipping the detonator cord lead, and that will cancel out the ignition for the spheres. The triggers will fire internally at their set time but won't detonate the C-4 in the spheres, just the ten pounds or so of Semtex that the maniac placed inside the box. Wait, I just noticed…now that's interesting, Chris, give me a minute."

The EOD chief backed away from the boxes and pulled a small notebook and pen from one of his pockets. He drew out a diagram of the ignition devices he'd just observed.

"Chris, we've reached the top rung of the risk ladder. This genius inserted something in the box that looks like a voltage drop sensor—something that can sense the slightest drop in the battery's power. A voltage drop of one-millionth of an ampere would be enough to cause the sensor to activate. The sensor has its own juice supply and will close the circuit. It's designed as a fail-safe against people like me."

He paced back and forth near the container, reciting possible solutions.

"But that's not all," he said, glancing at the small notebook containing the diagram he'd just made. "The last bridge to cross is the worst. I can get the triggers off the container wall, but I can't disable the microantenna that was installed. I can see the circuitry for it in the box. The microantenna is designed to transmit a low-frequency signal from the timer to a miniature receiver hidden in these spheres. Even if I remove the triggers, I can't get to the transmitter without hitting something called an *accelerator* that's soldered into the timer. This little gem speeds up the clock's digital counter—it can turn sixty seconds into one."

"Can you get the box off the container without setting the accelerator off?" asked Garcia.

"Affirmative, Chris, but we're still faced with the low-frequency transmitter. And we're running out of time."

Garcia sat still for a moment, trying to conceive of another option. He forced himself to concentrate, to focus. And in this process, a small particle of memory cell lit up and flashed a second's worth of history that had been catalogued and forgotten in his mental library. His mind went into playback mode as he remembered the scene.

• • •

He was serving his first tour of duty in the Coast Guard cutter *Lipan*. He'd been assigned as the officer of the deck for the midnight-to-four watch. They were conducting a search for a downed aircraft that had sunk in 185 feet of water near New Providence Island in the Bahamas. Its internal marker beacon was powered by a low-frequency radio transmitter.

They'd passed over a point twice that the sonar had identified as the site of the aircraft's wreckage. But they couldn't acquire the signal.

Finally, the CO arrived on the bridge and asked about the search status. Garcia, a young ensign, described their frustration in not being able to acquire the radio signal. The CO, a former enlisted radioman, looked at Garcia and said one word: "Attenuation."

He was referring to the weakening of radio-wave energy caused by the distance from the source and the scattering of the radio wave through different densities of water.

• • •

"We'll be right back to you, Chief. I think we may have a plan."

Garcia stood and leaned over the chart, looking at the track line that had been plotted by the master. He picked up a set of dividers and walked off different distances. Then he turned toward the master.

"Captain, we've got about twenty-five minutes before this vessel turns into a light show. How much water do we have under us now?"

The master stepped toward the series of digital screens near the steering station.

"Sixty-five feet under the keel," he replied.

Garcia glanced at the chart, looking at two areas of deep water that had caught his attention. The deepest trench was surrounded by shoal water that was too shallow for the *Mara VI* to approach and too far away. That left only one option, and Garcia measured off the shortest route to it.

"Leo, I'm going to ask the chief to remove the spare-parts boxes from the container walls. Are you ready for some fresh air and a fast boat ride?"

Montiel nodded his head and smiled.

"Señor Garcia, what a story we will have to tell our grandchildren."

Then Garcia turned toward the vessel's captain and the river pilot.

"Gentlemen, the EOD chief is a very competent man. We know he's found two bombs, but this is a big ship. These people could have planted more—we just don't know. Captain, I'd suggest you bring your vessel to all stop and prepare to abandon ship. At the least, she'll run herself aground on a mud bank and leave you out of harm's way. The choice is yours."

The master looked at Garcia for a moment and then out toward the smooth surface of the Delaware Bay.

"All I got to look forward to is a dull retirement. I'm going to proceed to the Fairton Shoal area. I suggest that you and Mr. Montiel get your collective asses in gear and have my crew evacuated ASAP. I can handle the navigation from the bridge."

Garcia walked to the steering console and picked up the handset connected to the VHF-FM radio, quickly depressing the transmit button.

"Coast Guard four-one-three-four-three, this is the *Mara Six*, channel sixteen—over."

"*Mara Six*, this is three-four-three. Go."

"Proceed to our port-side accommodation ladder and prepare to take off passengers—over."

"Roger, *Mara Six*. We'll arrive at your port-side accommodation ladder in one minute."

"Good copy, three-four-three. And have the UTB behind you come alongside to take off Mr. Montiel and myself."

"Roger. Out," replied the coxswain.

Garcia pushed the transmit button on his EOD headset.

"Chief, please stand by for us near the weather-deck ladder. Leo and I are going to relieve you of those triggers."

After the crew members had been evacuated, Garcia and Montiel descended the ladders from the bridge to the main deck.

41

The Price of Freedom...
Just Went Up

July 4
Near Cherry Hill, New Jersey
10:20 a.m.

The maid at the Starburst Motel had noticed the Do Not Disturb sign hooked over the doorknob when she had arrived in the morning, and it was still there. The occupant had asked for a nine o'clock wakeup call, but the receptionist reported that there had been no answer in the room. The maid knocked but received no response, so she slipped her pass card into the slot and entered the room.

• • •

The parking lot looked more like a used-car lot for police vehicles than a motel parking area. Seven New Jersey State Police cars, two state police forensic vans, three Cherry Hill PD vehicles, and three FBI sedans filled the area in front of Hamsa's room. And for some reason, the drug dealers, pimps, and their women had gone elsewhere.

The senior agent in charge of the FBI's Philadelphia office was on the secure phone inside his car briefing Sabinson. He'd described the scene and had sent him some graphic photos from his cell phone.

"We just got a positive ID on his prints, Colby. It's John Thomas Cronin, alias Abdul Hamsa. We also verified the fresh bullet wound he'd received yesterday. The Delaware trooper's bullet did a job on his left elbow."

"Any way of telling right now who did this or why?"

"No information on who may have done it. We canvassed the place for witnesses and got nothing. This is a pretty seedy location, not exactly Main Line Philadelphia. But the why may be explained by a hand-written note we found by the head on the dresser. It says, 'Abdul Hamsa—Blasphemer,' in Arabic."

"OK Mike, thanks for briefing me up…Wait a second; hold on."

Sabinson was back on the line in a minute.

"Have you heard the Riley news report?"

"No, we've been up to our necks with the Hamsa scene. What happened?"

"He was found dead in his cell this morning; they're dropping like flies! I've got my main intelligence guy, Chris Garcia, in a very tight spot right now, so I'd better sign off. Get your PIO to handle the media, and get back to me when you have an update."

Upper Delaware Bay
11:40 a.m.

"*Mara Six*, this is Coast Guard four-one-three-zero-three, ready to embark two passengers—over."

The second 41-foot UTB made its approach alongside to pick up Garcia and Montiel. Even though the huge containership was proceeding at a slow speed, the boat's coxswain could feel the strength of the suction zone that was created by the vessel's larger hull moving through the water. It was as if his smaller craft was being drawn toward its towering hull. The young coxswain could see the two figures walking carefully down the aluminum accommodation ladder.

• • •

Garcia descended in front of Montiel, carrying one of the metal spare-parts boxes upright. Montiel followed, carrying the second.

Although Garcia was now perspiring profusely in the humid ninety-degree air, he could feel the adrenaline surge kick in. He began to slow his pace, sensing the accommodation ladder swaying slightly as it was buffeted by the wind swirling past the *Mara VI*'s massive hull. He and Montiel finally boarded the small boat.

Garcia motioned for Montiel to follow him to the boat's stern. They both grasped the handrails tightly with their free hands. Then Garcia looked toward the coxswain.

"Boats, I need you to steer zero-five-five degrees, balls to the wall. In about six minutes, you should be in two hundred thirty feet of water. It's the only deep trench in the upper bay. Let us know when you get there."

"Roger, sir, steering zero-five-five degrees," the coxswain replied.

The UTB's twin diesels came to life, momentarily throwing both Garcia and Montiel off balance. They strained to hold on to the metal boxes as the boat's speed increased. Garcia raised his left wrist, glancing at his watch—11:53. He looked toward the open pilothouse door, where he could see the coxswain glued to the digital fathometer just above him.

"How about it, boats?" Garcia yelled.

The young man turned quickly in his pedestal chair, looking backward at Garcia.

"I have two hundred sixty-five feet under the keel, sir. This is it!"

Without replying, Garcia nodded toward Montiel, and they both began to lean over the boat's stern. Garcia shouted at Montiel, trying to make himself heard over the noise of the twin turbocharged diesels. He held the white box away from him, like some dangerous animal.

"I'm going to lay it in the wake's center; it should sink right away."

Garcia leaned his tall frame toward the water, releasing the glossy white box into the center of the boat's slick wake. It disappeared immediately. He then reached toward Montiel, taking the second box and releasing it in the same way.

Garcia glanced at his watch—11:57.

The two men gripped the tubular metal rail that surrounded the boat's well deck, staring out at the lengthening, flat wake and its frothy center. Montiel began to straighten up when the dark metallic waters half a mile behind them lit up. This was followed by an ear-piercing *whump* as two huge fountains of water erupted, erasing the boat's wake trail.

Garcia glanced at his watch.

"Leo! The damn guy was a minute early."

Montiel shot a glance at Garcia and pointed.

"Chris, take a look!" It was the *Mara VI*. She's still alive! God bless…what did you call it? Attenuation!"

Garcia stared at the *Mara VI* as the containership's profile grew smaller on the horizon. Then he turned to Montiel.

"How about a small Independence Day party when we get back? I think we've earned a few cold beers."

Cherry Hill Mall

12:01 p.m.

Simpson had a late breakfast in the mall's food court and spent the remainder of the time making some purchases: clothing, three Rolex watches, and two pairs of Bose headphones. At noon, he began making his way to the prearranged rendezvous with Campana in the mall's parking lot. He moved slowly under the load he carried.

• • •

There were now seven FBI vehicles packed with armed agents parked in various spaces throughout the northwest sector of the

292

mall's parking lot. Sabinson's instructions were clear. They were to make a felony stop of Campana's vehicle if he attempted to leave the area. On Garcia's advice, he wanted to catch all the remaining members of the plot.

• • •

Campana had arrived earlier and parked in the extreme north-west corner of the mall, facing the mall's entry doors. He selected an all-news channel, hoping to hear reports of his handiwork. What he heard was the first report on Hamsa, and now he was sure that the jihadists were planning to kill off all witnesses. No one would be left alive.

He saw Simpson walking out of one of the mall doors—a good three hundred yards away.

• • •

The FBI team leader raised his ten-by-fifty binoculars and adjusted the laser range setting until he could see the van's interior clearly.

"Campana is alone in the van. The black male who just exited the mall is our subject, Simpson—the one Campana picked up in Wilmington. Cherry Hill PD units are now in blocking position for all exits."

There were no replies, only the double-checking of weapons, protective vests, and ammunition.

• • •

Campana raised the armrest, retrieved his 10mm Colt, and jacked a round into the chamber. He placed it on the floor to his left, between his seat and the door.

• • •

The voice of the FBI team leader came across the tactical frequency almost in a whisper. "Something's up with the van's driver. He just displayed a handgun. It looks like he's getting ready."

"Son of a bitch," said one of the FBI agents, "these idiots may want to shoot their way out of their problem. I'm ready."

"I've been ready for this for over a year," said another agent as he pulled his Glock 31 from its holster.

• • •

Simpson made his way to Campana's van. He knocked on the double door's window, holding up his bags and pointing to the backseat. But Campana motioned that he wanted him to enter the passenger's side door.

Simpson entered the van with a puzzled look on his face.

"What's the deal?" he grumbled. "All I wanted to do was put my things in the back."

"That's reserved for Hamsa," Campana replied coldly.

Simpson glanced at his watch. "Where's Abdul?" he asked.

"You mean you don't know?"

"What's wrong with you?" Simpson shot back. "All I asked was—"

Simpson saw the semiautomatic pistol aimed at his head.

"You think I'm stupid," growled Campana. "You people killed Riley early this morning, and then you took out Hamsa. But I'm ready for you!"

Simpson looked at Campana in disbelief.

"Randy, please put that gun down! What the hell are you saying about Riley and Hamsa? I have been in the mall all morning, just like Abdul—"

"Shut up!" growled Campana. "You'd love for me to put the gun down, so you can finish the job. But that's not going to happen, and you're not—"

The sound of screeching tires interrupted him. He looked to the left and saw cars coming at his van from all directions. At that instant, Simpson snatched the weapon from Campana's grip and began firing through the van's windshield at a car coming directly at them.

An FBI agent made his way to the rear of the van. As Simpson continued firing, the agent stood and ran toward the front of the van. As he reached the passenger's side door, he raised his .44 magnum Desert Eagle, firing twice. Simpson disappeared from his sight picture, and he fired two more rounds, hitting Campana in the neck. It all happened in less than five seconds.

Coast Guard UTB 41303
1:10 p.m.

Garcia and Montiel stood in the cabin of the boat trying to stay out of the sun and sucking down as many bottles of water that their bodies could hold. The adrenalin high had long since passed and they were thirsty. Garcia had just sat down on one of the small jump seats when the coxswain handed him the secure phone's handset.

"It's Assistant Director Sabinson for you, Mr. Garcia."

"You guys showed some real brass balls today, Chris!" Sabinson shouted, "The *Mara Six*'s master finished his debrief about ten minutes ago. He thinks your team should be decorated by the President!"

"As long as the ceremony's at my ranch in Texas, we'll be there."

"But that's just the lead-in for the real purpose of my call. I didn't want to break your train of thought when you were on board the *Mara Six*, but there have been some advances in the case…"

• • •

Sabinson laid out the confidential information that the Bureau had on Hamsa, Campana, Riley and Simpson. As Sabinson

295

described the chain of events of the past forty-eight hours, a phrase swirled in Garcia's mind. He remembered reading about Christian Rothmund's fascination with the occult and the Book of Revelation in a Swiss intelligence report. It was Rothmund's favorite passage:

"and power was given to him... to take peace from the earth, and that they should kill one another..."

Sabinson ended with a positive accomplishment. They had defeated the plan to assassinate the President and all inhabitants living within a radius of three miles of Penn's Landing.

Coast Guard Base Penn's Landing
3: 15 p.m.

Garcia and Montiel made their way off the forty-one-foot UTB after it had arrived at its berth at the Penn's Landing Coast Guard Station.

Sabinson had called Garcia just before they arrived, describing Hamsa's end. Both Garcia and Montiel rejoiced at the news but still were unable to accept that it was all over.

They walked quickly, amid the hugs and uproar of an increasing number of well-wishers as the news of the morning's events spread throughout the base. Montiel put his arm around Garcia, out of sheer physical and emotional exhaustion, and they proceeded down the series of piers and past the Coast Guard patrol vessels.

"The coxswain told me they have a small club here," Montiel said, "so how about one of those famous Texas ten-gallon beers?"

Garcia nodded, and the two walked forward through a narrow pathway that was forming in the crowd's center.

They entered the refuge of the cool, dark base club. Those inside watching the home run derby stood and applauded as pitchers of beer were immediately brought to the corner table that had been reserved for them. Alex Khamis was already there waiting for them.

Garcia hugged Khamis tightly and then reached for the tall glass of icy beer, quaffing it in three slow gulps. Montiel was already two ahead of him.

Khamis motioned for Garcia and Montiel to gather closer. They huddled together in the corner.

"Colby said he briefed you guys on what happened to our four subjects."

They both nodded.

"I just can't shake the feeling that this is not over yet. I can't explain why, but I feel that there is something even worse waiting out there."

"You're not alone, Alex," Garcia said. "Leo and I talked about the same thing on the way in after Sabinson's call. We've only cut four of the Hydra's heads off; for every one cut off, two will grow back…until we finish the job."

"But everyone's celebrating like it's the final victory," said Khamis.

"I hope they're just blowing off steam," said Garcia, "because there are plenty more jihadists where those four came from!"

A Coast Guard lieutenant from the Public Affairs Office stepped forward, thrusting a cellular phone into Garcia's hands. "It's for you, Mr. Garcia," she said.

Garcia placed the phone to his right ear and immediately recognized Sabinson's voice.

"Chris, I just got off the phone with the president. You, Leo, and Alex have been invited to dinner tomorrow at the White House. I'll be there with the director. To put it mildly, the president is thrilled with what your team did."

"We couldn't have done it without your support, Colby."

"It all worked out, Chris. You guys came through."

"Thanks, Colby. We'll see you tomorrow!" Garcia shouted over the building noise in the club as he broke the connection.

The screen of the club's sixty-five-inch projection TV showed a tight shot of the president as he turned to speak with the Major

League Baseball commissioner. The crowd roared as David Ortiz stepped to the plate.

Immediately, the image of "Big Papi" Ortiz was replaced by a full-screen red banner that read, "Breaking News." The mug shots of four men appeared: Hamsa, Riley, Campana, and Simpson. In the background, the live feed showed a uniformed policeman lifting a yellow plastic tarp that covered a man's body sprawled on the pavement.

A reporter looked directly into the camera's lens and began speaking.

"The FBI has confirmed that one of the largest manhunts in their history has come to an end. Now confirmed dead is their most wanted fugitive, John Thomas Cronin. Cronin, who preferred the nom de guerre, Abdul Hamsa, was found dead in a motel outside of Cherry Hill, New Jersey, earlier today. Cronin was a homegrown terrorist who had conducted a bloody campaign against..."

Garcia sat back in his chair, having heard enough about Hamsa and terrorism for a while. Right now, he wanted two things: a beer so cold that it would hurt going down and a month's vacation on the ranch in Texas.

42

THE DESTROYER TAKES WING

Northwestern Pennsylvania
Upper Allegheny Valley
5:50 p.m.

A man stood in front of the lodge's oak entry doors. He was dressed in jeans, Nikes, and a white cotton polo shirt with a small embroidered American flag on its pocket.

Mahmud Fayad, al-Qaeda's operations chief, had prayed for the operation's success. But now, he had to accept defeat. New recruiting procedures would ensure that egomaniacs like Cronin would be filtered out. He would not allow this to happen again.

He closed the faceplate on his small cellular phone and slid it into the nylon holster clipped to his belt. An informant was reporting a heavy police presence on all interstate highways leading out of the Philadelphia area.

He turned and walked down the lodge's long hallway, toward the living room where seven men were seated around a large round table. As he approached the table, all seven men rose. He motioned for them to sit down.

"My brothers, you will hear the government crowing about their victories. But what have they won? Nothing. This was a trial-run of our capabilities. We learned from our mistakes. The infidel's arrogance will cause them to be caught sleeping. Our new plan will go forward. God is great."

The others repeated Fayad's reverence.

"Mohamed, your five years of hard work have earned the highest praise from my lord Osama and Sheik Omar," Fayad continued. "You have been selected as the lead pilot."

Mohamed Atta nodded, showing no emotion. His thin lips and dark, sunken eyes were devoid of any human warmth.

"Mahmud, we have dedicated our lives to this moment in time. May God be praised. I shall open the door to the bottomless pit, and its furnace will consume the infidels. The smoke from the fires shall darken the sun at midday, and the air shall turn foul!"

Fayad looked into the eyes and souls of each of the men and then turned his attention back to Atta.

"Have you selected a date?"

Before answering, Atta glanced down the long hallway. His gaze was fixed on a painting of a grotesque, web-winged angel flying high above the fiery pit of hell. In one hand, the angel held an upraised sword; in the other, a severed head. Mohamed Atta stood and bowed toward Fayad.

"It shall be the eleventh of September."

End

Other novels by the author:
The Scorpion's Dance (2013)
La Danza del Escorpión (2014) Spanish